The Perfect Alibi

CHRISTOPHER ST JOHN SPRIGG

 Moonstone Press

This edition published in 2019 by Moonstone Press
www.moonstonepress.co.uk

Originally published in 1934 by Eldon Press Ltd

Introduction copyright © 2019 Moonstone Press

ISBN: 978 1 8990 0003 6

A CIP catalogue record for this book is available from the British Library

Text designed and typeset by Tetragon, London
Cover illustration by Chrissie Winter and Charlie Fischer
Printed and bound by in Great Britain by TJ International, Padstow, Cornwall

Contents

At the heart of *The Perfect Alibi* is an "impossible crime" whose solution is pursued by both amateur sleuths and the local constabulary. The death of wealthy industrialist Antony Mullins initially appears to be an accident or suicide, but the signs of murder quickly mount. Good-natured Police Constable Sadler and his superior, Inspector Trenton, are alternately assisted and hampered by the efforts of the local residents to find the killer. Fortunately, journalist Charles Venables is on hand to help make sense of the conflicting and confusing evidence.

The book opens with a fire and a gruesome discovery that sets the village on edge. At first everyone appears to have a perfect alibi, but the more Sadler and Trenton probe, the murkier the picture becomes. It is soon apparent that everyone, including the victim, has something to hide, and what appears to be a clue might be exactly the opposite.

The Perfect Alibi was first published in 1934, the third detective novel by Christopher St. John Sprigg, and was well received by reviewers. Dorothy L. Sayers reviewed it in the *Sunday Times*, saying, "The characters in this book have a way of making acute and entertaining observations and that is the most attractive feature of a very attractive piece of work... If you like a book to be charmingly written and full of the sort of people you would like to meet you will enjoy this." A reviewer for the *New York Herald Tribune* wrote, "What we liked best was the carefree manner and the comic intention in back of everything—just enough so that you can take it or leave it, fun of an excellent restraint... Mr. Sprigg is so competent at writing and so amusing in his stride that probably he is someone else in disguise."

Born into a family of writers and journalists, Sprigg worked as newspaper reporter, short-story writer, magazine editor, advertising director, non-fiction author and poet before he published his first detective novel at the age of twenty-five. As editor of *Airways* magazine between 1925 and 1934, Sprigg wrote dozens of articles and book reviews, as well as several technical books on the aeronautical industry. He also wrote numerous short stories for other periodicals such as *Popular Flying* and the American *Detective Fiction Weekly*. By biographer James Whetter's estimation, the number of pieces Sprigg published in his "later" years—he died at twenty-nine—numbered in the high hundreds. He published six detective novels between 1933 and 1935: *Crime in Kensington, Fatality in Fleet Street, The Perfect Alibi, Death of an Airman, Death of a Queen* and *The Corpse with the Sunburnt Face*. A final crime novel, *The Six Queer Things*, was published posthumously in 1937.

Converting to Marxism, Sprigg spent his final years completing a work of literary criticism, *Illusion and Reality*, which linked the foundations of poetry to economic paradigms in British society. Shortly after the Spanish Civil War broke out in July 1936, Sprigg drove an ambulance to the loyalist troops in Barcelona, and then joined the International Brigade at Albacete. He was killed at the Battle of the Jarama River in February 1937. Six additional works of non-fiction and poetry were published after his death under the pseudonym Christopher Caudwell.

In *The Perfect Alibi*, Sprigg delivers a clever puzzle with a deft touch, surrounding his central crime with lively characters and an ingenious story. As with other Golden Age fiction, the period detail is also part of the charm, and Sprigg put his technical background to good use. It is a pleasure to bring this long forgotten book back into print.

Chapter One

CORPSE AT THE WHEEL

"That's a damned odd smell," remarked Miss Delfinage, looking up from the grooming of her racing mare, Jennie.

Her stable-maid sniffed, and nodded. "Perhaps it's Lord Overture," she suggested. "He's always burning queer things to save coal. Those old boots of his smelt very funny when he burned them the other day."

Miss Delfinage, however, had gone to the stable door. "Heavens," she exclaimed, "The Turrets is on fire!"

Several inhabitants of Fairview Estate (formerly Hake End), "Thameshire's Fairest Pleasaunce" (see the advertisements), noticed this at the same time as Miss Delfinage. So did P.C. Sadler, of Great Hake, wearily pushing his hated bicycle up Oak Avenue (formerly Bog Lane) on his daily round. He acted promptly. He walked quickly into Mrs. Murples' place, the New House, and phoned the Peppering Fire Brigade. He then sped on low gear up to The Turrets courtyard. The fire, happily, was not so serious as it looked, for The Turrets itself was not alight. It was the wooden garage beside it that was blazing, and this communicated with The Turrets only by a path covered with wooden roofing, borne on posts.

The wooden shed was flaming with all the fury of a petrol-fed fire, and no one could go within three yards of it. But P.C. Sadler could and did confine the fire to the garage by hacking down the posts supporting the roofing, with the help of The Turrets gardener. This done, they sprayed on to the flames a jet of water from a garden hose led out of the scullery window. In spite of the advice of practically all the inhabitants of the Estate now assembled, this jet had no effect whatever.

In a quarter of an hour the Peppering Fire Brigade arrived, followed by two errand-boys, three tradesmen's vans, several exhausted urchins and (five minutes later) a perspiring ice-cream tricycle.

Fairview Estate's faith in the Peppering Fire Brigade was shaken by what followed. There was a hydrant in the courtyard near the garage, but for some reason the Fire Brigade key did not fit it, and the united efforts of the firemen were unable to move the cock. After a long period, during which several hundred yards of fire-hose were pushed in and out of windows, accompanied by the shouts and arguments of the men, a jet was produced not much stronger than that already supplied by the garden hose. Under cover of this, the firemen began to hack at the doors with their axes.

An unsympathetic onlooker remarked loudly, "If you ask me, the fire brigade's doing more damage than the fire."

The captain of the brigade himself seemed to feel that some apology was needed.

"If only the Council would have let us have that foam extinguisher like I asked for, we'd have had this petrol fire out in two minutes," he explained to Mrs. Mullins, the young mistress of The Turrets.

She smiled nervously. "I'm not sure that I'm sorry. When my husband comes back from the office and finds our old car burned up, he'll simply have to buy that Bentley he's promised me so long. He'll probably accuse me of starting the fire myself!"

"Well, there's nothing like looking on the bright side of things, is there, madam? Now then, Simpson, what's the matter with you? You look as if you'd seen a ghost."

Simpson's face was white beneath the smuts of the smoke— alarmingly white.

"There's something in there," he said, with a limp gesture towards the splintered garage door. "In the driving-seat of the car—dead—all charred up..."

Miss Delfinage, with her usual coolness, caught Mrs. Mullins as she fell backwards with a stifled cry...

II

Miss Delfinage, too, was quite naturally with Mrs. Mullins when she called at Peppering Police Station to complete the dreadful task of identification. Samson, manager of Antony Mullins' firm, Morphopoulos & Mullins, Engineers, was also there, and together they looked at the charred remains beneath the sheet.

Inspector Trenton, who had been expecting a scene after the faint in the courtyard, admired her fortitude. Patricia Mullins' face was drained of its blood beneath her jet-black hair, and her voice trembled. But she looked as unflinchingly as Samson at what had once been alive, and at the melted pince-nez, and the charred clothes, and the pocket-book—and Samson's face was white enough.

"To think that he was joking with me when he left to go home for lunch this morning," Samson said, impressed as men so irrationally are by the unceremonious haste of death. He drew a handkerchief from the tails of his morning-coat and wiped his lips.

They joined Miss Delfinage in the waiting-room.

Trenton, the formalities of identification completed, was anxious to collect any information he could, unofficially.

"Oh, he told you he was going home?" he said, answering the other's remark.

Samson nodded.

"I can't understand it," murmured Mrs. Mullins. "He told me he wouldn't be home for lunch. He'd never come home before suddenly without at least phoning me!"

"Perhaps the phone was out of order," remarked Miss Delfinage. "You know what the Fairview Estate telephone lines are. A tree's always falling across them or something."

Inspector Trenton mentally noted Mrs. Mullins' remark and Miss Delfinage's comment. Already, beneath his sympathetic manner— genuine enough, for the dazed look in Mrs. Mullins' lovely eyes would wake pity in anyone—already Trenton was keenly debating possibilities. On him, after all, largely depended what the verdict recorded by Dr. Ogleby should be. A word with the manager on the financial health of Morphopoulos & Mullins would be necessary and helpful.

III

Although the manager's mind at the outset had recurred to his conventional last words with Mullins, they soon went farther back, to a conference they had had two days earlier.

Samson was not a fool. He was a shrewd business man, with that keen sense for character which is the real foundation of such shrewdness. There had been something fishy about that conference. There was something fishy about Mullins' death. Consequently the two things linked up in his mind.

The occasion of the conference was a decision to send Ralph Holliday, Mullins' nephew and junior partner, abroad. That was natural enough, for nearly all the firm's business was foreign. The oddity consisted in the instructions given to Holliday.

These in themselves would also have been capable of explanation.

Morphopoulos & Mullins were engineers, a conveniently general term which in their case meant the making of guns, tanks, rifles, machine-guns, bombs, shells and torpedoes in their Lanarkshire factory. Odd things happen in an armament business. Morphopoulos was a clever little Greek who had turned late in life from the business of drug peddling, with its dangers, to the wholly safe business of selling guns. He had entered into partnership with Mullins, who knew nothing about selling but was a brilliant engineer with more than a brilliance in invention. Mullins produced the guns, Morphopoulos sold them.

When Morphopoulos dropped down dead on his yacht in the Mediterranean, sentimentally enough leaving his share of the business to Mullins, he had built up an international system of graft, in all the smaller European countries, which was unique. Mullins had been content to leave all this to the agents appointed by Morphopoulos. That kind of thing worried him. But now, he had explained to Samson and Holliday at the conference, something ought to be done about the sales organization. His suggestion was that Holliday should go away for a year or two and travel round Europe, prying into their agents' affairs, and local affairs generally, to see if the organization could be improved.

It was quite natural to pick Holliday for this job. Samson was kept busy enough on routine, co-ordinating the London office and the Scottish factory, where he spent every other week with the foreign agencies. Mullins, as he himself had the sense to admit, was an engineer and nothing else, but Holliday had obvious assets for the task. He was young—thirty—and had an ingratiating manner. He could speak four languages. Five years in the Diplomatic Service had given him a knowledge of the currents of European society and, presumably, a certain experience of intrigue.

The odd part consisted in Mullins' instructions. "You must work in the dark. Take an assumed name in Paris and shed your present identity. Don't present your credentials to any of our agents until you have found out all you can about the Defence Ministry's affairs in that particular country—perhaps not even then. I'm quite sure some of our agents are no longer *persona grata*, and if so we must shed them quite ruthlessly. Find out.

"But before you go I want you to promise that you will communicate with no one in this country except through this office, and only then in letters written in our private code."

Why the devil shouldn't Holliday write to anyone over here, Samson had thought, and Holliday had thought the same.

Mullins had been adamant on this point, giving only the flimsiest of reasons about it being essential for no third party to know where their secret agent was. Holliday had objected violently. There had been a quarrel, and quite suddenly Samson had sensed a bitter antagonism between the two men, something nothing at all to do with armaments.

Mullins had quite steadily persisted. And he was in a very strong position. He had rescued Holliday when the latter, his patrimony lost in a company crash, had resigned from the Service. He had installed him as a very junior partner at a salary far beyond what any other firm would give him as a matter of business. And Mullins could just as easily unmake the partner he had made. He gave Holliday clearly to understand that he must comply with his instructions in their entirety or cease to belong to Morphopoulos & Mullins.

Holliday had given in. Given in with an ugly sneer which had made the older man look disconcerted. It was a sneer that said, "Well, you've won. You've got me out of the country for a time. But you must be damned afraid of me."

To Inspector Trenton this conversation was exciting. Samson had recounted it to him very darkly. The manager had a vague circling manner when it came to dealing with anything less concrete than business details, and he circled vaguely round this conference for close on an hour. At last the irritation visible on Trenton's pinched little face broke out.

"Please be explicit, Mr. Samson! This is a privileged occasion and you can be frank. What earthly reason, that you know of, had these two men for animosity?"

This made Samson mumble worse than ever. Trenton turned red with exasperation.

"Yes, yes, yes! I understand this is all suspicion. I know you've no real grounds for your belief. All I want to know is, what did you suspect?"

The suspicion, when it came, was obvious enough. Mullins had married a woman of twenty-five, more than twenty years his junior. Holliday had met her at Mullins' house and had been a frequent visitor. Quite suddenly his visits had stopped.

Rumour suggested he had been forbidden the house.

In business the two men had continued to meet on easy terms. But they never met outside business. Soon Samson had heard other rumours. Holliday and Mrs. Mullins had been seen out together, at restaurants and theatres.

"Naturally," said Samson, "I suspected the motive behind this mission of Holliday's. It was to separate him completely from Mrs. Mullins. In either case Mullins held the aces. If Holliday refused to leave the country he could legitimately cut off his livelihood. If Holliday agreed, then absence ought to end what any self-respecting husband would suppose was only a temporary infatuation."

Here was real treasure for Trenton. Two possibilities immediately emerged.

Suicide. (Perhaps Mrs. Mullins had told her husband she would follow Holliday abroad.) A vague possibility, barely hinted even to himself, until he had learned more about Holliday—murder!

Chapter Two

APPEARANCE OF A DETECTIVE

The Turrets was imposing from a distance. It was, apparently, a grey pile of ancient stone, with a vast courtyard, soaring windows, and a great colonnaded loggia from which could be seen miles of Thameshire countryside, only hazily blighted by the contagion of London smoke.

At one side a tower soared upwards, with a crenellated top pierced by slits of windows and embraced by ivy.

Closer inspection revealed that the whole thing was an early Victorian fake. The walls were built of cheap brick covered with stucco. Bits of cast plaster decoration were stuck on to the façade.

However, it had been the family seat of the Overtures, and it had its legends. The first Lord Overture had married the prettiest girl in Peppering, or, for that matter, in Great Hake. At forty he had fallen off his horse when riding to hounds and become a cripple, confined for ever to the house. At this time it had no tower.

Lord Overture was a keen architect of an amateur Gothic sort. The mansion had originally been built under his own supervision.

He came to the conclusion his wife was walking out in the woods too much. Kind friends told him she had repeatedly been seen talking there to the handsome young doctor at Great Hake. His manservant helped him on to the roof when next she took a walk, and he followed her progress with an old telescope. She disappeared over the hill.

The next day he called in the builder and had the tower designed. Staggering round on two sticks, he urged on the work. His wife smilingly congratulated him on his new interest in life.

Soon after it was completed, he was found lying dead at the foot, his telescope still clasped in his hand, his head shattered. Local scandal pleasantly suggested that the young doctor had secretly climbed up the tower and pushed him off the edge. There was no evidence. It was easier to suppose that the crippled man had toppled off the edge in the course of his observations of the countryside.

Lady Overture never married the young doctor, so perhaps the whole story was merely local gossip. A model wife, she brought up the second Lord Overture in an atmosphere of respectability, and passed over to him his estate unimpaired. The second Lord Overture rapidly impaired it with the aid of slow horses and fast women, with their usual accompaniment of high living in low company.

The third Lord Overture, left with nothing but the family estate, determined to recover the family fortunes. When the Mullinses came to Fairview he was grey-haired, but still optimistic. The Turrets had been successively a school, a country club, a film studio, a block of flats, a home for mental cases, a sun-bathing centre; and had finally been let to Antony Mullins. Lord Overture considered he had let it to Mullins extraordinarily cheap; but he had his reasons. He pictured the wealthy engineer as a perpetual source of capital—a little private gold mine near at hand. Lord Overture was always in need of capital.

There was, of course, old Mrs. Murples. But she was, as even Lord Overture, in his pathetically gentle way, remarked, a "little odd, poor lady." She was worth a quarter of a million, but she only used her money to back young pugilists. The "Battling Bantam" was training at her house at the time of the tragedy. As she was seventy, an eccentricity of this sort was at least pardonable, and did not give the estate Lord Overture was now exploiting a bad name, such as might frighten off respectable young married couples hoping to settle down.

Miss Delfinage, two days after the murder, was standing in the courtyard of The Turrets, near the garage, and (she reflected) almost on the traditional spot where the first Lord Overture had been dashed into oblivion. She turned to find a thick-set young fellow, with a strong face full of character, and untidy black hair, staring at her with a sullen expression. The sullenness was possibly habitual.

"Well?" asked Miss Delfinage.

"I was thinking that I ought to have painted you at the same time as I painted Jennie," he said seriously. "You've got more chin and cheekbone than I realized."

Miss Delfinage looked annoyed. "As the mare you painted looked as much like me as it did any living object, I suppose I should look like a mare. No thanks. My ideas of painting are old-fashioned. I know what I like, and I like things to look like what they're meant to be."

The young man sneered. "Why stop at that? If my painting of a horse must look exactly like one, why shouldn't it smell like it as well?"

Evidently the bad terms between the two were habitual.

Miss Delfinage glared in indignation. "If you'd been spanked when you were small and made to earn your living when you grew up, you might be as much use as a horse."

The artist refused to he ruffled. "I suppose you think I should be painting signs, or doing comic strips for a daily paper, and incidentally doing another comic strip artist out of a job? Or perhaps you think I ought to be getting rich in such useful businesses as dealing in murder for instance, like the late Mullins did."

Miss Delfinage placed her hands on the hips of her smartly cut breeches with an air of determination. "Look here, Filson, you can be as rude as you like about my face and my horses, but you'll speak decently about Mullins. He gave me my start here; he lent me the money; he let me have the paddock; and he was my best customer."

Filson shrugged his shoulders. "I've no grudge against him." He looked at her meaningly. "But I wonder who had?"

"What do you mean?"

"Good God, you don't think it was an accident?"

A strange voice said in a tone of cool detachment: "Really, why not, may I ask?"

They both started. The third person was a lean young man, above the average height. He fixed a monocle in his eye and leaned forward ingratiatingly. He then repeated his question.

"Where have you sprung from, anyway?" asked Filson.

"Oh, from Mrs. Murples' place," the other explained casually. "I butted into your conversation because I knew of a bloke who gassed himself in a garage when he was looking for a leaking gasket. He fell on top of the engine, with his jacket pressing against the red-hot manifold. The jacket caught fire and everything went up in flames. In his case, though, he was pulled out and pulled to. It occurred to me that might have happened here."

"Something like that probably happened," said the girl reflectively. "There is one thing that is a little odd, though, and I'll admit it. Why did he lock the door?"

"He didn't," said Filson briefly.

The monocled stranger looked from one to the other. "Conflict of opinion." He turned to the girl. "How do you know it was locked?"

"The firemen tried the handle and had to burst open the door. I thought it queer at the time."

"And you?" he turned to Filson. "Not that it matters much, but I suppose the police will want to know."

Filson seemed a shade embarrassed. "I could have sworn it was unlocked. Somebody must have said it, I think. I remember now; they did break down the door." He looked puzzled.

The other indicated the ruins of the garage with his monocle. "Can one go inside and have a look round?"

Filson looked disgusted. "If you want to, I suppose. It's not my property. I warn you that our local bobby, Sadler, is inside. He'll probably arrest you."

"Well, it's all experience." He smiled pleasantly at the other's tone, and walked round the corner and into the charred pile.

"Damned cheek, that fellow," grunted Filson. "Must be an awful bounder, nosing into a show like this."

"We're doing the same," pointed out Miss Delfinage. "I think he's rather amusing."

I I

P.C. Sadler was sitting on a can of oil gazing reflectively at the scorched and twisted motor-car. He looked at the intruder, and their eyes met.

"I've seen you before, officer," remarked the latter. "Now where?"

The policeman laughed sardonically. "Take that piece of glass out of your eye and you might be able to see better. Considering, Venables, that for three months you were number 2 and I was number 4 in the same eight, your remark is confoundedly insulting."

Venables started in genuine surprise. "Sadler, by all that's holy! What are you doing under that helmet? No wonder I didn't recognize you!"

"The fact is," explained the other with a certain amount of embarrassment, "when the pater died, while I was still up, we were left with hardly a bean. You remember I left Magdalen the second year. Then my confounded uncle, who's Chief Constable in this part of the world, got bitten by Trenchard's idea for drafting an officer class into the police forces, and talked me into this job. His theory was that being a true Sadler, I should rapidly distinguish myself, so giving him the excuse to promote me. Unfortunately," added the young man gloomily, "I've led a completely undistinguished two years in one of the most peaceful and law-abiding parts of Thameshire. Apart from two prosecutions for unrenewed dog licences and one for playing football in the street, I have nothing to my name at all. Great joy on the part of Trenton, my superior, who reports on me as 'Very honest and conscientious, but without initiative!' To be perfectly candid, I was thinking of chucking the whole thing, but now this old bean has gone up in flames, there's just a faint chance I may do something."

Venables nodded. "There is. I don't mind telling you there's something squiffy about the case from the look of it."

Sadler looked interested. "You're on the case professionally, are you? Did Trenton give you the tip there's more in it than meets the eye? He's been as close as an oyster with me."

"No, to be honest I'm here by accident. I oughtn't to be here at all really. I'm busy full time on this Aeroplane Mystery, you know—did he fall or was he pushed? However, as I was driving out to Badlands aerodrome, I promised to give our sports man, Addison, a lift as far as Mrs. Murples', for him to get a line on the Battling Bantam's fight on Thursday. While he was shooting the works I thought I would nose round here."

"Oh, well, nose round if you like," said Sadler, relapsing into boredom again. "I'm damned if I could find anything."

Venables methodically explored the ruins for a quarter of an hour. In doing so he followed the remains of the wooden shelter to the kitchen. Not without mild surprise, Sadler saw him try the handle, open the door and disappear. He returned in ten minutes, a smile on his face.

"Well?" asked Sadler expectantly. "Discovered anything?"

"Lots. There's possibilities here. I wish I could throw up my aeroplane victim. But I'm hot on the trail there."

"I'll take over for you," said Sadler. He grinned disarmingly. "Credit and all. What happened? Have you a clue?"

Venables drew something from his pocket. "Here is the clue."

Sadler took it. It was about an inch of copper wire, twisted at the ends.

"To appreciate it," said Venables, "you must find out whose business it is to switch on the light outside the garage."

Sadler stared. "I'm damned if I see. Why so mysterious?"

"Because, old chap, if you don't find out the implications from the clue I've given you, you'll never be any good at policing, and you may as well chuck your hand in. If you perceive in time what they mean, here are two further warnings. If the show looks like suicide, be sure it's murder. If it looks like murder, it's suicide. Well, I must be off now. Cheerio. See you all of a sudden. Probably look in on my way back."

Sadler sat down, replaced his helmet, which he had removed, back on his head, and stared fixedly at a piece of copper wire for the space of fifteen minutes.

Chapter Three

MURDER OR SUICIDE?

Inspector Trenton looked at P.C. Sadler with dislike. He suspected the young man of covertly mocking at him, which was quite unjust, for Sadler had a high opinion of Trenton's ability. The trouble was that Sadler took most of his duties with a certain air of gaiety, which is all right as between people with the same common upbringing, but is likely to cause awkwardness in business between men with different backgrounds. Trenton had neither gaiety nor humour, but he had perhaps more brains than his subordinate. Sadler, however, possessed determination and plenty of *savoir-faire* which, as will be proven, may occasionally be more useful than mere intelligence.

The immediate cause of Trenton's present dislike was that the Chief Constable had asked him to make use of Sadler's services in the investigation of the Mullins business. The Chief Constable felt himself justified in the request, for his nephew, after all, had found the fire and, as was admitted, behaved with perfect correctness in the emergency. Trenton thought himself justified in resenting the request because he felt that, if the investigation was a success, Sadler would get the lion's share of credit, while if it was a failure, he himself would have to take the knock. However, the request had been passed on with deceitful offhandedness by his immediate superior, Superintendent Mercer, so he could do nothing but acquiesce.

They were now discussing the report of the pathologist who had examined the mortal remains of the engineer. The report guardedly stated that the body was too much damaged to state with certainty the cause of death but—

The "but" was of some importance. A bullet had been found, which had penetrated the brain in such a way that it would, if Mullins were alive when it was fired, have caused instant death.

"In other words," explained Inspector Trenton, "he was shot. Obviously. No one could have got into the garage to shoot him while it was in flames—anyway, there would be no point in doing it. Therefore it was done before he was burned. Therefore he was murdered."

Venables' conversation floated through Sadler's mind. Well, Venables at any rate had solved two first-class murder mysteries, which was more than Trenton had ever done. Why not back his opinion? The copper wire still reposed in his pocket. He had not yet had time to make the inquiries suggested, but here was what Venables had hinted at—suicide that looked like murder.

"I think it might have been suicide, sir," he said solemnly.

Trenton looked at the other suspiciously to see if this was one of his jokes. Then he frowned. "Very well. Go over my remarks and point out the flaws in the reasoning? Then give your own reasons."

As yet Sadler had none. His good-humoured face bore a placatory air as he ventured, "Well, what I had in mind was this. He might have shot himself and then some third party might have arranged to have his body burned to disguise the fact. His wife for instance. There are insurance policies that are invalidated by suicide."

Trenton smiled in cold disgust.

"Three ifs! A fine theory for a policeman to put up in a coroner's court."

I I

Sadler explained his point of view to Miss Delfinage, a better listener than Trenton. The confidence was natural, for ever since the young policeman had chased Jennie one sultry day on his bicycle over ten miles of country, Miss Delfinage had been grateful. A closer sympathy followed. Sadler was good-looking, with his tanned open features and golden hair. Add to that the fact that, like her, he had been born to leisure and later compelled to earn his living by hard work. How different from her pet aversion, Francis Filson, who skulked in his studio, at the end of Oak Avenue (formerly Bog Lane), and never, so far as she knew, engaged in any manly diversion, but merely lived in idleness daubing upon canvas. There was something deliberately rude even in the way he had named his house "One," for the Oak Avenue houses weren't numbered, and the numeral was, as she could well see, an implied sneer at the suburban minds of his neighbours, who had given their homes appealing, individual names. Her cottage for instance was called "Newmarket."

Sadler as naturally found Miss Delfinage congenial. She may have had plenty of chin and cheekbone, as Filson had rudely remarked, but take it or leave it, her face was pleasant, and could, Sadler reflected sometimes with a tinge of regret, be made quite a lot of. A damned nice girl, and decent as they make them.

"I must say I rather agree with Trenton, Laurence," replied Miss Delfinage. "Why wasn't he murdered? I can't imagine him committing suicide, anyway."

Sadler explained about the conversation with Venables.

"So that's who that fellow was!" exclaimed Miss Delfinage with delight. "How thrilling! If only I had known!"

"Oh, he's all right," grunted Sadler unenthusiastically. "However, the point is, what did he mean by giving me this bit of copper wire? Also what did he mean by his question about whose business it was to switch on the light outside the garage?"

"As a matter of fact, it was nobody's business. Mullins was always complaining about having to grope about in the dark, and six months ago he fixed up a time-switch, so that the light went on automatically after dark."

Sadler thought for a moment. "I suppose that washes out the importance of the question. Even so, what did Venables mean about this piece of electric wire? I suppose it's electric wire of some kind. They don't use bare copper as a rule for lighting though, as far as I can remember. Does it suggest anything to you, Sandy?"

Miss Delfinage, it may be explained, was "Sandy" to her intimates. The name had no reference to her hair, which was irreproachably black. It was a corruption of her Christian name, Sandra, given to her by her mother, who had Italian leanings, and hoped that Miss Delfinage might grow up to look pre-Raphaelite. Sandra hardly suited Miss Delfinage's style. Sandy did.

"It suggests nothing," she replied. "I'm a complete dub at that sort of thing. I always have to send for someone even if the fuse goes."

Sadler got up suddenly. "Bless you, that's given me an idea. By Jove, what a fool I was not to see it!"

He dashed out of the room, and Miss Delfinage, slightly dazed, saw his long strides up the path to The Turrets, in an altogether unpoliceman-like haste.

III

When Sadler next met Trenton, the Inspector had returned from a visit to London, where he had been investigating Mullins' personal affair. He was unprepared for Sadler's jubilation.

"I've discovered how the fire originated, sir," said the young man. He produced a rough sketch. "The light outside the garage here, which lights up the pathway from the garage to the house, is controlled by an automatic time-switch—as a matter of fact, of a type produced by Mullins' own firm. I soon discovered that for the last six months the switch has been set regularly, on the first of each month, to come on at dusk during that month.

"The time-switch itself is installed in the alcove behind the kitchen door. Dusk occurs this month at about half-past five in the afternoon. I found the switch set for quarter to three, or just about the time the fire broke out."

"Odd, certainly, but I don't see what bearing it has on the case."

"Take it in conjunction with this," went on Sadler, producing the piece of copper wire. "This came from the fuse-box, which is just beside the automatic time-switch. It was in place of the ordinary fuse wire, and is, of course, quite useless for that purpose, because its thickness is such that instead of melting away and breaking the circuit when it is overloaded, as a fuse wire should, it would be the last wire in the circuit to go. Even the mains or district fuses would go first.

"Supposing the wiring of the light was tampered with where it ran along the wooden wall of the garage. For instance if the two wires were bared, so that the naked metal nearly touched, nothing would happen as long as there was no current through the wire. Directly the time-switch made the wire 'live,' however, there would be a 'short.' In the ordinary way the fuse wires would melt and relieve the 'short.' But as we have seen, they had in this case been replaced by thick wire. The 'shorting' wires would get white hot before the mains fuses went, and would set fire to the wood. If the wood had been soaked in petrol or oil and a certain amount of petrol or incendiary material scattered around, then the whole place would go up at once."

"That's sound," agreed the Inspector, a little surprised by the other's complete presentation. "What do you make of it? What's the reason?"

"My idea is that Mullins shot himself," answered Sadler, "having previously arranged his little time-bomb to go up soon *after* he had shot himself. After all, it may need resolution to shoot oneself, but think what it would mean to let oneself be burnt alive. Anxious as he was to make his death appear an accident, we may fairly assume that Mullins could not face cremation alive. Hence the elaborate precautions. The motive is obscure, but I'm inclined to think either he wanted to avoid the disgrace of suicide, or because of an insurance policy, or for some motive we may discover on investigation."

Trenton listened to his subordinate with close attention. "You've discovered something big, Sadler," he said, with ungrudging enthusiasm. "We may certainly assume that the time-switch caused the fire. But you are wrong about the motive. Mullins would have realized that we should have a post-mortem, and that the bullet would be discovered. Then it would be obvious the fire was a blind. Point number one. Secondly, the new facts you have discovered are still more strongly in favour of murder. Here is an ideal way of getting rid of a body with a foolproof alibi. Point number two. For the murderer would reason: I may by this method completely destroy the body. Alternatively the police may find the bullet in the body. In either case I can prove an alibi for the time of the fire."

"Can't be much of an alibi if Mullins left the office at 12.30 p.m. The earliest he could get home was 1.30 p.m. Supposing the murderer waited for him in the garage and shot him at once, and that all the time-switch jugglery had been done. Even then he only had about an hour to get well away from the scene of the fire. Not much margin for an alibi."

"Quite enough margin. After all, the longer the time between the murder and getting rid of the body, the greater the risk of its being found. An hour just gives him time for a cast-iron alibi and reduces to a minimum the danger of detection."

"All the same, sir, there may be something in my suicide theory. Mullins may have thought that even if you did discover the bullet, then (supposing you knew nothing of the time-switch arrangement) the subsequent burning would absolutely convince you that the affair was murder. In other words he may have planned for you to find the bullet, planned for you to think it murder."

Trenton reflected. He pulled viciously at his small grey moustache, and then his bird-like face smiled mischievously. "You've forgotten two points. The door was locked. We've searched the garage and haven't found the key. How could he get in without a key, or get rid of it once he had locked himself in? How could he shoot himself and then get rid of the revolver?"

I V

Venables was matching pennies with the Art Editor that evening when he was called to the phone. The voice was Sadler's.

"Hello, Venables. Thanks for the tip. I discovered the time-switch and the fuse-box! But look here, your advice doesn't quite pan out. What exactly do you mean by your final cryptic message? If it looks like suicide it's murder; but if it looks like murder it's suicide? You see it looks as if Mullins may have killed himself; but it also looks just as likely that he may have been murdered. So which the devil is it?"

Venables laughed. "In that case, old chap, it's neither." Sadler gave an exclamation of disgust. "Have a heart! Do you seriously suggest a man could first have shot himself then burned himself by accident?"

"Stranger things have happened. Reflect!"

Sadler, after reflection, considered the twopence he had spent on the phone call completely wasted.

Chapter Four

THE DEAD HAND POINTS

T renton found himself making use of Sadler, in spite of his initial prejudices. There were advantages in a man who, in plain clothes, did not look too obviously a policeman. Fortunately Trenton did not realize that in admitting this to himself, he was perhaps endorsing Lord Trenchard's dreadful heresies, the infection of which had spread from the Metropolis to so many constabularies.

At any rate, that is why Laurence Sadler was trusted with the task of interviewing Mullins' solicitor and bank manager in London, sixteen miles from Great Hake.

Randall, the bank manager, had been a personal friend of Mullins. After an initial expression of surprise when his quiet young visitor in the well-cut (if shiny) lounge suit announced himself a policeman, he became frank enough.

"Mullins was a rich man. I've thought over the case, from what I could find in the papers, and I guessed inquiries of that sort would be made. There can be no question of financial worry. We handle here both the firm's account and Mr. Mullins' personal account. Naturally Morphopoulos & Mullins are not making the profits that were made when the old man was alive. Who is? But even at the worst there was always more coming out of the business than Mullins ever spent." The manager looked knowing. "I emphasize all this because I know from previous experience that you gentlemen generally search for a financial motive if there is any possibility of suicide."

"It is part of the routine," admitted Sadler. "Was there anything at all unusual in any of his financial transactions during (say) the six months before his death?"

The manager hesitated. "Well, like everyone else, he was selling all his more doubtful securities and investing in gilt-edged. But apart from that his account was as conventional as you could wish. No mysterious blackmailer. Not even a Miss or Mrs. 'X'."

I I

Mr. Grazier, of Hope, Dimity & Hope, had handled the dead man's affairs. Sadler passed through a dingy office in which two venerable old ladies were filing letters by the helpful process of scattering them on the floor and crawling among them on their knees, then on into a dark room already littered with the effects and deed-boxes of "Antony Mullins, Decd."

Mr. Grazier, comparatively youthful, belonged to the bright new generation of lawyers, with conviviality and shrewdness written clearly on his alert and confident face.

They discussed the dead man and the police's progress in general terms. Then Grazier placed the tips of his fingers together and smiled meaningly. Yet he seemed a little uneasy.

"Well, Mr. Sadler, I think I know as well as you do the sort of information you want from me. My relations with my client were perfectly ordinary except on two occasions. Once, a month ago, he consulted me on the precise legal position arising from his partnership agreement with Mr. Holliday. In brief, what he wanted to know was what grounds were necessary for him to proceed with success to a dissolution of his partnership with Holliday. Holliday was, of course, the junior partner, and the agreement provided for various circumstances in which this could be done, and on the bearing of which I advised him."

"Did any one of these circumstances seem to him particularly appropriate?"

"He did not offer any explanation of why he wanted the information. But he put forward many hypothetical cases likely to be affected by a certain clause. This clause provides that the agreement can be terminated in the event of Holliday refusing to comply with any just and reasonable instructions given by the senior partner and the general manager jointly, if such orders were given in the interests of the firm."

"I see. And what was the other occasion on which he consulted you?"

"The other occasion was when he came to make a new will. I may say that at the time this testament surprised me, for I never remember hearing of one couched in the same terms. Directly I heard of my client's death the will seemed to me even more remarkable. In fact, I think I may hazard a guess that it will have a profound influence on your investigations."

Sadler found it difficult to preserve the attitude of stolid calm he had adopted as a proper mask for a criminal investigator. The lawyer also was unable to conceal a certain quiver of eagerness as he unlocked a safe and drew out the document.

"A year or two after his marriage," said the lawyer, rustling the document, "my client made a will in which he left certain small bequests, in no case amounting to more than five hundred pounds, to various friends, distant relatives, and employees, one large bequest of fifty thousand pounds to his nephew, Holliday, and the remainder of his estate to his wife. Six months ago, however, he came to me and made a fresh will. In this the small bequests remain unaltered, but he cut Holliday completely out of his will, and left a life interest in his estate to his wife only so long as she remained unmarried, and subject to an extraordinary proviso." The lawyer seemed a trifle embarrassed. "This proviso was only to operate if there were an inquest on his death. In the case of such an inquest, the will was to stand as mentioned, if a verdict of death from natural causes was returned. If, however, there was any other verdict, then there was to be no life interest in the estate, which in its entirety (apart from the small bequests previously referred to), was to pass at once to the Society for the Promotion of Scientific Research, a body which, I should add, was in any case to receive the reversion of his estate on the death or marriage of his wife."

Sadler now appreciated the embarrassment. This was hardly a will that a solicitor would draft without protest.

"Good heavens, what an amazing testament! Did he give any reason?"

"None at all. I sounded him tactfully, but he merely said sharply: 'I'm not a fool, Grazier, and I've got a reason for this. If you like to think me a fool, well, damn your eyes! It's your job to express my wishes, not your opinion.' All of which, of course, was perfectly true. I pointed out to him that the proviso, as drafted by him, would have the effect of depriving his wife of the income even if the verdict was *felo de se*, 'suicide while of unsound mind,' or 'death by misadventure,' and he only laughed. 'Exactly what I want,' he said; 'either I die peacefully in my bed or the coroner says I died from natural causes. If I don't, the proviso must take effect.' I may say," went on Grazier, "that I was a little worried about so novel a clause, and before I drafted the testament in its present form I looked up the authorities and also took counsel's opinion. As a result, I decided that the will, even with such a proviso, was a good one, unless, of course, upset on grounds of insanity at the time of execution, which proposition might well be raised, though not, I think, upheld."

Sadler turned the matter over in his mind. Surely the lawyer knew more than he had said?

"This is a queer story, Mr. Grazier. Let us be quite frank. You would have seen that in whatever circumstances Mr. Mullins died, the proving of such a will would place his wife in a terrible position in the eyes of the world. Naturally, as his adviser, you pointed this out to him?"

Grazier banged the table excitedly.

"I did. I emphasized the point. Mullins was a personal friend of mine, and I was, in fact, able to go a little farther even than a mere legal adviser could have done. He heard me out quite calmly. Then he said in a low voice, 'Grazier, if you'd been in my shoes during the last three months, you'd realize this will is more than justified! My God, I even have to be careful of what I eat—' Then he suddenly pulled himself up and laughed, with a sly expression on his face. 'There, old man,' he said, 'that's my business. And you stick to yours. I'm consulting you as a legal adviser now, not as a friend. As a friend of the family you must know nothing about this will. As my legal adviser either draw it up as I want, or be damned to you, and I'll go to a man who will.'" Grazier shrugged his shoulders. "If you had met Mullins in one of his obstinate moods you would realize why I argued no more. But I can tell you that I have thought over this affair more than once since and it worried me. You can imagine the shock when I picked up a paper and saw the headlines!"

Sadler had been glancing through the document, and he now returned it. "There's only one inference for a reasonable man, and that is that Mullins suspected his wife of trying to kill him, or get him killed. Why on earth then didn't he tell someone so, or even tell her for that matter? To tell a murderer you suspected him would be enough in this country, I imagine, if the murderer wasn't a maniac. However, the point is, do you know the slightest reason why he should have such a suspicion?"

"None," said Grazier with finality. "Frankly, I thought at the time that he suffered from the mental trouble you meet occasionally in men of his age and brilliance, deeply in love with a young wife. Not madness, you know, but acute and uncontrollable nervous jealousy. As for Mrs. Mullins, anyone who knew her would realize how absurd Mullins' suspicions were. In fact I wish that, whatever he said, I had argued with him, and tried to win him round, for when I prove this will the situation will be awful for her. To be candid, I intended to leave the matter for a year, and then ring him up and remind him about his will. By that time I calculated he would have found out what a fool he'd been. And then this happened!"

"And then this happened," repeated Sadler thoughtfully.

III

Before he returned to Great Hake, Sadler decided to call on James Constant, the Secretary of the Society for the Promotion of Scientific Research. Grazier had told him that the legacy had been discussed at an earlier date between Mullins and Constant.

The offices of the Society were in Victoria Street, and proved to be small but respectable. As soon as Sadler had sent in his name, Constant sent out word that he would see him.

The Secretary was a short, bearded man, with bright eyes behind large spectacles, and a nose full of character. He apologized for the darkness of the room, lit only indirectly.

"Possibly our new benefaction will justify us in housing ourselves more efficiently!" he said.

Evidently Constant wished everything to be above board.

"You knew of the legacy then?" said Sadler, taking the point.

"Certainly. And I may say that I did my utmost to get Mullins to alter his mind. I told him I was deeply grateful for his thought for the Society, but that I would give anything to have him spare

us so invidious a bequest. I said we would be more than content
with a legacy of, say, fifty thousand pounds without any conditions.
I must say that I thought he was not quite sane about the subject.
He refused to alter a word of his will, and made me swear that if we
accepted the bequest at all, we would make no *ex gratia* payments to
his relatives. I agreed, for he was determined, and I thought that in
a year or two he would see reason." Constant looked at the young
policeman keenly. "Then this tragic affair occurred. You may be
sure I wondered whether, after all, my old friend was not right;
whether some premonition, who knows how, had not given him a
warning, perhaps misunderstood."

Sadler went to the point. "Did he give you any tangible reason
for his extraordinary attitude to his wife?"

"None. He muttered about plots, and that no one could make
a fool of him. He certainly was frightened of something, and yet
I had the impression he was more infuriated than afraid. This I can
believe, for he was not the man to be afraid without good cause,
but he was easily irritated."

"You had known him long then?"

"Yes, several years, although I had never met his wife or, in
fact, entered his home circle. Ours was not so much a business as
an intellectual friendship. In fact the founding of this Society was
largely his inspiration. He provided the initial funds, gave generous
donations, and by his influence made me secretary, with much wider
powers and a more handsome salary than is usual in such a post
with societies of this nature. He always believed that this Society
would one day do great things.

"I should explain," said the Secretary, brightening, "that our
object is the promotion of fundamental research. As you know,
most engineering research is subsidized commercially, and therefore
ad hoc. It is designed to find out particular things—directed along
lines of obvious commercial value—unfadable dyes, for instance,

or imperishable rubber. Mr. Mullins believed that more research was required into the fundamentals of physics and engineering, with no immediate gain in mind. If any discoveries were made of commercial value, well and good, they could be quite frankly commercialized on a royalty basis, with special terms to those firms who have supported the S.P.S.R. by subscriptions. In this way it was hoped to secure support from industrial organizations who would not be able, as business firms, to support a purely academic organization. I may say that so far Morphopoulos & Mullins have been almost alone as a firm in according us this support to any generous extent, but were we once to stumble on any principle of value, firms would, I think, fall over each other to subscribe. I hope great things of our first Institute, which the Mullins legacy will enable us to complete and fully staff far earlier than I ever believed possible."

The Secretary came to earth from his dream with a start.

"I am afraid I am boring you," he said.

"Not at all," answered Sadler untruthfully.

Chapter Five

DR. MARABOUT SEES THE DEVIL

"**G**oing to see a pretty lady to-day, I suppose!"

Pierced by this unerring shaft of insight from his wife, Inspector Trenton stopped smirking into the mirror. He had not realized that his wife had noticed either the smirk or the careful anointing of hair and moustache.

"Don't be silly, my dear. A man in my position has to keep himself smart. As a matter of fact I shall be occupied all day in investigating the Mullins case."

He then went out and called on Patricia Mullins.

Trenton had debated for some time whether he would see Mrs. Mullins alone or supported by one of his henchmen. Finally he decided that he would feel less hampered alone. It was going to be a delicate business, he reflected, sweating gently under his collar. It was.

Patricia Mullins received him in a room expensively decorated but, so he felt, lacking homeliness. These chromium-plated chairs now. He admitted grudgingly, as he dropped into one, that they were comfortable enough. A more fitting criticism would have been the way in which they clashed with the fake Gothic of The Turrets architecture. Nothing but equally fake Jacobean reproductions or perhaps imitation refectory tables would have harmonized with that. But Trenton was concerned only with human values.

Beyond the formal words of welcome, Patricia Mullins volunteered nothing. Trenton was good enough psychologist to permit an awkward pause while he studied her face. Its delicate oval was accentuated by the silver glint of her very blonde hair. Her features were regular and the mouth, the Inspector noted, was full and generous. No cruelty or bitterness here.

She was a pretty lady, he thought, recollecting his wife's phrase, but there was something that lingered in her expression more touching than mere prettiness—a shadow of suffering of the kind that makes a child's pain so poignant, because there is no selfish complaint, but only surprise that such things should be. Perhaps the Inspector did not, in that short period, analyse Mrs. Mullins' half-shadowed face to that extent, but he felt the emotions in the rough. Lest his psychological pause should be turned by his susceptibilities upon himself and prejudice him in favour of someone he already classed in his mind as a suspect, he broke the silence summarily.

"It is a bad business this, Mrs. Mullins."

She looked at him enigmatically. "Perhaps you will tell me what you mean. Ever since this dreadful thing happened there has been whispering. Why has the inquest been adjourned? What does it mean? What do you suspect? I tell you it is absurd to suggest that Tony could have—killed himself. If you thought so, why haven't you told me why? Surely I should be told?"

"We have told you so little because we are sure of so little." The Inspector spoke quietly. "No, Mrs. Mullins. your husband did not commit suicide. He was shot, and he was already dead when he was burned."

"Shot," she repeated, in horror, as if there was something unspeakably dreadful in the idea. He saw her hands tremble and her cheeks go white. He remembered that she had fainted once before, but she waved away his proffered hand with a little irritation. "All right. I'm not going to do anything silly!"

There was a pause during which he wondered what her next question would be. It was practical enough. "Have you any idea who shot him? Surely a thing like that could not happen without some suspicion..."

"No, Mrs. Mullins, we have no suspicion. That is why I have come to you to ask you if you can tell us anything that would throw any light on it."

She shook her head. "It is unthinkable to me that such a thing should have happened to Tony. I never knew he had come back from the office even. I was with Mr. Filson up to the time we heard the shouts outside and found there was a fire."

"Where is the key of the garage door?" asked Inspector Trenton suddenly.

The question startled her so visibly that for a minute she was unable to compose her lips to reply. "Why do you ask? I don't know! My husband had it always."

"The door was locked, and the key was not in his clothes!"

There was another silence.

The Inspector drew a fresh covert. "When did you last see Mr. Holliday?"

If he had expected any discomposure such as had been produced by his question about the key, he was disappointed. She seemed slightly surprised at the irrelevance of the question; nothing more.

"On the Wednesday afternoon Tony ran him back to the station in his car. About five. He came just before tea-time."

The Inspector continued his policy of unrelated questions. "Whose duty was it to put out the garage lights?"

Again she seemed surprised. "I don't know that it was settled. I can't drive and never went to the garage. I suppose Tony put them on and off himself."

Was she shamming, or did she really know nothing about the time-switch?

"Did you hear any shot, or noise that sounded like a shot, while you were with Mr. Filson?"

"I don't remember any. But truthfully, so much shooting goes on in the coverts behind the paddock that I might not notice it, so long after, if there was a noise."

"Do you know of a revolver in this house, Mrs. Mullins?"

Here was something that got behind her reserve. She looked uneasy again, but gave no reason for it in her slow answer. "I don't know of any revolver in the house."

"Mrs. Mullins, you say you were with Mr. Filson at the time of the fire? For how long had he been with you, and had there been any interruption?"

She answered the question almost without thinking. "He is painting me, you know. I had been sitting for him in the North Room with just one break since twelve o'clock. The break was for lunch, which we ate in the room, and that was all."

The Inspector hesitated before playing his final card. "Do you know what was in your husband's will?"

She looked surprised. "I don't think there was any secret about it. Apart from one large bequest to his nephew, Mr. Holliday, Tony left everything to me."

Very gently the Inspector told her of the new will.

A burning blush suffused her face when she grasped the nature of the alteration. "No!" she exclaimed. "He didn't write that! He couldn't have. It is terrible, wicked. He must have been mad, surely. He never did such a dreadful thing. He never even hinted at it. Inspector, what will people say?" Fresh waves of crimson swept over her face as different implications of the situation struck her. The Inspector felt acutely embarrassed as she looked at him with that odd, child-like expression of pain. "What does it mean?" she asked in a low voice. "Do you understand why he did it? Is there something I haven't realized behind all this?"

The Inspector rose to his feet. There was no more to be learned for the moment. "We know no more than you do. This will was a surprise to us. Of course it has shocked you, Mrs. Mullins, and I don't think it is fair to question you till you have thought things over."

II

Dr. Eustace Marabout, who lived at "Trismegistus," also in Oak Avenue (formerly Bog Lane), refused to be relieved of his dried alligator when he sat down to tea with Miss Delfinage. Sandy was used to his idiosyncrasies and made no comment, but Dr. Marabout was too polite to place the object on the table without some explanation.

"The alligator is a sovereign remedy against vampires," he explained. "There are an enormous number of them in England to-day, and they are still increasing. I have written several times to the Ministry of Health about it, but although the Minister acknowledged my letter, there has been no action taken. I am trying to get the local M.P. to take the matter up."

"Good heavens! Surely there aren't any on Fairview Estate?"

"Nothing would surprise me less," answered Dr. Marabout, with a worried expression. "I have noticed two individuals, whose names I need not mention, whose eyebrows meet, or nearly so, which as you well know is an infallible sign of a vampire. I have taken the precaution of planting garlic in my garden which will prevent them reaching my threshold. The herb is objectionable on the person, however, and I prefer to carry round this baby alligator. Knowing the cunning of this class of demoniac, I take care never to let the reptile out of my sight."

Dr. Marabout, Doctor of Philosophy of the University of London, was a materialist when he first started the occult studies which made his name famous. At that time his intention was merely to document the various superstitions of mankind. Soon, however, he was impressed by the overwhelming documentary evidence in favour of witches, vampires, possession, overlooking, lycanthropy and allied subjects, which had persisted unchanged throughout the ages. "Unless," he once wrote, "we are to put no trust at all in history, and refuse to accept any man's testimony as to historic fact, we are bound to accept the almost unanimous statement of our forefathers that there were once witches and werwolves. There is no alternative. Either the evidence of impartial and honest men is to be admitted, if numerous enough, or we must sweep away all history as founded on quicksand." The Doctor preferred to accept the verity of historic evidence, and having accepted it, was forced to believe in the existence at one time of werwolves and vampires. If then, why not now? However, I need not expand his point of view. It was fully recorded in the press when Dr. Marabout was sued for the value of an Alsatian dog, which he had shot dead with sanctified silver bullets under the impression that it was Mrs. Murples. "Had I noticed the animal was not a bitch I should at once have realized my mistake," he explained to the court.

It must not be assumed that Dr. Marabout is not rational. Possibly his failing is an excess of reason. Tall and spare, with the typical scholar's face, pursed and wrinkled with reflection, but lit readily by a kindly smile, his views on life are philosophical and balanced; and he only disagrees with the wiser judgments of mankind on his own subject, on which, after all, he may claim to know more than most.

"I sometimes think that we are the only sane people on the Estate," he remarked to Sandy, carefully making the sign *Fylfot* on his bread and butter before putting it in his mouth, in case it was bewitched.

Sandy reflected. "Well, there certainly are some odd people here, but then it's an odd estate. Still you can't say the Eytons are anything but sane."

"Ah, yes, there is always the Eyton family. Delightful people if only the mother was not so criminally careless. Little Peter, I am sure, was being overlooked last winter when he was so ill, but Mrs. Eyton refused to stew up in his milk the toad I gave her. As a result Peter was months before he got well, and in fact it was not until I gave Mrs. Murples a clear hint that I knew what her game was that the child recovered at all."

Sandy could imagine Mrs. Eyton faced with the toad. She changed the subject.

"I suppose you have heard that the police now think poor Mr. Mullins was murdered?"

"I have heard the theory."

"Who on earth do you think could have done the thing?"

"Probably the Devil," answered Dr. Marabout seriously. "I thought I saw him coming from the garage the day before the murder."

Dr. Marabout may have had odd ideas about what it was he saw, but he never claimed to see things that weren't there. Consequently his remark surprised Sandy.

"What was he like?"

"A little shabby," replied Dr. Marabout "He was shorter than I would have expected, and had a small flaxen beard and horn-rimmed spectacles. I did not, of course, realize who he was at the time. This was about five o'clock. Next day, between quarter- and half-past one, I saw him coming from the garage. At least I imagine it was the same devil, but I only saw his back. However, both creatures were short and stocky, so I expect they were the same. I went back home and only a few minutes afterwards the fire must have occurred. The fire at once made me suspicious. The Devil can't help playing with fire."

In the course of tea their conversation drifted on to other subjects, and Dr. Marabout gave her a lucid analysis of the political

situation in Germany, explained the causes affecting the dollar-
pound exchange, advised her of a good lock-up in industrials for
her small savings, and discussed the chances of the favourite for
the November Handicap. But her mind was not in the conversation. For one thing seemed to her crystal clear. Antony Mullins
must have been home about half-past one. Perhaps he was already
murdered. Who but his murderer could have been coming from
the garage at that time?

Chapter Six

INTERROGATION OF A WIDOW

Inspector Trenton and P.C. Laurence Sadler faced the Chief Constable. Trenton, of course, had an easy chair. Laurence, to show there was no favouritism, had been given by his uncle the most uncomfortable seat in the room.

"What exactly do we really know?" asked the Chief Constable, suspending a pencil over a note-pad.

"We know," said Trenton, "that at 12.30 p.m. on Thursday Mullins left his office in Broadway, Westminster. At a quarter to three on the same day a time-switch was set to go off and fire his garage at The Turrets on Fairview Estate. A fire was actually raging at three, and Mullins' body was in the garage. The time available can be narrowed further. Before he left, Mullins mentioned to Samson that he had parked his car in a two-hour park and therefore must hurry. Hence we can assume that he had brought his car up and therefore must have returned in it. It is impossible to do the journey from Westminster to Fairview Estate in less than an hour between noon and two. Therefore we know with certainty that as he left town at twelve-thirty, Mullins was killed between half-past one and three, or, if we accept the time-switch evidence, as I think we must, at a quarter to three. Just over an hour. Very little time, incidentally, for the murderer to make his arrangements."

"I agree," said the Chief Constable. "In fact, if he had done the arrangement of the wiring *after* he had killed Mullins, he was protracting the risk of discovery. I think we ought to expect that this was fixed up beforehand."

"It could not have been arranged more than twenty-four hours before the murder," pointed out Laurence. "Otherwise when the time-switch, which was a twenty-four hour one, went on in the usual way there would have been a 'short.' Also, if the time-switch had been altered more than twenty-four hours before, the fact would almost certainly have been noticed directly Mullins went to put his car away, for it would have been dark."

"Yes," confirmed the Inspector. "We know from Mrs. Mullins that her husband used the car after dark to take Holliday back to his train. The light must have been functioning then."

"Good!" said the Chief Constable. "Here is something settled. The murder took place between half-past one and a quarter to three. So the murderer must have been on the spot then. He must also have been there at some previous time, but not earlier than the preceding evening, to rearrange the wiring, unless we think him someone rash enough to run risks. However, he obviously isn't, from the careful scheme he evolved to get rid of the body. By the way, how the devil did he know he would have an opportunity of murdering Mullins that day? The time-switch, once tampered with, was bound to be discovered within twenty-four hours, as we have previously agreed."

"Perhaps he had made a rendezvous with Mullins before he fixed it up. Or perhaps he phoned him from Great Hake with some story to make him return."

During all this time Laurence had been wriggling uncomfortably in his chair. Finally he summoned up courage enough to say what he wanted. As with all outbursts prompted by courage, the remark sounded rude.

"Supposing we are all up the pole."

The Chief Constable looked at him in surprised reproof. "Up the pole, Laurie! What do you mean?"

"I don't know; but it all seems fishy to me. Why all this burning business? Obviously a post-mortem was bound to find the bullet.

No fire would get rid of that, short of a furnace. It all seems so silly to me. I mean to say," he trailed off, "why muck about with wires and so forth for nothing?"

The Inspector smiled grimly. "Your nephew formed the idea, at an early stage in the case, that Mullins killed himself. I admire his tenacity. However, the fact remains that we found the door locked and no revolver inside."

The Chief Constable looked official. "Don't be a fool, my boy. You're not the first policeman I've seen make a fool of himself through not wanting to accept the obvious conclusion. And, in point of fact, the coroner very nearly decided not to have a post-mortem. If it had been someone less important than Antony Mullins, I don't think he would have. So your murderer wasn't so silly as you think in going to so much trouble."

The two resumed their discussion, and Laurence felt himself edged gently out of it.

"We've established two important things, then," stated the Chief. "First, the time during which the murder must have taken place; second, the fact that the murderer must have spent at an earlier date nearly an hour undisturbed on the premises. That would give him time to fix everything. Now we get down to the real business. Whom do you suspect?"

"In the face of the will, the thing sticks out a mile," answered Trenton happily. "Mullins feared his wife. Incredible it may seem, yet if his hints to Grazier are to be trusted, he not only suspected that attempts would be made on his life, but believed they had already been made. In his new will he therefore cut Holliday out altogether and penalized his wife if he were to die violently. We may take it that these were two people that he hated and feared. In case we might think Holliday's disinheritance due to other reasons, we have the additional evidence of his using his authority as senior partner to send Holliday abroad on business. We have a third slant on it, inasmuch as it was already becoming notorious that there was something between his wife and Holliday. We may therefore assume that Mullins wished to get Holliday out of the country both to keep him away from his wife and to safeguard himself. We know from Samson the pressure he brought to bear on Holliday and how Holliday resented it. Everything fits in."

"It seems to me clean-cut. God bless my soul!" the Chief said reflectively, "we've strung natives up in bunches for less than that in India. Not, of course, but they've not had the laugh on us once or twice when the real murderer has confessed afterwards. Or would have had the laugh, I should have said; because, of course, they were beyond laughing. Well, anyway, here you've got a man expecting to be done in. (Why the devil he didn't tell us so is a complete mystery.) He fears the man who's making love to his wife, or his wife, or both. He tries to send the man out of the country. And next day he's done in."

"Exactly, sir, which means that we've got to go bald-headed for Holliday."

"Supposing he was in Berlin all the time," said Laurence, who, after his last deflation, had only with difficulty been blowing himself up again. "Rather a sell for us, eh?"

The Chief Constable at once pushed in another pin. "My boy, we neither think Holliday guilty nor innocent. I hope he will survive our scrutiny. The point happens to be that he is the obvious suspect, and we go for him first. If he comes out of it, we go for the woman."

A faint pang touched Inspector Trenton, and in his mind's eye he saw that look of child-like suffering framed in a halo of lighter-than-gold hair. "She has an alibi," he said rather quickly. "She was sitting with Filson during the whole time of the murder."

"Did she volunteer that?" snapped his Chief.

"Yes, sir, I think she did."

"Ha! Probe it, Trenton, probe it! We had a good axiom in India. Distrust every alibi unless it is one the suspect tries to conceal from you. Remember it."

"One curious thing has cropped up. A fellow was seen at the garage the preceding evening, and again coming out of there not long before the fire."

The Chief Constable jumped. "But that must certainly have been the murderer! This is vital! Have you followed it up?"

"The only difficulty is that the witness is a little unreliable. He thought this man was the Devil."

"Good heavens!" exclaimed the Chief Constable. "Is there a lunatic asylum there?"

"That's Dr. Marabout," interjected Laurence. "He's quite sane really."

"He sounds it," remarked his uncle with heavy irony.

"He's potty on vampires and werwolves, of course. He has pentacles embroidered over his underwear to keep off spells. But Sandy—Miss Delfinage—who knows him quite well, says he would never say he saw something he did not, though he might imagine it was a witch or a sylph or something."

"Fine in the witness-box!" commented the Chief. "But go on!"

"Well, I back Miss Delfinage because she seems to know every little thing that goes on in the Estate. Not nosy, you know, but people like her and tell her things. It was really she who told me about the time-switch and so put me on the track of how the fire was started. Anyway, Dr. Marabout told her about this man. I've seen Marabout since, and got a vague description out of him. Assuming the two people he saw were the same, it was a short, stocky, bearded person—he only saw the beard on the first occasion, but he was definitely shortish and thick-set on both occasions."

"H'm. What's Holliday like?"

"Tall and clean-shaven," answered the Inspector. "However, he's broad-built and that type of person might look short from a distance," he added hopefully.

"Pshaw! I shouldn't take much notice of this vampire creature if I were you," snorted the Chief Constable.

"Miss Delfinage says——" began Laurence.

"Who is this Delfinage girl?" asked his uncle querulously. "Is she a sweetie of yours or something?"

"Good Lord, no! I see a lot of her up at the Estate, of course—on my beat. I caught a pony of hers for her once, that's how I got on speaking terms. She runs a riding school. Quite a good kid."

"Well, it doesn't matter, anyway," said the Chief Constable, still looking at him with a certain amount of suspicion. "Keep in with her. She seems a useful source of information."

I I

Miss Delfinage called on Mrs. Mullins to offer her condolence and help. Whether there was any human curiosity prompting her visit it would be rude to inquire. Also unnecessary.

Mrs. Mullins was looking less crushed than when the Inspector had seen her. It might be that the two blows she had received in quick succession had, instead of prostrating her, awakened her fighting spirit. Or was it, Sandy wondered, that one had cancelled the other? The death of her husband perhaps had been ameliorated by the knowledge of his cruel will. But surely she must have known something of his feelings.

"What's this I hear about the will?" she therefore asked, in the first long pause that followed the usual condolences and reassurances.

"What's all what?" replied Patricia Mullins blankly.

Sandy, accustomed (as she afterwards explained) to read in a vicious horse's eye exactly when it was going to bite, saw precisely what was passing through Mrs. Mullins' mind, as follows.

"How does this girl know about the will? Perhaps she heard it from my husband. He wouldn't have told her unless they were fairly friendly. Now I come to think of it, he started her in the riding school and was always riding... A little strange. Perhaps she has given her little game away..."

While Sandy sensed this, her own mind was working rapidly. She must give some credible reason for knowing that there *was* something odd about the will. She could not say that Laurence had told her about it. It might get him into trouble.

"I gather there's something funny about it," she told Mrs. Mullins with composure. "The police asked me if I had heard anything about a will, and whether your husband had told me anything about his."

The suspicion died in Patricia's eyes. Yet Sandy accounted that suspicion as telling in her favour. A guilty person, she reflected, is rarely keenly suspicious. He is too busy thinking of how he can ward suspicion from himself.

Patricia told her the story of the will. The Inspector, had he seen her face, would again have seen it invested with that hurt and child-like misery. Sandy read in it nothing but a sulky bitterness. Neither perhaps was wholly right.

"Who is this Secretary of the Society for the Promotion of Scientific Research?" asked Sandy, when Mrs. Mullins had explained the provisions of the will.

"I never met him," answered Patricia. "My solicitor went to see him, though, and he says he is a sly little creature with a silly beard and piggy eyes. I'm sure he got round Tony and made a fool of him with his precious Society. I wouldn't have minded if he'd left his money to his relatives, but to a Society—ugh!" She shuddered with a woman's instinctive contempt for corporate bodies.

Mrs. Mullins' solicitor might have been a little surprised at his client's rendering of his description of Constant. It had been, "A typical scientific little Johnny. Pretty shrewd-looking, with a little beard and sharp eyes."

Miss Delfinage suddenly gave a gurgle. "Good heavens, he's the man!"

"What do you mean?"

"He's the man Dr. Marabout saw leaving the garage the day before the murder and then again just before the fire. Think of it! Who else had so much to gain as he? It explains everything. You know there isn't a single person on the Estate with a beard except Lord Overture, and goodness knows he'd be the last person, seeing your husband was his best tenant. But Constant! That would fit in with everything."

Mrs. Mullins smiled tolerantly. "A little fantastic, surely."

"What's your theory then?" asked Sandy, more than ever convinced of her guess, now it was lightly received.

"I think he did it on purpose to throw suspicion on me," Mrs. Mullins said coolly. She paused. Sandy's eyes were regarding her without encouragement. Her carefully retained control tottered for a moment. "Oh, don't think I don't know what the police think, and what you think, and what the whole of England will be thinking as soon as the will is made known! It's like him. I can imagine him chuckling with laughter now, at the success of his scheme." She shuddered. "Just a cold, quiet chuckle. He never laughed out loud. It's all so like him. I wouldn't have minded so much if he'd been angry and hit me, as a man of his character might, or cursed me, or left me. But it was that cold, simmering fury of his, that never showed on the surface. He would go out of his way to hurt and humiliate me, with ingenious schemes, so that no one would ever pity me; just as I'm hurt and humiliated now. For God's sake, girl, don't look at me like that!" The woman's eyes blazed with indignation. "I know what you are thinking. But I tell you, long before I ever looked at another man, I knew he hated me. He drove me to it. And then he hated in me what he had caused himself. He knew he was being unfair and he revelled in it."

Her head sank forward. She seemed suddenly tired. "But there, how absurd it is to try and make anyone believe it. Such a complicated way of committing suicide! They don't realize that he was an inventor; and that all the complication is just what he would have planned to get his aim, and fool the world."

Sandy murmured a few words of condolence. She granted the woman in front of her the sympathy that was demanded by her tortured voice, by the obvious anguish. But she did not grant any credence to her story.

"I'm not so sure she is innocent," she reflected. "Mullins was a damn good scout. Look at the way he helped me with my school. Not the slightest need to do it unless there was something decent in his nature, instead of which, she tries to make me believe he is a sadist. Of course she's probably humbugged herself into believing her own story. Having wronged him, she at once tries to imagine that there was some excuse for her. Hence all this business of secret cruelty, and making her seem in the wrong. I never did like that soapy blighter, Holliday, anyway. Never looked at another man! My God, why do we women use these damn silly expressions?"

"My dear," she said aloud to Mrs. Mullins, "you simply must not let your mind run on these things."

Chapter Seven

A SHOT IN THE DARK

T he postman, as he plonked down on the general office counter the usual bundle of letters for Morphopoulos & Mullins, would surely, for mere pity's sake, have abstracted from it a letter which bore a Berlin postmark, had he only known that it would cause infinite suffering to Inspector Trenton and his Chief Constable, so that they would damn themselves, each other and the policeman's lot, that it would impede for a long time the solution of the Burning Garage Mystery, that it would cause endless misunderstanding and wasted activity, and finally result in the production of this book.

The letter from Berlin was a hasty note scrawled on the firm's note-paper. It ran as follows:

"As arranged on the phone this morning I have communicated with Messerschmidt and told him that in view of the change in the political situation I will leave the matter in his hands. It would obviously be unwise to hold the conference he suggests. With regard to the other question I am surprised at Volterra taking the attitude he does, for we definitely promised him ten per cent on the net and not on the gross."

This letter was written and signed by Holliday.

How it became a thorn in the flesh of the investigators was as follows. Trenton, probing Holliday's alibi, had interviewed Samson. Samson had said at once that Holliday had been in Berlin on the morning of the murder. Trenton, playing the jocular investigator, which never sorted very well with his acidulous visage, here remarked playfully:

"Ha! ha! Mr. Samson, you'll never make a detective! He may have *said* he was going to Berlin. He may have been *seen* leaving for Berlin. But that doesn't prove he *was* in Berlin."

Samson rather took the wind out of his sails by saying curtly that Holliday had phoned Mullins from Berlin.

The Inspector leaped on him again. "How do you know it really was from Berlin?"

Samson replied that he had been in the room with Mullins when his secretary had said, "Call coming through from Berlin for you." He had then heard Mullins discuss with Holliday the situation which had arisen by reason of the fall of the German War Minister in disgrace a week ago, and heard him tell Holliday, in view of the temper of things in Germany, to get into touch with Messerschmidt and cancel the conference. Mullins had also appealed to him about the vexed matter of Volterra's commission because of Holliday's dealings with Volterra.

Worse followed for the Inspector. Samson rummaged in the bundle of Mullins' opened but respectfully replaced letters, still in their envelopes, as if waiting for the dead man's ghost to return to deal with them, and extracted from them this letter of Holliday's, whose envelope bore, as Trenton sadly noticed, the postmark "*Berlin, 2.30 p.m.*," and the date of the murder.

The Inspector ground his teeth and ceased to be jocular. The alibi could not be more perfect if it had been made for the purpose. Yes, echoed the Inspector suspiciously, if it had been made for the purpose.

The Inspector did not let it rest there. Fortunately Morphopoulos & Mullins knew what hotel Holliday had been staying at in Berlin— the Atlantic. He had, of course, left it by now, they added, and gone on to Kossovia, the next country in his itinerary. But they did not know under what name he had registered in Berlin, except that it would be one of the dozen or so for which passports had been given to Holliday. Yes, they admitted shamelessly, such things were part of the stock-in-trade of Morphopoulos & Mullins.

Provided with these names, Trenton went to Berlin, visited the hotel, and traced one of the names on the list as registering for one night. Hotel servants could only give a vague description of a pleasant-spoken young Englishman bearing the name. Trenton wished that he had been able to obtain a photograph of Holliday until the need was removed by the tracing of a phone call to England—to the very number of Morphopoulos & Mullins—in the record of long-distance calls kept by the hotel operator. The time of the call agreed with the time Holliday's phone call came through the other end. To make absolutely certain, however, he called on Messerschmidt, Morphopoulos & Mullins' Berlin agent, who confirmed the story of the conference. In fact he produced a letter from Holliday, brought by hand on the day of the murder, oddly enough in typewriting (perhaps Holliday carried a portable for business communications?) but signed.

The borrowed services of a graphologist, available by courtesy of the C.I.D., completed the chain of evidence exculpating Holliday. The signature to the typed letter to Messerschmidt was certainly Holliday's. The letter written in handwriting to Mullins confirming the phone conversation was all Holliday's ("except," added the handwriting expert, "that I should at once have suspected the signature if the rest of the letters were not palpably in Holliday's writing. It is, of course, more difficult to counterfeit free handwriting than a stylized signature"). "These experts!" commented Trenton. The envelope of this letter was typewritten, not handwritten, but the typewriter was the same as that used for the letter to Messerschmidt.

Now the sum total of this, as Trenton and the Chief admitted, was that it let Holliday out as completely as if he had been surrounded by a convocation of bishops with linked hands throughout the Thursday of the murder. For if Holliday was able to post in Berlin, a quarter of an hour before the murder was discovered and two hours after Mullins was last seen alive, a letter containing a reference to a telephone conversation held over the long-distance phone with Mullins half an hour before he was last seen alive (such conversation being vouched for by Samson and, so far as the fact of the call was concerned, by two telephone operators), then the alibi was watertight. They assumed the most fantastic improbabilities. For instance, that the hotel guest was an agent of Holliday's successfully counterfeiting his voice over the phone to his uncle—even so, how could that agent post a letter in Holliday's handwriting dealing with matters discussed over the telephone an hour before? Trenton had had a wild idea that the thing might be workable by aeroplane, but had been laughed out of the Air Ministry by a sleek young man who assured him that even with an autogiro landing on Fairview Estate, and yet capable of the fastest speed ever recorded for any aircraft, the thing was impossible. So there it was. Holliday had a clean bill of health.

"It's the woman, as I said all along," remarked the Chief Constable untruly. "Go after her alibi. There's something fishy about an alibi which depends on the word of an artist."

I I

Next evening Laurence was strolling amiably down Oak Avenue (formerly Bog Lane) when he heard a loud report behind him, accompanied by a whizzing noise past his left ear. It was already dark, so though he turned instantly towards the trees from which he had heard the report come, he saw nothing moving. Now being a youth of resource he did not shout, blow his whistle, or rush madly into the trees among which his assailant was presumably lurking. He merely stayed still, one arm raised to his head as if the shot had turned him into a stone. After the lapse of five minutes—during which he heard nothing but the sudden opening of a window in "Trismegistus," Dr. Marabout's residence, the house nearest to him, about a hundred yards away—he was rewarded by the sound of a furtive scuffle, some fifty feet to the left of where he had thought the report of the firearm had come from. He leapt towards the spot.

Although it was getting dark, there was still sufficient light to see objects dimly, and directly he had got near the apparent source of the scuffle, Laurence saw a figure in full flight among the shrubs and saplings which covered the unsold land between the built-on plots in Oak Avenue. He noted, not without relief, that the figure appeared to be somewhat smaller than his own. He therefore gave chase with great vigour, at the same time yelling, and blowing his whistle. The figure tripped up, with an appalling oath, over a fallen sapling, and Laurence seized it with the approved Peel House grip. Unfortunately he had underestimated his opponent's strength, for the unknown freed himself and then did something which gave Laurence the impression of walking gently into a wall of cotton-wool studded with electric light bulbs. He became unconscious...

He came to himself, with a singing head, in a lighted room, dimly wondering why a goat of all things should be bending over him. With full consciousness the goat turned out to be the anxious face of Lord Overture, last of the Overtures, whose thin, bearded face was regarding him anxiously.

"There," said Lord Overture, with relief, "I'm glad you've come to. I was afraid I should have to give you some brandy."

"What happened?" asked Laurence conventionally.

"Really, I was going to ask you the same," said the other, a little aggrieved. "I heard a gun go off and someone yelling and blowing

a whistle, and then I found you flat on your back and quite unconscious. What hit you?"

"A mule, I fancy," answered the young policeman, cautiously
exploring his jaw.

"No, surely not a mule!" exclaimed Lord Overture literally.
"I am sure there is not a mule on the Estate. Besides, could you be
sure in that light? Perhaps it was one of Miss Delfinage's horses.
But then it could hardly have shot you, could it?"

"Did you see anyone near me?"

"No horses. No animal of any sort, not even a rabbit," Lord
Overture, who had a one-track mind, answered positively.

"Not horses, people! Persons! Small men with horseshoes in
their fists."

"No, nothing like that, I assure you. How odd! Is it supposed
to be lucky to carry a horseshoe? Very awkward, I should think.
After all, one can't carry them in one's hand all the time, and it
must be awfully bad for the hang of one's coat. My tailor complains
even of the nutcrackers I carry round in the autumn." His lordship
reflected. "You must have mistaken a revolver for a horseshoe,
I think. I distinctly heard a firearm of some kind..."

It will be gathered therefore that Sadler got no helpful information from Lord Overture, and he left the Lodge bitterly vowing
vengeance, and not without a certain amount of alarm at the new
turn of events.

III

"I'm worried about this attack on you, Sadler," said the Inspector.
"I can't understand it. The man who murdered Mullins must be a
maniac who's ready to murder anyone at sight; and yet that seems

all wrong in view of the ingenuity with which the crime was planned. Or else we've got so near the heart of the mystery that the murderer is alarmed about his own safety. So much so that he'll take the risk of potting at people and nearly getting caught. I don't know, it doesn't seem to hang together somehow."

"I suppose we *are* right in assuming the bloke who had a stab at me was the murderer. It couldn't have been someone with a grudge against me, do you think?"

"Still reluctant to admit that there is a murder, Sadler?" remarked the Inspector acidly. "People with grudges wouldn't choose a time like this. Besides, this isn't Ireland. It isn't that madman Marabout with his sanctified silver bullets, by any chance, is it?"

"Lord, no. I don't think even he would see anything occult about a policeman."

"Well, anyway, I don't think you ought to go about the Estate alone after dark."

"Neither do I."

The Inspector was immersed in a gloomy silence. "I'm blowed if I know where to turn to next. I wish the Chief would take my advice and call in Scotland Yard. But you know what he is. He said he'd rather have a few murders than have those blighters nosing round in his area…"

"Good for uncle! I say. Miss Delfinage has got rather a bright theory. You know Constant?"

"Constant? Oh, of course, he's the legatee. What about it?"

"She thinks he did it. You know Marabout saw a bearded fellow come out of the garage the day before the murder; and then the same fellow was wandering round there next day just before the time of the fire. Well, the only bearded fellow on the Estate is that old billy-goat Overture; but Constant *has* got a beard. Of course it's a bit fantastic."

"This Delfinage girl seems to do more detecting on that con-founded Estate than all our constabulary put together," commented the Inspector peevishly. "Still it is a good idea, and worth following up. Look here, Sadler. Run up to town to-morrow; have another interview with Constant, and find what he was doing at the material times. You'll find him quite an affable bird."

He was. In fact he roared with laughter when Laurence, as he thought very airily and subtly, hinted at the value of knowing the movements on the day of the murder of everyone who knew the victim. Before he got as far as explaining his carefully thought-out reasons for this, Constant had exploded.

"How priceless! So the police think I did poor old Mullins in. Don't look embarrassed. I absolutely agree with you. I'm the ideal murderer. My Society—and therefore I as its highly paid secretary—stands to gain more than anyone else by the murder. Also I've the cold and calculating scientific mind. What more could you want? Unfortunately, old chap, I was in my office all day!" He rung the bell on his desk. A bored-looking young man came in.

"Binns, this is Mr. Sadler, of the Police. As a matter of form he wants to check up my movements on the day of poor Mullins' sudden death. Will you give him full facilities to question the staff?"

Laurence did so. It appeared that at ten minutes to one, or possibly earlier, certainly before one, Constant had arrived at the office apologizing for his lateness. There was a considerable accumulation of work to deal with, and Constant had in fact been in the office, without going out for lunch (he had sent out for some sandwiches), until six that evening. His staff had been in and out of his room most of the time, and it was absolutely impossible, in view of their evidence, to suppose that he had left it between the time he arrived and the time he left.

"Sorry to disappoint you," Constant said when Laurence came to thank him. They were alone. Constant's eyes gleamed cruelly for a moment behind their glasses, and his great beak of a nose suddenly seemed menacing as he leaned nearer to Sadler. "Try looking a little nearer home," he whispered. Then the curtain was dropped as suddenly as it had been raised and he laughed. "You may discover a hole in my alibi yet, young man. I have a very devoted staff who might easily be rehearsing a prearranged story."

Laurence, however, expressed to Trenton his scepticism of finding the hole. "He's safe. Of course theoretically he might have waited for Mullins in Mullins' car—their offices are near together—shot him, and had an accomplice ready to drive the body out to Great Hake to pop it in the garage before the time-switch went off. Then he could stroll casually into his office before one o'clock all right. I think we can dismiss that, however. One doesn't have accomplices in this country in a premeditated murder; it is not exactly easy to murder people in the middle of the day in Westminster; and—apart from using an accomplice—it is not possible to murder a man at Great Hake who has left Westminster at twelve-thirty and be back in one's office before one."

Trenton agreed dismally. "I'm inclined to go back to the theory I formed when I first heard about this bearded blighter wandering round the garage. I think it was the murderer all right, but I think the beard was a false one, intended to disguise him should he meet anyone. A fairly obvious precaution after all. It suggests that the murderer was someone well known on the Estate, but of course that does not inevitably follow. He may only have been thinking of avoiding possible identification at a later date."

Chapter Eight

AN ALIBI IS SHAKEN

Laurence Sadler was peremptorily called to the bedside of his suffering superior, Inspector Trenton. Trenton, in a white tie and tails, had been investigating one of the notorious riverside haunts of Great Hake. Here, "from information received," he had reason to suppose" that drinks were being provided after licensing hours. Both his wife and he had agreed that he looked very gentlemanly in the smartest cut of a Peppering tailor.

At the "Yellow Sunshade," a charming young creature in modest black had made advances towards him, which in the course of his duty he had accepted. They were both sitting side by side in a punt moored to the river frontage of the establishment, at a quarter to one in the night, when the young person had asked him whether he would like a drink. Concealing his inward elation, the devoted man had agreed. Unfortunately, as soon as she reached the bank, there had been a loud cry of "Take a drink of this, you —— copper!" and unidentifiable helpers had overturned the punt and abandoned the Inspector, gasping, in the water.

The result, apart from ruined evening dress, had been a heavy cold, which prevented the Inspector speaking, except in a tomb-like whisper. Obviously this was no voice with which to elicit statements, and he was compelled, therefore, to let Laurence interview Mrs. Mullins.

The ducking had made him cynical about the female kind. "She's a plausible, pathetic sort of body," he warned Laurence, "and those are the most brazen liars of the lot."

Patricia Mullins smiled pleasantly, but surely not seductively, at Laurence. She seemed, in fact, preoccupied. "You're rather younger than I expected," she said. "I've seen you before, but then, of course, you had your helmet on. Perhaps it was that."

"That, of course, is one of the uses of the helmet. It also breaks the force of the bandit's blow, pacifies lost children, intimidates hooligans, and provides a convenient space above the crown of the head for stowing small articles. The latter is not encouraged by the authorities..."

Laurence pulled himself up. "H'm. In the matter of this business. You will realize that we have to make a few more inquiries to establish the movements of the principal actors. You will guess this is only formal by the fact that I am making the inquiries." He grinned deprecatingly.

Mrs. Mullins laughed delightedly. "Are you a serious policeman? Excuse me; but you remind me irresistibly of a revue I saw. Don't be offended, the comparison is more complimentary than it sounds."

Laurence endeavoured to look annoyed, but the smile in Patricia's eyes was dangerously infectious. "Ronald Vernon, the young policeman hero of *Time for Another*," he said bitterly. "I know, you're not the first."

He was unable to prevent himself adding: "The matter I have come on is fairly serious."

The smile died at once from her eyes, and she regarded him with composure. "There are not many minutes of the day in which I forget that. What is it you want to ask me?"

"Exactly what did you do from the time your husband left you that morning?"

"He left me at nine. He went, so far as I know, straight from the breakfast table to the garage. At any rate, he said he was going there. I sat at the table for a few minutes, and then the housekeeper came in and we went over the housekeeping books."

"For how long?"

"For about half an hour. Then I went upstairs and changed. That would take about half an hour. I then went out for a stroll with Tango, my Bedlington, you know. I was back before eleven. I read for some time, and I know it was five minutes past eleven when Mr. Filson came to work on my portrait in the North Room."

"Where is that?"

"Beside the tower. It is the other side of the building from the rooms we live in, but it has the ideal light for painting. As a matter of fact, we gave Mr. Filson permission to use it whenever he liked. He said he would earn the favour by painting me, and that was how the portrait began. When he arrived we went at once to the North Room and got on with the portrait. Mr. Filson was in good form, and we worked steadily, until I said that not being inspired I simply must have some lunch, so I rang the bell for some food to be brought in and we had it. Then we heard shouts, and we went outside to see what it was, and found the garage on fire."

"Can anyone else confirm your story, besides, of course, Mr. Filson?"

She did not resent the question. "Bridget let Mr. Filson in and out, and also brought in lunch to us. I'll ring for her."

He raised his hand. "In a moment, Mrs. Mullins, if you please. I should like to look at the North Room first, if I may."

They went down a long corridor dreary with the sort of oil paintings one finds in long corridors. The North Room, cold in its sunless light, contained the usual impedimenta of an artist's studio. He walked up to an easel and pulled off the cloth covering the canvas. "This, I suppose, is the portrait."

Then he turned and looked at her keenly. "Not a very fast worker, is he?"

Not a single brush of paint had been put on the canvas. A few rapid strokes of charcoal outlined a sketch of Mrs. Mullins, in which her eyes were almond-shaped and gleamed with the malevolence of modern art. This was the preliminary groundwork for the painting. It had obviously been sketched at a sitting, by an artist who had suddenly been inspired by a striking aspect of his sitter. Laurence found it difficult to believe that any painter could take two hours over it. It was essentially the thing an artist, in a sudden white heat, would dash off and, the virtue gone out of him, say radiantly to his sitter: "We've made a splendid start. Come back to-morrow."

Mrs. Mullins read something of the sort in his eyes. "He doesn't work very quickly. Of course he only started the portrait that day, and naturally I've been too upset to sit for it since."

Laurence followed her thoughtfully to the sitting-room again. "Shall I ring for Bridget now?" she said.

"Does Bridget dress you?"

She looked at him with a faint uneasiness. "Of course not; Bridget is a parlourmaid. Simpson looks after my things."

"I should like to speak to Simpson. Do you mind?"

"It is not the sort of request one can, in fact, refuse, is it?"

While the maid was being sent for, Laurence spoke again. "You, of course, realize that when I report to my superiors the result of any statements I take from your servants, they will naturally want to be assured that they were completely uninfluenced."

She looked at him scornfully. "I understand. Why not see her alone?"

"Please remain. I don't think either of us need be afraid of the result of what I am going to ask."

She handed Simpson over to Laurence with a brief sentence.

He endeavoured to reassure the maid. "The fact is, your mistress and I have had a little argument as to whether my memory is better than hers. It is about the dress she was wearing when this dreadful thing happened to your master. Of course I saw her near the garage, but she tells me that I was wrong in what I thought she was wearing." He leaned forward confidingly. "Now you can imagine that it wouldn't do me any good in my job if it was found I was wrong in my memory of what happened on an important occasion like that, so your mistress has suggested we settle it for good and all. Do you remember what dress she was wearing?"

Simpson's frank face looked pleased. "Of course I can remember. Why, I could lay my hands on it this moment."

"Splendid. Can you bring it here?"

In the pause that followed Simpson's departure, Mrs. Mullins looked at him coldly. "You must have a remarkable memory. I have completely forgotten what dress I wore on that day. And can it really be important? Or was it merely a gesture to impress?"

He returned her glance gravely. "Neither have I the faintest recollection of what you wore. Yet such things are sometimes important, and this may be more important than either of us yet realize."

Simpson returned with the dress. Laurence took it, looked at it closely, and then returned it with a smile. "I am wrong, I thought the dress she was wearing was—" and he described in his blundering, masculine way the dress Mrs. Mullins wore in the sketch he had just seen in the North Room.

"You certainly are wrong, Mr. Sadler," giggled Simpson. "Madam gave me that dress some time ago. Why, I wore it my evening out just before the fire."

"Thank you, Simpson. That will be all."

The purpose of his questioning was now plain, but as Laurence met Mrs. Mullins' eyes when the door shut on Simpson, she refused to allow them to show any knowledge of his drift. "Would you like to question Bridget?" she asked, with utter coldness.

"Bridget," he repeated. "Irish, I suppose. May I ask if she was your maid before you were married?"

"She was. She came to me from my mother's house in Ireland."

"Exactly. Mrs. Mullins, when a person is certain to tell you a lie, it is a mistake to question them. Whatever they answer then, they generally determine to stick to through thick and thin, and that can cause trouble in a witness-box. So it is better, you understand, to leave questioning till you suppose the witness to be in a more reasonable frame of mind. I will see Bridget, if I may, on a later visit."

She flushed. "Are you being purposely offensive? Or is it that men in your position are automatically relieved of the need for courtesy towards women?"

"I think, Mrs. Mullins," he said wearily, "if you reflect, you will see I might now retort in almost exactly the same form of words. And should we be any farther? When I asked Simpson to produce the dress you were wearing on that day, I had every belief that she would produce the dress you wear in that sketch in the North Room. I see you look incredulous. I read the incident of the portrait thus. I thought, 'Mrs. Mullins must have seen at first glance that the portrait does not appear to account for two hours' hard work. Yet for some reason suppose it did. Suppose the artist was talking most of the time. It would have been the easiest thing in the world to get him to do more work on it later. Instead of which, because she was absolutely honest, perhaps she let it stand there, and scorned to tell anything but the truth.' Somewhat foolishly, but because my business is not to throw suspicion on anyone but to find out the truth, I brought up the matter of the dress, believing it would be an independent witness to the truth of your story. In fact it proved that the story was a fabrication. Had I guessed that would be the result, I would have seen Simpson privately, for by seeing her in your presence you know now as much as I do."

He looked at her keenly. "I wonder if you believe me—that I never guessed, till just now, that the story Bridget will tell me if I ask her, and the story you have told me, is—not honest?"

She did not reply to his question directly. There was no scorn in her face now, only a kind of wonder. "What do you think now?"

He looked genuinely perplexed. "I have not learned to distrust my judgment yet. I should have said that you were the last woman to make up an ingenious little story to get you out of a difficulty. Particularly," he added meaningly, "a minor difficulty."

She returned his look gravely. "I thought I was not that kind of woman too. And yet..." She hesitated on the verge of giving him her confidence.

"And yet, Mrs. Mullins?"

She rose abruptly. "It's no good." Her voice was suddenly cold. "You have heard my story and, I suppose, taken it down. I do not wish to change it in any way. Good morning."

He found himself walking down The Turrets drive, completely puzzled. The sensation, though painful, was probably good for him.

Chapter Nine

PUZZLE OF A PUGILIST

Inspector Trenton was still snuffling in bed when his assistant was stopped by a peremptory umbrella, placed across his path as he strolled down Oak Avenue (formerly Bog Lane). The umbrella was wielded by Mrs. Murples.

"Young man in a hurry," she said, in her crisp clear voice, "your chin is swollen!"

Laurence looked at her. She reminded him at the moment of a pre-dynastic mummy, with a wrinkled, dark monkey face and preposterously scant grey hair. Swaying slightly with suppressed laughter, she put both hands on her umbrella, which was a large and masculine one, evidently used as a stick, and regarded him mockingly.

"I walked into something in the dark," he said crossly.

She hooted with laughter. "I should think you did! One of the smartest uppercuts I've ever seen, I should imagine, from the look of it. Just like a dream, I expect, wasn't it?"

"I don't quite follow you, Mrs. Murples."

She wagged the point of her umbrella six inches under the nose of the irritated young policeman.

"Can you see that?"

"I can."

"Well, young man, if you can see that, you ought to be able to guess what hit you." She relapsed into laughter again. "So you tried to get the better of the Battling Bantam, did you? I'm glad he socked you. You ought to know better than to leap on to pugilists in the dark at your age, my boy. If you really want to try yourself against the Bantam—welter weight though you are—come round to the gym to-morrow, about eleven!"

Speechless for the moment, Laurence stared at her, but Mrs. Murples was now waving vigorously with her umbrella at a white-sweatered figure in the distance, whom he recognized as the Bantam's trainer.

"Wait for me before you start," she squawked, and rapidly trotted towards him.

It was only because other duties detained him that Laurence did not turn up earlier than eleven next morning to follow Mrs. Murples' hint. For Laurence was kept busy enough, even though his new position as Trenton's personal assistant in the Mullins investigation carried with it temporary release from such hum-drum duties as beat-pacing, following up defaulting dog and wireless licencees, and controlling traffic. There was the matter of the bullet which had shot Mullins, for instance. The Home Office firearms expert had reported on it, not very helpfully. He had been able to suggest at once the type of revolver from which it came, or rather the six possible types. Unfortunately, as he told Trenton at the same time that these particular types accounted for about fifty per cent of the total revolver sales in this country, the information was not so useful as it might be. However, Laurence was slowly working through the local shops, with their records of the names of recent purchasers of firearms, in the hope that one of the names might be in some way linked with the chief suspects in the murder.

His thoughts were on firearms therefore as he strolled slowly up the side path to the New House—a disgustingly ugly mansion which Mrs. Murples had fitted with every convenience likely to appeal to boxers, from swimming-pools, gymnasiums and punch-balls to a billiards-room. He wouldn't, reflected Laurence gloom-ily, even be offered a drink, since it was common knowledge that

Mrs. Murples domineered ruthlessly over the boxers she backed financially, and permitted no alcohol to pass the threshold when training was in progress.

When Laurence arrived the Battling Bantam was toying with an equally small sparring partner in an open-air ring. Mrs. Murples, seated comfortably in a high-winged chair near one corner of the ring and swathed in innumerable fur rugs, was recording points on a small pad in her lap. As Laurence approached from behind she seized a megaphone.

"Footwork, Battler!" she shrieked down it. "Where's your footwork? We know you haven't any brains in your head, but why aren't there some in your legs? Dance! Balance yourself! Think with your toes!"

She grunted in exasperation as Norris, the sparring partner, tapped the Battler playfully on the nose.

"Wallop him, man, wallop him! Imagine he's pinched your best girl. (He probably has, by the way.) Wake him up."

"That's right!" she yelled, as Norris succeeded in getting a fast one in over his opponent's heart. A wicked look came into the Battler's eye.

"Go on now, Battler!" she shrieked. "Wipe the floor with him! Tear him up! That's what we pay him for! Damn, that's two minutes," and she seized a hand-bell which stood near her and shook it vigorously.

Both combatants climbed through the ropes and stood before her while she gave an incisive lecture on boxing which Laurence (in spite of his instinctive dislike of the wizened little creature) was forced to admit was masterly. The Battler endeavoured to give it his full attention, but his eyes returned uneasily to Laurence, only to switch them away instantly when Laurence returned the gaze.

The Battling Bantam, born Montague Tompkins, seemed a well-meaning if not particularly bright specimen of potted muscularity.

There was no doubt he was visibly disturbed about something, and Mrs. Murples watched his embarrassment with a grin.

"You'll have to have it out, you two," she said imperiously, waving Laurence forward.

"Look 'ere," said the Battler dismally, "you didn't ought to have told him what I told you. Gawd knows what sort of trouble you'll get me into. I think——"

"You never have been and never will be capable of thinking, Battler," interrupted Mrs. Murples peremptorily. "Your nerves are on edge about this nonsense, and you'll have to settle it with Mr. Sadler before your fight comes off. I'll go bail if there's any trouble. They won't put you in prison before the fight anyway."

"Ow, I say," whined the pugilist.

She ignored him and addressed Laurence. "What was it all about? As far as I can make out, the Battler was strolling down this path towards Oak Avenue when suddenly he heard a gun go off. He thought somebody was shooting nearby, and as he didn't wish to be mistaken for a rabbit, he stayed still. Then something came charging towards him, and the Battler having about as much courage as a two-year-old in the dark—don't look sulky, Battler, you know it's perfectly true—started to run in the opposite direction. Then he was seized. He naturally enough defended himself and laid his attacker out. A neat uppercut to the point, and a jab on the jowl as you were falling just to complete it. Of course when he found out he'd hit a policeman he lost his nerve and didn't want to say anything about it. However, I can't have him worrying just before a big match and getting his nerves on edge, so you must settle the whole thing one way or the other."

Sadler interrogated the pugilist, but he stuck closely to his story. What was Laurence to do? Quite likely the story was true. There seemed no earthly object in the Battler taking pot-shots at him.

However, a little investigation about the possession or otherwise of firearms, if made discreetly among the staff of the New House, might be useful and bear fruit. It would also be as well to make some inquiries about the pugilist's movements on the day of the murder, just in case. Meanwhile the last thing to do was to alarm him, the more so if he were implicated.

On the whole Laurence felt inclined to believe that the Bantam was not responsible for the shot. At the same time he took the liberty of doubting the boxer's story of his aimless stroll down the path. It was, after all, possible to suppose that the boxer, for some guilty reason, was spying on him without any lethal intent.

He said some reassuring words, not unmixed with reproof, and left the trio.

"Good-bye, young man," hooted Mrs. Murples, as he strolled away. "And don't walk into anything again in the dark! And don't you laugh, Battler, either. You'd have walked into Norris's fist twice this morning if he'd taken the opportunities you gave him. Come on now, another round, and remember those are feet on the end of your legs, not turnips. Shake them and see."

As Laurence strode back up the path, with the stately tread that he had acquired after two years of assiduous practice, his thoughts were still running on firearms. Should one be able to tell the sound of a revolver from other weapons, for instance? Or did all small arms sound much the same? An obvious thing a criminal investigator ought to know. So immersed was he on the subject that he realized, with a start, that his eyes had been resting on a revolver in the path in front of him for at least three seconds without the fact registering. He bent down and picked it up.

Yes, this was one of the six types that the Home Office expert had pointed to in his little museum as possibly responsible for the bullet in the dead man's head. He looked at it thoughtfully. Odd. He didn't remember looking closely at the path as he came down it, but could he possibly have missed such a thing; slap bang in the middle of the path? Could anyone else have missed it? Yet the path was constantly in use. He was holding it reverently by the extreme muzzle—finger-prints were possible—and so holding it, he went back to the police station in Peppering deep in thought.

I I

The proving of Mullins' extraordinary will had aroused universal discussion. Naturally comment in the daily press was restricted by the penalties of libel, but those of slander did not prevent gossip, and gossip led to speculation so widespread that it stung the Chief Constable to action.

"Just like that fool Trenton to go and get ill. Think how damned silly it sounds! 'How is the investigation going on, Chief Constable?' 'Unfortunately, sir or madam, our detective has caught a cold.' 'About the only thing he can catch apparently, ha, ha!'"

Laurence gave him a brief résumé of the progress of the investigations. The result of the interview with Mrs. Mullins made his uncle jubilant. "I always knew it was that woman. Get the truth out of her!"

"It's all very well, but you know what our limitations are. We've got to be confoundedly careful about interrogating her, particularly as with that will published she is for all practical purposes suspect No. 1."

"What do you propose to do then?"

"Try and get some slants on it from other angles first. I doubt very much, in fact I'm certain, she didn't do it—alone, at any rate. I mean no woman would fix up the time-switch and so forth. It needs a mechanically minded person, and whereas most men would be capable of evolving it, not one woman in a thousand would think along those lines. It would be poison every time."

"I don't care. She's a liar, and that means you must keep on her track. Obviously this Filson man is her accomplice. Why, the fellow's an artist."

Laurence would have liked to quarrel with the word "liar," but didn't see how he could. After all, she *had* lied, demonstrably.

"One suspects the Filson fellow, of course. He's the obvious line. But I want to get a little more on him. Miss Delfinage—"

His uncle snorted. "The girl again! It seems to me you do all your investigation in 'Epsom' or whatever the place is called."

Laurence ignored the remark. "Miss Delfinage can probably tell me the worst about him. She dislikes him heartily."

"H'm, what's this extraordinary story Trenton told me about people potting at you from hedges?"

Laurence told him.

"Well, no offence to you; but I shouldn't be surprised if the whole thing's a mare's nest. Probably some bloke doing a bit of quiet poaching and not even knowing you were there. Then you leap into the woods and grab this pug, and the fat's in the fire. You must expect an occasional pot-shot anyway," he added cheerfully. "By Jove, in India beggars were shooting at us every time we put our heads out of the window. They never hit you except by accident. Hand dithers so much, you know."

"They managed to hit Mullins," replied Laurence grimly. He decided to tell his uncle nothing about the revolver found on the path. For, at the moment, he was a little puzzled by it.

When he got to the police station again he found an anonymous note in the post for him. Scrawled on a sheet of paper in big block capitals were the following words:

"Where's the pistol that shot Mullins, Mr. Detective? Try looking near home. What about Mrs. Murples' grounds, for instance? Not, of course, that it means anything if it is found there, but still it is a bit odd, isn't it, that the Battling Bantam should be always hanging round The Turrets?

"NOSEY."

"Nosey," repeated Laurence. "I shouldn't mind making a guess at who Nosey is."

Chapter Ten

ARGUMENT WITH AN ARTIST

Three days after the will was proved Samson received a letter from Holliday written on the note-paper of a Madrid hotel. It was brief.

> "Sorry to hear of the old man's death. Ought I to come home? I can hardly pretend to be the dutiful nephew after he's cut me out of his will; and I am on to some big possibilities here, if only the Ministry isn't turned out again. Anyway, if you think I ought to come back, put in a small ad. in *La Libertad* in the next few days.
> "R. HOLLIDAY."

Samson saw no reason for recalling Holliday. It was notorious that their Spanish agent was *persona non grata* with the republic, and it would be excellent business if Holliday could establish fresh contacts.

Trenton, however, very much wanted to see Holliday, for he still felt he might be able to throw light upon Mullins' last movements.

Samson proved unexpectedly obstinate. "If you want to see him, put an advertisement in yourself. I'm not going to bring him home for your convenience. It's to the firm's interest for him to stay where he is."

Trenton therefore advertised as follows:

> "R.H. Would like to see you in official capacity for interview *re* Mullins. You could give us valuable help. Any time or place.—
> INSPECTOR TRENTON."

To this advertisement no reply was received.

Meanwhile, Laurence asked, oughtn't they to wipe Holliday off their books altogether as a suspect? His alibi was cast-iron. Moreover, instead of rushing home to Patricia Mullins as soon as Mullins was out of the way, which was what one would expect if half the scandal talked about them was true, he had remained in Spain pegging away at the firm's business. Moreover, all Mrs. Mullins' correspondence had been surreptitiously opened since the day after the murder, yet there had been no trace of a communication from Holliday. All of which went to show that he had acted and was acting perfectly honourably.

At the same time, Trenton replied, there was something in itself almost suspicious in so clear a suspect being able to produce so perfect an alibi. But this was not very helpful.

I I

Trenton had given Laurence latitude to follow up any immediate developments on the Estate, and Laurence felt he could consider himself entitled to a little more probing into the matter of the revolver and the anonymous note, to say nothing of the midnight assault. Of course it might be that they were in no way related; but he thought otherwise.

By now they had obtained a list of all the persons whose names were recorded as purchasers of firearms from shops at Peppering, Great Hake, and the local market town of Queensbridge. Now it was not without interest that two of the dwellers of Fairview Estate were in this list. What is more, they were purchasers of revolvers of the pattern which he had picked up in Mrs. Murples' grounds.

The names were—George Eyton and Francis Filson.

Of course this meant nothing in the way of direct evidence; perhaps it went the other way. Surely no intelligent murderer would use a weapon which could be so easily traced to him. Yet if the subsequent fate of these two weapons could be accurately traced, it might throw some light on the circumstances of the murder.

The artist was in when Laurence knocked on the bright blue door of "One," and himself flung open the door. "Oh, it's you, is it!" he said shortly. "This murder business, I suppose. Come in."

They went into a room furnished with horsehair chairs and sofa, a table covered with a plum-red plush tablecloth, a much-flowered carpet, and an ornamental gilt clock. Filson saw the policeman's eyes rest on the various outrages.

"Horrible, isn't it?" He glowered round him. "I find it acts as a stimulant. One hour of sitting in this room, and I rush out and work like a slave at painting."

"I saw your portrait of Mrs. Mullins at The Turrets," said Laurence conversationally.

"Oh, that's just a rough sketch, you know. The idea came suddenly, as it does, but things have been so upset, I've never really been able to start it again."

"Indeed?"

The young man's strong face became suddenly overcast. "Of course there's a good deal of work in that sketch."

"Really?"

"Yes. By Jove, we were doing it while poor old Mullins was being killed. Awful, isn't it?"

"Awful, if it were so."

"What the devil do you mean?"

"Merely that he *might* have been killed at some other time, after all. We can never be certain of a thing like that." The policeman's tone was casual.

Filson's eyes were fixed closely on his face. "I still don't see where the doubt is. Mullins left town at twelve-thirty. He was found dead at three. He couldn't have got to the Estate from town before half-past one. So I don't see how there can be doubt as to when he died."

"There is always doubt about anything that is not actually seen by a trustworthy witness," said Laurence gravely.

The other gave an exclamation of disgust.

"Just to show how uncertain evidence is," went on Laurence, ignoring Filson's snort, "can you tell me the dress Mrs. Mullins is wearing in your sketch?"

"Certainly." Filson described it accurately.

"Thank you," said Laurence amiably. "That, I think, indicates the vagaries of the human mind. For in this brief sketch that you made during your two hours, you drew with complete accuracy a dress your sitter was not only not wearing, but had given away some time before. I see you want to say something. No doubt you will tell me that you were painting from memory. Incidentally, I am rather puzzled to find that Mrs. Mullins has not put you on your guard against this particular trap. I fully expected to meet an ingenious excuse."

Filson got up. His face was purple with passion. "What the devil do you think you are? Do you suggest that both Mrs. Mullins and I are lying?"

"I suggest nothing," answered Laurence pleasantly. "I cannot help it, however, if things suggest themselves. By the way, have you ever seen this before?" He produced the revolver.

The artist looked at it. His tongue shot out and caressed his lips. But his answer was elaborately careless. "Never. I say, is that the weapon which did the trick?"

Laurence looked him straight in the eye. "Good Lord, no!" He answered as innocently.

The other's face bore an expression of increasing wariness.

Laurence balanced the revolver in his hand. "You haven't answered my question. Have you ever seen this revolver before?"

"Never."

"Sure?"

"Certain."

There was a pause.

"Can I see the revolver you bought from Parsons in Queensbridge on August 8th of this year?"

Behind Filson's watchful gaze, Laurence now felt sure he could detect a trace of apprehension.

"I—that was stolen some time ago. I forget exactly when."

"Really. You reported the loss to the police?"

"No. I didn't think it worth while."

"How was it stolen?"

"Eh?"

"I mean, in what circumstances?"

"Oh, it just—vanished."

"No suspicions?"

"No. None. I left it about rather carelessly, I am afraid."

"Did you have a licence for it?"

"I'm afraid not. I suppose I am liable to be fined?"

Laurence made no reply. "Did you send me this?" he asked suddenly, thrusting forward the anonymous letter.

Filson took it and read it slowly. Then he returned it. "This is simply silly. Do you really think I should send you such piffle?"

"I asked you the question, Mr. Filson."

"No. Of course not."

Laurence sighed. "I am afraid your attitude is not going to be very helpful to yourself or to Mrs. Mullins. We have had a man at the local post office ever since the murder, and naturally if certain persons post a letter we go through the contents of the box to find out what letter they have posted. By a process of elimination it is fairly easy to find, as it must be among the letters lying on the top of the pile."

There was an undoubted look of apprehension now in Filson's face, but he made no physical movement betraying his confusion, and remained silent.

Laurence again reverted to the revolver. "What distinguishes this from the revolver you lost?"

"What do you mean?"

"Surely you know it is exactly the same pattern as the one you lost?"

Filson's smouldering eyes turned slowly to the object. "Even if it is, what then?"

"Exactly the same type; yet you know it is not yours at once. So I ask you, what is the distinguishing mark?"

"I know it isn't mine. Isn't that enough?"

"Nothing more, Mr. Filson?"

"Nothing, confound you!"

Laurence put the revolver away with a smile. He drew out his note-book and glanced at a page. Then he looked up. "What were you doing in the garage at half-past one on the day of the murder?"

"What nonsense are you talking? I have already told you where I was at that time. I suppose these are the police methods of questioning one reads so much about."

Laurence smiled. "Of course, you were sketching Mrs. Mullins at that time. Yet someone is ready to swear he saw you leaving the garage at half-past one."

Filson's lips curled in scorn. "The usual police trap! Well, I don't fall for it."

Laurence shook his head. "You are wrong, Mr. Filson. Someone saw you leaving the garage and I have his evidence here. However, you have made your attitude quite plain." He snapped the band on to his note-book and rose to go. "Someone was seen to leave the garage at half-past one. Someone, long after the murder, threw this revolver into Mrs. Murples' garden. Someone sent me an anonymous letter telling me where the revolver was to be found." He paused. The other's eyes were fixed burningly on him. "Someone perhaps (but so far we are not certain) had a motive for murdering Mullins. When we are sure of that we shall have a complete story and—"

"And?" the other sneered.

"And then we shall want to speak to you again, Mr. Filson."

As Laurence went the artist was standing in front of the mantel-piece. His hands were thrust into the pockets of his paint-smeared flannel trousers, and Laurence suddenly realized the strength latent in those powerful shoulders. But it was the face that puzzled him. It was sulky, angry, worried; yet, for a moment Laurence thought, it was almost like the expression of a furious schoolboy rather than of a dangerous man.

Filson thrust back his dishevelled hair from his forehead with an angry gesture. "I can give you any motive you want right now," he said defiantly. "Mullins was an unmitigated swine. And every man on this Estate who met him knows that."

III

The Mullins inquest was conducted by Dr. Heckmondwike, who thus obtained his first opportunity to figure prominently in the Press since his tenure of office as Coroner for the County Borough of Queensbridge had begun.

The police brought forward as evidence only the following: That Mullins was seen alive at 12.30 p.m. in London, and found dead on Fairview Estate at 3 p.m. of the same day. That death was due to a bullet wound. That the door of the garage was locked and the key missing when he was found dead. They desired a verdict of "Murder by a Person or Persons Unknown." This evidence, they felt, would be sufficient to procure it.

It wasn't. On the second morning Dr. Heckmondwike came into court with an expression of foxlike cunning on his wrinkled face. Inspector Trenton, who had seen it before, groaned.

"Inspector Trenton!" said the Coroner. "I understand that the body was too charred for the medical evidence to ascertain whether or no the wound was such as to be self-inflicted."

"That is so."

"Is there any reason why the wound should not have been self-inflicted?"

"Yes. We were unable to find either the key of the garage or the weapon, although the garage was locked when the body was found," answered the Inspector wonderingly.

Dr. Heckmondwike's head went forward on its rubbery neck. "Indeed, Inspector, and what is to prevent somebody going in, finding the body—for reasons of his own deciding to conceal the suicide—removing the weapon and the key from the dead man, setting fire to the garage, and locking the door as he went out?"

Laurence, in the well of the court, could barely refrain from laughing aloud at the Inspector's chagrined face. "It is possible, of course, sir; but it is unlikely."

"I am the judge of that," said the Coroner nastily. "Have you endeavoured to trace the key of the garage?"

"We have," said the Inspector, "without success."

"Thank you. Stand down, Inspector."

Dr. Heckmondwike, who was sitting without a jury, returned an open verdict.

Chapter Eleven

EVIDENCE OF A DIABOLIST

W hen, next day, Laurence met Dr. Marabout mooning gently at the end of his garden, he remembered that it was, after all, Dr. Marabout's description of a short, stocky man coming out of the garage which had made him, at a venture, accuse Filson of being there at the material time. Marabout, as he watched him, pulled up a plant and carefully shook the earth from its roots.

He greeted the savant with a smile. "A new herb?" he asked.

"Dittany," answered the other gravely. "It used to be eaten by deer when pierced by an arrow, as it caused the arrow to fall out. Do you think it would have the same effect with bullets?"

"Frankly, no."

"Neither do I," replied the other unexpectedly. He placed the plant in his capacious side pocket, which was already bulging. "By the way, I saw you speaking to Mrs. Murples. What did the old woman want?"

Laurence laughed. "Oh, nothing much!"

"Nothing about a person attempting to shoot you in the dark?"

Laurence started. "What made you ask that?"

"Come inside and perhaps I can tell you something." They went through the door of "Trismegistus," its lintel protected by a horse-shoe and a pentacle, straight into the library, with its thousands of dusty calf-bound quartos and folios.

Marabout motioned him to a chair. His eyes were enigmatic as he looked calmly at Laurence.

"You think that because I happen to follow purely rational processes in my evaluation of evidence I am a dreamer. Young man, you make a great mistake. You of the new generation have tried to fit the world into a preconceived plan. I do not. I assume it will follow the plan recorded by the countless millions of our forefathers. It is a mad world; and only madmen expect it to behave according to reason. Reasonable creatures like myself expect it to behave *sui generis*. Therefore we are not surprised at the hourly petty triumphs of evil, at the shifting of shapes, at the malignity of hate, at the power of herbs and words, at sudden death!" He folded his hands and nodded.

Laurence shifted restively in his chair. "No doubt all this is true. At the moment, however, I am interested in nothing but evidence. You know something about the attack on me? What is it?" He smiled. "Did you see it in a crystal?"

The other scowled. "Even in jest do not suggest that I engage in the infernal practice of reading the future." He said sternly, "Have you read your *Macbeth*, Mr. Sadler? That is the wisest thing ever written about fortune-telling. No, I saw it with my eyes, leaning out of my window in the evening!"

"What did you see?"

Marabout hesitated. "The light was dim, but I feel fairly certain of what took place. I saw Lord Overture sitting on the branch of a tree. He leaned out and shot at you with a two-barrelled shot-gun."

"I say you know," Laurence expostulated, "Lord Overture! Why, he took me into the lodge?"

"Certainly," answered the other calmly. "I watched you chase some strange shape. Whether it was human or supernatural I could not see in the dusk. You fell. Lord Overture got down the tree very quickly, went into the lodge without the gun, came out a moment later with his servant, and they both dragged you in."

Laurence was amazed. There was a verisimilitude about the account which almost certainly rang true. And after all, "Trismegistus" was the nearest house to the scene of the occurrence.

The doctor smiled complacently. "Did you arrest Filson, by the way?"

This time Laurence was really startled. He began to feel there was something genuinely eerie about this creature, in spite of his spells and his dried alligators. "What on earth made you think I would?"

Marabout lifted one eyebrow quizzically and drew Laurence to the window. "You see that path there. It is the back path leading to Mrs. Murples' house. One of these days I shall see her come snuffling down there on all fours, rub herself against that tree, and change into human shape. The second time she comes along there I shall shoot her before the change takes place. If only I can produce a dead werwolf my arguments will at least be accepted by this unbelieving and yet credulous generation. As I was watching this path the other day, I saw Filson, with a guilty air, throw a revolver down. A little later I saw you pick it up. The inference was natural, but I hope not justified in the event?"

"Can you swear to that?" Laurence asked jubilantly.

"Certainly."

"By Jove, that makes my case."

The doctor regarded him for a moment under his shaggy eyebrows. "You mustn't arrest him!" he said with finality.

"Why on earth not?"

"Do you really want to know?"

Laurence smiled. "Of course!"

For the first time Laurence realized that Dr. Marabout had hitherto been evading his direct gaze. Now he looked Laurence directly in the eyes, and they were piercing eyes, chilled with knowledge. They gave Laurence almost the feeling of a physical shock.

The doctor spoke coldly and clearly. "Can't you realize the sort of man Filson is? Then I will tell you. He is nothing but a boy who plays at life. He plays at being an artist. He plays at being in love.

He plays at experiencing all the dangerous and vicious emotions. But it is only play. Such a man will experience everything but reality. He cannot kill."

Dr. Marabout tapped on the table in his urgency. "Listen! You think he is in love with Patricia Mullins. But he is playing at that too. I tell you, until you understand that woman, you will never lay your hands on the central knot of this crime. I sometimes think of her as the most dangerous woman I have met. Oh, if only you young men would read your story-books, which tell us all we need to know about human beings. For human beings do not change, and men have written and spoken about each other for fifty thousand years. You have heard of Deirdre, whom all men loved. Mrs. Mullins is a Deirdre. And I will tell you the truth about Deirdre. She is the eternal romantic illusion. She is the women every man *thinks* he is in love with. And that is the most dangerous kind of love. Why? Because when a man and woman are really in love illusion vanishes, and they know each other as they really are, and do not mind. But when a man thinks he is in love, he is really in love with the dreams of a hundred generations, with all the huge and terrible things that have been written and spoken about love. Because of that illusion he will believe anything but the truth. Now there are six men who of my own knowledge are and have been in love with that woman"—once again his piercing gaze fell upon his hearer—"and by heaven, young man, you are the seventh!"

Laurence was unable to help himself smiling. "I say, you know, as a poet you are magnificent, but I'm afraid I can't agree with your psychology. I admire Mrs. Mullins certainly. But as for being in love, no. Aren't you forgetting I'm only the village policeman?"

The doctor shook his head. "Remember my words. If ever you find I am right, remember this. That woman is so dangerous because of her generosity. Watch her mouth. I know nothing about the detection of crime, but I tell you this: you are a fool if you are only looking for alibis and keys and pistols. Look in human hearts! And I tell you further, Filson believes himself in love with this woman, so he will escape the brunt of it. But you do not, and so you will not escape."

Laurence studied him for a moment in silence. "I believe thoroughly," he said at last, "that my business is in the end with minds and not alibis. But how can one check up on the mind? Can you probe it like an alibi?"

Marabout shrugged his shoulder. The fire was gone out of his eyes. "I am afraid I am not really interested as to whether the murderer is found. I early formed the opinion that Mullins was better dead."

"I have heard something like that before. Yet why should Mullins be so hated? What did he do?" Marabout dismissed the subject with a wave. "Nothing that I know of. A man with eyes like his was capable of anything. He is better dead, before he does any real harm."

Laurence refused to let the other slide into vagueness. "What manner of man are you, Dr. Marabout?" he asked curiously. "Will you think me impertinent if I ask you, is there, after all, something of a gesture in this creed of yours?"

The other laughed. "You think I am a charlatan." He raised his hand to silence the other's protests. "No. Then I will put your question into kinder words. Am I perhaps showing my contempt of the world, exposing perhaps the unreason of reason, by clinging to a position which is logically sound but ridiculous in fact?"

He gave a slow smile. "And do you really expect me to answer such a question?"

I I

The same afternoon Francis Filson met Mrs. Mullins in the garden of The Turrets.

"You have been avoiding me!" he accused.

"I have been avoiding everyone," she answered gently. "Can't you understand that?"

"You might at least have put yourself to the trouble of telling me about that confounded policeman. Why didn't you warn me he had found out I wasn't painting you on the day of the murder?"

She was silent for a moment. Then she spoke wearily. "What's the use? When one has been found out in one lie it is rather late to tell another, isn't it?"

He laughed contemptuously. "Don't tell me that's the reason, Pat! It's too weak even to convince yourself. You know perfectly well you've placed me in an infernally awkward position. There must have been some reason."

She gave a pathetic little gesture of despair. "I don't know. Oh, it's no use, I honestly don't know, Frank." She sat down on a garden seat and gazed gloomily ahead. "Why did you drag me into all this?"

The artist gave a theatrical laugh. "My God, it takes a woman to make a remark like that! Why? Oh, only for your sake! Foolish, wasn't it! Such an inadequate reason!"

"I sometimes wonder," she said slowly, "if you really do love me. I sometimes think you live in a dream-world, and the woman you love and think is me is one of the characters in it. One day you'll come down to earth. You'll wake up. And then perhaps you'll see me as I really am."

He leaned forward eagerly. "But don't you see I *do* see you as you really are. I am the only man perhaps who has seen your"—he paused for a word—"your essential *wickedness*—yes, that's the word, though it makes you wince. The same lovely wickedness that made the women of the Renaissance the most fascinating that have ever lived, those glittering Borgias, ruthless as splendid serpents—"

The woman gave a low laugh. "Your awakening will come then when you see the good in me."

He shook his head. "There is none. Think of what you have done," he said ruthlessly. "You have killed one man: you have ruined the career of another: you've made a fool of a faithful husband—of the ideal husband. Yes, I know about Eyton all right, so don't look startled. Finally, see what you've done to me."

"It sounds very dreadful, as you say it. And in a measure it's true. And yet it's just as untrue. For I've done nothing at all, nothing, that any human being in the same conditions couldn't be expected to do. Is that my tragedy? Or is it just a comedy of Fate?"

He laughed mockingly. "It's you. And if it were otherwise it wouldn't be you. Oh, I know you couldn't help playing with Holliday, and Eyton, and myself. You couldn't help us making the fools we did with ourselves. You did nothing but smile your enchanting smile. That absolves you from all responsibility. And it's a mere accident, isn't it, that the one man you couldn't play with is—dead!"

"I think you're unjust, Frank. But I suppose it sounds a little silly to talk of justice. After all, did I ask you to do what you did?"

"No, you didn't ask me. It wouldn't be like you to commit yourself! You've always evaded that. You've kept all three of us on a string without even so much as needing to say a word to us. But there are other ways of asking a man besides giving him a written request, and you know that no man who loves you as I do could help acting as I did."

She sighed. "I think if you loved me as you say you do, you would be rather more understanding." She paused. "Oh, Frank, you've no need to answer that, I can answer it myself. What right have I to talk of love, who never loved myself? You see that was the cause of the whole tragedy. When I married Tony it was that or starve, and for mother to starve too. I was perfectly frank about it. Perhaps that was where I made the mistake. For if I had only pretended a little, Tony might never have had that abominable jealousy that made him into a wild beast. And he might never have realized the hold he had over me, either. Well, I suppose all this is my punishment."

He took her hand. "Look at me, Pat. One day I'll make you confess you love me."

"You've earned the right to demand it. But all this seems to matter nothing now. I feel as if I wasn't a part of the world any longer. Just drifting..."

He shook his head. "That's just a mood," he said confidently. "You're tough enough, thank God, to throw this off. Take a cold-blooded view. The swine's dead. He deserved to be."

She shuddered and got up abruptly. "Don't." She looked at him with tortured eyes. "I know the truth; and it was silly of me to hide it. We can never be happy with this secret between us, never. Don't you see?"

"I don't. It seems to me a tie between us."

She laughed hysterically. "A common guilt! Oh, don't shake your head. I know we're equally guilty in the sight of our souls and the sight of the law. What we both wished has come about. I wished for it from the moment I asked for a revolver, and you wished for it from the moment you gave it to me. And I tell you the moment may come when we shall hate each other because of this."

He smiled tolerantly. "Pat, you're hopelessly over-wrought! We are both completely amoral beings fundamentally. This child-ish dread is pure nerves. Try and think of the practical side of the business. What are we going to say to the police now?"

She passed her hand wearily over her forehead. "We must stick to our story, that is all. We were together all the time of the murder.

They can't prove we weren't by direct evidence. Have you got rid of the revolver?"

"Yes!"

"No one saw you?"

"No. That was all right."

"You know, Frank, we mustn't meet like this. We mustn't be seen together."

"Nonsense; it doesn't prove anything."

"I don't care what it doesn't prove. I won't see you. I don't want to. Please, not till things are more—definite!"

He shrugged his shoulders in acquiescence. "As you will. But I've earned the right to know one thing—to ask one thing."

"And that is?"

"The affair with Holliday. Is that—over?"

She laughed bitterly. "It was over before it was begun, as far as I'm concerned. And now I fancy he's come to the same conclusion. I never thought it was serious. He tried to persuade me it was; but it seems to me to have been one of those immortal passions that can't survive a hundred miles of travel. I haven't heard from him since he left. Well, it's better it should be so.

"Perhaps he guesses what has happened," she added sombrely. "Anyway, none of these things matter very much. We're bound together, we two."

"And I'm glad of it."

She looked at him curiously. "I may grow to hate the bonds."

"Never!"

"No more meetings, then. I've got to get used to this kind of thing. It's not easy, you know." Her eyes were haunted as she met his. "Remember, this is definite, we mustn't meet again—not until I write to you and say we may."

Chapter Twelve

STRANGE BEHAVIOUR OF A PEER

"Now what evidence have we really got?" asked the Chief Constable. "Boil it down. Summarize it. You can always give the material facts in a few words. I must say that brevity has always been the guiding rule of my life, and I've never known it let me down. Sum up; and at once you know where you are. Why, I remember in India—h'm. Well, I'll tell you about that another time. Carry on, Trenton."

"The situation, sir, as the result of Sadler's able investigations, is pretty much as follows. We know the alibis of Filson and Mrs. Mullins won't hold water. We can take it, in fact, that they have no alibi for the material time. We can take it also, I think, that it was really Filson with whom Mrs. Mullins was having an affair, not Holliday as we first thought. Finally, we know that Filson attempted to dispose of a revolver which could have fired the bullet that killed Mullins. We can trace, as apparently Filson did not realize we should be able to, the original purchase of the revolver by him. Moreover, we have a witness as to his disposing of it. We can, I think, also assume that he wrote the childish anonymous letter which was intended, I suppose, to divert suspicion to someone else."

"Excellent, Trenton! I think this is a strong enough case to take action."

"I don't know, sir," answered the Inspector doubtfully. "You see, our weakness is that we cannot prove that either of them was anywhere near Mullins at the critical time. It would make all the difference between certainty and doubt if we could."

"You have Marabout's evidence about the short fellow who was seen there at the time of the murder and the evening before. That was Filson."

Trenton nodded. "Exactly—Marabout's evidence. That's the trouble, if you ask me, sir. Marabout is our only witness. And I ask you what sort of figure will he make in the box—under cross-examination by Freeth-Jones, for instance? It would be pitiful! And yet it is on his evidence that the whole case against these two will really turn."

"I think you're making a mountain out of a molehill, Trenton. It's your first murder case, isn't it? I thought so. Well, we're all a little liable to get cold feet when we think we've got to produce enough evidence to have one of our fellow-men killed. But you'll soon get used to it. By Jove, when I think of the hundreds of poor devils I've sent to Kingdom Come! Only Indians, of course, but still they're human beings more or less. Now what you've got to look at in this case is, is the evidence enough to convince you had it been a case of burglary or larceny? Of course it is."

"I *have* got cold feet," confessed the Inspector. "I still think the case is weak. A great deal depends on the kind of statements we can badger them into giving. I suppose, by the way, we'd charge them both—a kind of Bywaters and Edith Thompson business?"

The Chief Constable nodded. "I'm afraid we can't expect any luck, though, like that bundle of letters. But I don't know. It's the same with all these cases in my experience. If you're on the right track, you'll get plenty of supporting evidence as you go on. People who saw nothing before, suddenly remember having seen things after the arrest. Then there are the servants. When they see their mistress in prison they soon start talking. I feel we ought to act as soon as possible. Before the scent gets cold."

"We ought to wait, surely, for the Home Office report?" queried Laurence, who, like the legendary Duchess, up to now had taken no part in the conversation.

"Eh, what report is that?"

"Sadler is right, sir. We're waiting for the Home Office report on Filson's revolver. You know the modern method of bullet identification? If the expert is ready to swear that the bullet came from Filson's revolver, I should feel much happier about the case. Of course, sometimes the bullet has no marked characteristics at all microscopically, but if it has, and it supports our theory, then we are in a strong position. You see, at present there is no link between Filson's revolver and the bullet in Mullins' head except a purely hypothetical one. It might just as well have been any other revolver. Eyton's, for instance. We know he purchased one."

"All right. Have it your own way. But watch, mind, that they don't skip the country. Have you been able to get in touch with Holliday, incidentally?"

"No. He's evidently determined to have nothing to do with the business. And I don't blame him. He'll feel even less inclined to get mixed up in it after we arrest these two."

"At the risk of seeming a little self-centred," chimed in Laurence. "What about this business of people taking pot-shots at me? Rather selfish and conceited, of course, to worry about it, but why should people want to be so impolite?"

"You probably annoyed Filson," said his uncle. "After all, you already knew too much when it happened, and Filson must have known it."

"Unfortunately Marabout, as I told you, distinctly stated that he saw Lord Overture do the dirty deed. And as Marabout is our principal witness, it hardly does to suppose that he was mistaken."

"They're an odd family," remarked the Chief reflectively. "Lady Irene Overture threw a roll at me once in the Savoy Grill Room. She didn't know me from Adam then either. She couldn't stand seeing me eat spaghetti, she said. The suspense was too awful."

"If her brother had merely thrown rolls at me or even loaves," pointed out Laurence, "it wouldn't have been so bad. But shooting at people is a bit different."

The Chief Constable shrugged his shoulders. "Well, I leave it to you. If Marabout will stand to his story, we'll take proceedings against Overture. Still, if I were you I should go round to Overture and frighten hell out of the old fool."

"I don't mind confessing to you, Sadler," said Trenton, as they left the Chief Constable, "that I'm even more worried about this business than I told the Chief. We know that the woman and Filson are lying like hell, but that's a long way from murder. Look at the thing impartially. This murder was perfectly planned in execution. I mean the time-switch, and the fire, and the fitting in of the times. Now why should two people who'd planned such a neat piece of work produce such a clumsy alibi? Is there anything more suspicious to start with than an alibi that depends on the evidence of the two suspected parties? And it must be full of possible holes. The evidence of the painting upset it, for instance. The servant's evidence will probably smash it. I feel sure there's something fishy about this case that we don't even guess yet."

"I agree with you, sir. In fact I think our investigations have only just started. And when and where they'll end the Lord only knows, for I can't see any possible ending except the one we're working on now."

They walked together a few paces, and the Inspector appeared to be struggling internally. Then he spoke, slightly red in the face.

"Er, Sadler, when we first started this business I perhaps resented a little your being recommended as my assistant. Natural, I think, and perhaps I showed my feelings. Well, I want to say that I see I was quite mistaken. Quite mistaken. You've done some very good work. In fact I've spoken very highly of you in my last report, and I think you may expect to see some tangible results of that recommendation."

II

Lord Overture rose from his knees as Laurence approached. He had been engaged in embedding in the clayey soil of Fairview Estate a rectangle of posts, stapled to receive wire. He surveyed the result proudly.

"What do you think of it, officer? Quite neat, eh?"

Laurence looked at it closely and confessed himself puzzled. "I'm afraid I don't quite see what it's for."

"Of course not," answered Lord Overture proudly. "It's the very latest idea. I saw it in an article in an American paper. The article was, I think, called 'Nifty Gadgets.'"

"It certainly is very—er—nifty."

"It's a play-pen," stated Lord Overture.

"Oh, yes, a play-pen. Quite. What exactly is a play-pen? I expect I used to know, but I'm afraid I've forgotten."

"My dear fellow, you couldn't be expected to know. Now as a policeman you'll appreciate the value of this. It's for mothers to park their children in while they're shopping. You fill the centre with sand, and the little things play about there quite safely without running any danger from traffic."

Laurence looked about him. Apart from the seven buildings already in existence on Fairview Estate, the landscape was innocent of buildings as far as where, on the skyline, the little cluster of roofs that was Great Hake could be seen. Between stretched an unspoiled countryside of pasture and covert.

"Surely it's rather a long way for mothers to bring their children?"

Lord Overture laughed tolerantly. "Of course, I forgot to tell you. Look at this plan." He unrolled a smeared and tattered drawing from his pocket. "I spent all Sunday working this out. You see as far as that elm tree there, with the broken branch. A street of busy shops is going to stretch to there. Possibly farther, but we mustn't overdo it. The wide avenues of houses will branch off at right angles from this street. Half-way down there will be the cinema. Opposite the cinema I am arranging for a car park—very important nowadays—and a garage. I shall sell the concession for a garage on the Estate at my own figure."

Becoming still more enthusiastic, Lord Overture waved his transforming hand over the landscape. "The Turrets, of course, must become a country club. I really blush when I think of the paltry sum for which I let it to Mullins. Then we must have an ice skating-rink—or do you think," he said, turning anxiously to Laurence, "that the vogue for ice skating has passed?"

"I don't think so," answered Laurence gravely.

"Good, then we must have the rink. And lastly, of course, the play-pen."

"I should have thought that it might have been really better to wait a little, till the shops were built, before you started on the play-pen, don't you think?"

"That," replied Lord Overture, "is where you are wrong. The play-pen is the easiest thing. That's why I start on it. I always believe in starting the easiest thing first. Then if the harder things prove too hard, well, one has got the easier thing, at any rate, hasn't one?

"In any case," he added, "one could always use this for something. A goat would look rather well in it, don't you think? However, I am afraid I am wasting your time. You came to ask me something. I can see it. You must pardon me. I get enthusiastic."

"I did want to ask you something, Lord Overture," said Laurence in a different tone of voice. "I came to ask you what explanation you propose to give for shooting at me at half-past six on Wednesday evening."

Lord Overture looked him straight in the eyes. "I deny it completely."

"You deny it?" said Laurence, astonished.

"I deny it, completely, entirely, and *in toto*. On the word of an Overture."

"Can you then explain the fact that Dr. Marabout is prepared to swear that he saw you, actually saw you, shooting at me?"

"I can explain it quite simply. Marabout is a damned old fool. He might just as easily have said that he saw a cow elephant in tartans puffing at you with a pea-shooter."

Laurence felt annoyed. "I didn't expect you to take this attitude, Lord Overture. I may say that I was fully prepared to entertain any acceptable explanation of your action, had you felt inclined to give it to me. I might add that my superiors are perfectly satisfied with Dr. Marabout's evidence, and so, I think, will be any court of law. In view of your attitude we shall certainly press the matter, so I may as well caution you now and say that any statement you make may be used in evidence against you."

Lord Overture drew himself up with simple dignity. "Officer, you are offensive. You may, if you please, suggest that I am a liar. You may, if you will, accuse me of murderous assault. No one respects the police more than I do. But if you dare to suggest that I, an Overture, who have shot Peppering Coverts for forty years, could miss someone your size with a shot-gun at a distance of five yards—then, sir, policeman or no policeman, I have half a mind to give myself the satisfaction of pulling your nose."

"Indeed. So you appear to know it was a shot-gun?"

"Of course."

"How do you know that if you didn't fire it?"

"I did fire it," replied Lord Overture simply. "Did I ever deny it?"

"Do you mean that you now admit shooting at me?"

An expression of cunning crossed the peer's goat-like countenance. "On the contrary, I deny it. I never shot at you. I shouldn't dream of it. But if you had asked me whether I shot near you, or over

you, at the time in question, then I should have replied, 'Certainly.'
I did! I admit it! I have never told a lie in my life—except, of course,
in the way of business."

"I see. May one ask why on earth you shot at or near me?"

Lord Overture's face became suffused with passion. "Certainly
you may! I did it to frighten you! I'm tired of you police nosing
round into this business, and getting the Estate into the Gutter
Press. Do you realize what you are doing? No less than fifteen
different clients with whom I was in touch with a view to selling plots on this Estate have, because of the publicity, cancelled
their negotiations! Fifteen! All because you weren't content to
let the matter rest at suicide. Of course it's suicide. Mullins was
practically asking to be murdered. And if he was murdered after
asking for it that's suicide, isn't it? Instead of which you come
round here raking up all this mud and scandalizing one of the
fairest pleasaunces in the Home Counties. I tell you, if it hadn't
been for that old fool Marabout I'd've put the fear of God into
you and Trenton within the next few days. No," he added, as
he saw Laurence struggling to speak, "it's no use apologizing.
The mischief's done as far as the good name of the Estate is
concerned!"

Even after Laurence had warned him of the possible conse-
quence of his action and threatened him with the penalties of an
outraged law, Lord Overture was unperturbed.

"On the contrary, I am of the opinion that I might succeed in
a claim against the Chief Constable for the loss of those fifteen
possible clients..."

III

There was a curious expression on Inspector Trenton's face when Laurence returned to the station. He thrust across a letter. "From the Home Office," he said. "About the revolver."

The letter ran as follows:

"INSPECTOR R. TRENTON,
THAMESHIRE COUNTY CONSTABULARY,
QUEENSBRIDGE.

"DEAR SIR,——We have now received the report of Mr. Samuel Entourage on the bullet and revolver sent under cover of your communication of the 12th instant. He reports as follows:

"'The bullet, as is not always the case, has clearly defined markings, which must have been produced by firing through the barrel of a somewhat corroded revolver. The corrosions would, of course, only be visible microscopically. These markings do not give any support to the hypothesis that the bullet was fired by the revolver sent me for examination at the same time. In fact I should be prepared to state, with every emphasis, that it was totally impossible for the bullet to have been fired by the firearm in question.'

"I have the honour to be,
"Your obedient servant…"

Trenton reclaimed the letter. "You see! Filson's revolver never fired the shot which killed Mullins. So there collapses our case. There's no more hope of getting a conviction on that evidence than there is for a celluloid cat in hell."

Chapter Thirteen

A HORSEWOMAN ON THE WARPATH

"The truth is, Laurence, that you police have made a hopeless mess of the whole business!" Sandy, after seeing nothing of Laurence for several days, and therefore suffering torments of curiosity, was in no mood to be charitable.

Laurence caved in without a protest. "I'm afraid you're right. Damned if I know what X does here. I wonder what Venables would do in a case like this?"

"Venables, my dear, is far too clever to get involved in a case like this. If not, why doesn't he give us a hand? The *Mercury*'s full of his aeroplane murder triumph this morning. But as far as I can see, it was only a case of following the obvious clues. Now this, I admit, is a bit difficult, and you can bet your life Venables will keep out of it."

"You know, I still have a lingering belief in the suicide theory."

"Rot!" said Sandy kindly. "Mullins would never have killed himself. He wasn't that kind of man. The whole trouble is that Pat is throwing dust in everyone's eyes. I must admit she is doing it very cleverly. All this cruelty business, for instance. Personally, I don't think men can be trusted with detecting where a woman's concerned. At any rate not if she's got a complexion like Pat's. Of course it's easy enough if you stay indoors all day instead of living in the open air."

"We weren't, however, discussing complexions," said Laurence mildly.

"Possibly I am wandering off the point a little. Anyway, I am tired of the police. I warn you, Police Constable Sadler, that I propose to solve this mystery. I shall begin my investigations right away."

"Good God," expostulated Laurence, aghast. "I say, you know you can't do that kind of thing. You'll be stirring up all sorts of bother."

"Nonsense," said Sandy firmly. "Do you think I have no tact?"

"I've never said that. But you conceal it very well."

"Somebody on the Estate did it," pursued Sandy, ignoring the remark. "Probably someone absolutely virtuous and respected like Eyton. I never did trust these ostentatiously faithful and devoted husbands. It's so rude to other women, don't you think? Oh, don't look so scared! You needn't worry. *I* shan't get potted at from trees or involved in fights with professional pugilists."

"I absolutely wash my hands of you," said Laurence despairingly. "May I remind you that your first choice of the murderer was not very happy?"

"What precisely are you referring to?"

"To Constant, the worthy Secretary. You remember you picked him as the murderer. Unfortunately he was in his office all day."

"He's probably thrown dust in your eyes. I'm not sure that I may not go up to town and check Mr. Constant's alibi. It sounds very fishy to me. So does Holliday's for that matter. The kind they work out for people in detective stories, only I can never be bothered to check them up to see whether the author has made a mistake."

"You can't do any harm, I suppose. And you may conceivably do some good. More than I shall, with my present job—checking up on all revolvers bought locally. I'm sick of the sight of them. The original revolver must be at the bottom of the Thames by now unless the murderer is a complete ass."

I I

The first steps in Sandy's personal researches took her to "One." This, as she confessed, was a little odd, because she had not origi-nally intended to go there. But as she went down Oak Avenue, past the "play-pen," the bright blue door of Filson's cottage struck her eye; and in a moment she found herself going up the path.

"One should follow one's intuition," she reflected.

Filson apparently did not believe in intuition. His welcome was freezing. In fact his whole appearance was something of a surprise for Sandy. His face was pasty; there were lines from the nostrils to the corners of his mouth and his hair was unbrushed. It was also obvious that he hadn't shaved.

"Good God, what do you want?" he said angrily when he opened the door.

"Pleasant social call," replied Sandy with exaggerated cheer-fulness. "I should leave two cards, I believe. Perhaps three. The books don't deal with the etiquette for a young unmarried lady calling upon a bachelor. I say," she added, peering into the room, "you seem to have been having a hell of a party. That, no doubt, accounts for the wild and woolly appearance and general bad temper."

"What do you mean, bad-tempered?" asked Filson crossly.

The cottage was certainly the worse for habitation. Papers, books, gramophone records and half-opened tins of salmon were scattered about the rooms. Several sardines were distributed over the hearth-rug of the lounge, the remainder being in process of absorption by a melancholy cat, eating delicately out of the open tin.

"So you've started to bring the morals and manners of Bloomsbury to our Estate! Shame on you!"

"If you don't like it you know where to go," answered Filson somewhat weakly. He passed his hand over his forehead. "What do you want, anyway?"

Sandy started to clear up some of the debris.

> "When pain and anguish rack our brow
> A ministering angel thou!"

she hummed. "What on earth has happened to Mrs. Wimpole?"

"Oh, she gave notice, the silly old cow!"

"Really. Any reason?"

"No, none at all. I don't know—she may have been a little peeved because I chucked a cup of tea at her."

"A mere pleasantry. And yet she left. Wasn't there anything else?"

"Well, she'd got out of the room before I could chuck anything else. Pretty quick on her feet."

"Odd that she should have minded. No sense of humour, these women. However, don't try throwing cups of tea at me because I have a sense of repartee and probably a straighter eye than you." She placed the rubbish on a tray and started to carry it out.

"Look here, what are you doing all this for?" he said ungraciously. "Very nice of you, of course. But still I'm quite capable of looking after myself."

"It hardly looks like it. Anyway, I've come to have my portrait painted."

"Oh, have you?"

"Don't you remember? You said you would like to."

"I don't remember. Yes, I do. Still, I can tell you I never felt less like working than at the moment."

"Why not?"

"In all politeness, may I ask whether it is any of your business?"

"In all insolence, I reply, it is! I will now tell you really why I came here. I've decided to find out who killed Mullins. You see he helped me once, and I feel he's been unfairly treated. No one seems to care a damn whether he's dead or not. Oh, don't look at me with that injured air. Everyone's the same. Nobody worries who the murderer is. All they seem to be afraid of is that they'll be implicated in some way. It's perfectly disgusting."

A flush darkened the artist's cheeks. "Look here, be careful you are not taken seriously. This isn't a matter for acting."

Sandy smiled with forced sweetness. "Fortunately, I don't take you as seriously as the police."

"What do you mean?"

"I mean, young man, that as near as nothing the police nabbed you the other day."

Filson laughed, not with great success. "Don't talk rot."

"Fact." She looked at him keenly. "Do you know what got you off?"

Filson was unable to prevent himself replying with a note of eagerness. "What?"

Sandy didn't answer for a moment, but walked into the kitchen adjoining the lounge. Then she spoke casually through the open door. "The police know that your revolver did not kill Mullins."

He laughed again and followed her into the kitchen. "Indeed. And that disappointed you, I suppose?"

"It neither disappointed nor surprised me. Yes, I even confess I was relieved."

"That was very nice of you."

"It was. Now you are out of trouble, I should stay out."

"Meaning?"

"Meaning stay away from it. Oh, don't look so innocent. Goodness knows I like Pat, but she certainly seems to mean trouble for her friends."

Filson exploded. "Look here, Sandy, this is a bit too thick—"

"Calm yourself. You know it's true. Now look here. I know you didn't murder Mullins."

"Very nice of you, I'm sure."

"It is. Although you didn't mean it. I'm probably the only person who doesn't think you've done it. The police do really; though this discovery of theirs about the revolver has pulled them up on their haunches for a moment."

Filson looked at her without antagonism for a moment. "Look here; if it isn't curiosity, why are you worrying about this?"

"Supposing I said it was to get you out of your present trouble, would you believe it?"

"I'm afraid not."

"No, on second thoughts it doesn't sound very convincing! So I am afraid you must fall back on idle curiosity after all. Now will you answer the few questions I came to ask you?"

"What are they?"

"First of all. Do you know who killed Mullins?"

Filson hesitated.

"Now then, don't dither! It is obvious you think you do, anyway, without my asking you."

"Yes," he said in a low voice.

"I doubt it. Did you see it done?"

"No. I don't know why I answer your questions, all the same. I think you know too much, Sandy. You'd better be careful!"

She laughed sardonically. "I shall be careful enough. Now tell me something else that has puzzled me. Do you know of anybody else on the Estate who loved Pat as romantically as you?"

"Damn it, what the devil right do you think you have to ask such a question? Did you really think I would answer it?"

"You have answered it," said Sandy calmly. "Take that dish-cloth and help me dry these things up."

III

Sandy took advantage of a long-standing invitation of Mrs. Murples' to call in at the New House to tea. This was a famous function. All resident boxers, trainers and sparring partners were expected to turn up, and any impoliteness such as swearing, eating two sandwiches at one mouthful, or noisiness with the tea, would call forth a rebuke from Mrs. Murples which would effectually prevent the offence being repeated for some time. In fact the Battler himself had a scar on his forehead where he had been struck by a plate, sent skimming through the air by a judicious flick of his hostess's wrist after he had expectorated reflectively on the carpet.

"My dear," said Mrs. Murples as Sandy was shown into the drawing-room where tea had already begun. "This is a pleasure. Don't apologize. It's my fault for not telling you we're having tea half an hour earlier now the light goes so early. You know Mr. Tompkins, I think. Also his trainer, Mr. Norris. You are just in time before the Bantam eats all the buttered toast. Very bad for the wind, as you ought to know, Battler. Well, now, I really mean it when I say I'm glad you came, Miss Delfinage, for you seem to know everything that goes on, you clever little thing, and you simply must tell us the latest news about the murder of that Mullins man. For of course it was murder, wasn't it?"

"The police seem to think so."

Mrs. Murples gave a sinister smile. "I'm sure you can think of a better reason than that. But now tell me, why on earth can't they find the murderer? I always thought it was simple in a case like this."

"I think the trouble is that everyone who knows anything is keeping dark to try and save their skins. If some of the witnesses would speak, the police would be farther advanced. And I think they will make them speak pretty soon."

The Battler, never an adept at dissimulation, shied perceptibly. Sandy at once fixed him with a penetrating gaze. Mrs. Murples did the same. Under the combined gaze of two formidable females, in the uneasy surroundings of a room crowded with upsettable what-nots, he began to dither.

"Can I 'ave another cup of tea?" he asked in a choked voice.

"You already have half a cup left," remarked Mrs. Murples acidly.

The pugilist started violently. "Blimey, so I 'ave."

Mrs. Murples gave a gesture of despair. "Upon my soul, I some-times envy you your horses, Miss Delfinage. Any more tempera-mental creatures than bantam-weights I've never met in my life! Just a bundle of nerves. Look at him!"

"Now you don't want to say that, Mrs. Murples," he protested weakly.

"I do and have," she replied sharply.

"He does seem upset about something," said Sandy, cruelly continuing to stare at him fixedly. "Really it is quite unnecessary. Although, of course, the police do suspect him; they don't propose to do anything immediately."

"Ow, I say. Really, miss! I think it's a bit 'ard."

"You drive me frantic, Battler, sometimes," said Mrs. Murples, making a clawing gesture with her hands. "What have you been up to again? You've had something on your mind the last few days. I thought it was that affair with the policeman, but it doesn't seem to be that. Surely you can't really have been such a fool as to do Mullins in?"

"Ow, I say, Mrs. Murples!"

"You've said that before," remarked the lady testily. "Make some intelligent contribution to the conversation."

"Make what?"

"Speak, *say something*!" yelled Mrs. Murples suddenly picking up the silver teapot.

The Battler jumped as if he had been jabbed on the mark. He raised one hand defensively. "All right, I understand you. You don't want to get violent. But look here, if I tell, 'ow do I know this lady 'ere won't go and tell the police?"

Mrs. Murples looked at Sandy and winked surreptitiously. "You don't think any more of the police than I do, I expect." She turned to Battler. "That's all right. I'll answer for Miss Delfinage. She'll probably be able to give you better advice than I can."

"Well, look here, it was like this," began the Battler, groping round for the threads of the story. "I was up at the Castle with a friend."

"Bridget!" exclaimed Sandy suddenly.

The Battler looked embarrassed. "'Ow did you guess?"

"She's not blind," Mrs. Murples replied shortly. "But go on."

"Well, this was on the morning of the murder, do you see? About one, I suppose it would be. I was reckoning on having a bit of lunch with Bridget. She's a good kid, and I've 'ad a meal there before. Mrs. Mullins doesn't mind. Well, there we were, in the room just beside the front door, when there was a bang on the door. Bridget popped out to answer it, and she left the door of this room open, so that I could 'ear 'er speak when she opened it. At least I could just 'ear 'er speak, and the man she opened the door to fair shouted."

"What did they say?" asked Sandy.

"'Arf a moment. I'm coming to that. 'Where's your mistress?' 'e said. 'I must see 'er.' 'I'm sorry, sir, but she is not at 'ome,' Bridget answers. 'Where is she?' 'e repeats in a overwrought sort of voice. 'Well, she's not at 'ome,' says Bridget politely. 'She is. She must be,' 'e says. 'Take my name in, Bridget, there's a good girl. I must see 'er.' 'Well, sir,' she answers, 'I'll see if she's come in, but I'm pretty sure she 'asn't.' Now when she was gone I 'eard 'im groaning and muttering to 'imself. Well, about a minute later Mrs. Mullins came along the corridor. 'What do you want, George?' she asked in a sort of weary voice. Not annoyed if you understand me, but not liking 'im worrying 'er. 'Are you all right?' 'e asks. 'Of course I am. What are you rushing back 'ere at this time for?' Then 'e sort of sighed and said, 'I guess I lost my 'ead. Pat, when did you last see your 'usband?' 'This morning,' she said. 'Why did you ask me that?' And it seemed to me that she was scared of something. 'And was 'e all right then?' this bloke says. 'Of course. Surely you didn't come all the way round 'ere to ask me how my 'usband was. I don't know what's come over you, George. I'm giving Filson a sitting for my portrait. You've interrupted it just as it was going well!' He gave a sort of bitter laugh and said, 'Well, things won't go on well for ever.' She said, 'What do you mean?' And 'e said, 'Nothing, I suppose. I've done a foolish thing. Forget about it, Pat. I think I've been a little mad these last three hours. Why did you 'ide from me?' 'I've already told you what I was doing,' she said short-like. 'I didn't mean to be unkind, George, but you mustn't do that sort of thing. Now run back to the office. Then 'e went and I 'eard 'er speak to Bridget and say: 'Look 'ere, Bridget, whatever you do don't you let anyone know that Mr. Eyton called round 'ere.' And of course Bridget promised. Now when she got back, Bridget saw that I knew. Bridget would go through fire and water for 'er mistress and she made me swear by Gawd knows 'ow many saints that I wouldn't breathe a word. Said she'd chuck a bottle of vitriol over me if I ever let out a squeak. But what I says is, there's something fishy about this business. Accessors after the crime, that's what we are more likely than not from wot I can tell and I don't like it, not 'arf I don't."

Mrs. Murples looked at Sandy.

"Can you make head or tail of what this man has said?" she asked despairingly. "Because I'm blest if I can."

"The police will try to make only one thing out of it," Sandy replied. "And it's not a very nice thing. Commonly known as a rope."

"Battler!" said Mrs. Murples sharply, "you've spilt tea all over your knees."

Chapter Fourteen

SO HE SHOT MULLINS

"Flossie, get off the sofa!"

"Peter, put down your father's pipe!"

"Enid, leave Kitty alone!"

"Tommy, wipe your boots before you come in!"

"Veronica, you must let Peter play with his own train!"

Mrs. Eyton tossed off these remarks at the same time as she welcomed Sandy to the "Nook," with hardly any change in her voice and, seemingly, without taking her eyes off her visitor's face. It was a knack gained by practice, and Sandy had seen her, while knitting and reading simultaneously, keep under full control her numerous offspring and their attendant Labradors, spaniels, cats, and rabbits. No doubt long experience of this sort of thing also accounted for a certain vagueness in Mrs. Eyton's manner of speech, which was inclined to drift gently to and fro in the subconscious. Sandy always felt she ought to admire Mrs. Eyton, and just as obstinately was unable to. Model wife, devoted parent, never ruffled, always even-tempered, only gossiping as much as politeness demanded, though she was all these, Sandy finally decided that she was too damned patronizing. These women with model husbands generally are, she reflected. Was George Eyton really anything to be proud of? A shepherd might as well be proud of the lack of pugnacity of his sheep. And as she now suspected, George Eyton was, in fact, not a model husband at all.

To-day Mrs. Eyton looked tired and even vaguer than usual. A man might conceivably have felt a pang of compassion. Sandy, belonging to the tougher sex, thought of Antony Mullins, her helper, and the wife who had involved him in a knot of doom. Quite simply, she hoped for vengeance.

"My dear," exclaimed Mrs. Eyton, "now you've come in you simply must stop to tea; you know, I've meant to ask you so many times. You've been so nice to Enid. Tommy, wipe your nose, dear. Veronica will lend you her handkerchief. Just fancy, Sandy, Lord Overture came round and asked me if he could borrow my children to put in his play-pen. Can you credit the impudence of the man! He said he'd have offered to pay for them, but this m-u-r-d-e-r had affected the Estate so much he hadn't two round coins to rub together. Perhaps I'd better call it umpety-umpety, the children are so knowing. Do tell me, dear, you know all about the umpety-umpety, have they found the man yet? It is so very upsetting, you know, to think there is an umpety-umpetyer on the Estate. After all, there's no knowing whom he might start on next, is there?"

Now this, thought Sandy, watching the speaker's eyes, is something in which she is really interested.

"No, there isn't," she answered off-handedly. "But tell me about Lord Overture. What on earth was his idea?"

"Really I don't know, dear. You know how odd these peers are. Do you think the Duke of Wapping will get his divorce from that dreadful woman? Of course I think these titles are so absurd, don't you? Although they do say there aren't really many Chinamen there, and it's quite a nice place to live in. Wapping, I mean. Of course the co-respondent is probably as anxious that the divorce shouldn't go through as the Duke is that it should, from what one hears of the woman. But I never did like the Thames. We're near it here, of course, but somehow I never think of the river as the Thames; I mean punts are so different to barges. Do you think they really have the slightest idea?"

"Who?" asked Sandy, momentarily baffled.

"The police, of course, dear. Weren't you listening? I suppose I do babble a bit. George always says so. But as I say, he never utters a word but sits there smoking his foul old pipe, and naturally someone must provide the conversation. But you haven't answered my question."

"I really don't know what the police think."

"Mysterious creature," answered Mrs. Eyton with an unbelieving smile. "Still, perhaps you are right. One shouldn't give away these confidences."

"What exactly do you mean?"

"There now, Kitty's scratched you, Enid! That will be a lesson to you. What does the child think she's doing, rubbing it with a piece of india-rubber! Well, I'm only joking, of course, but I can't believe you haven't some inside information from young Mr. Sadler. A very nice young man, too. I can never believe he is a real policeman, even with his helmet on, though, of course, being a nephew of the Chief Constable makes it all right. Stop Flossie rubbing against the chair, Veronica! You know her hair drops off when she's moulting, and it makes your father so annoyed when they come off on his black jacket."

"I'd really rather not discuss the umpety-umpety," said Sandy carefully.

"Of course, Mr. Mullins was a good friend of yours. It's upset George terribly too. You know he was a friend of Mullins as well. Always round at The Turrets. Tommy, if you upset those tadpole-things on the carpet, I'll give you such a spanking! My dear, do tell me if you have heard anything which—well, I mean anything you think I ought to know." For a moment Mrs. Eyton was too overcome by some secret thought to continue with her knitting. She put it down.

Sandy was ruthless. "You must know that's a very awkward question, darling."

Mrs. Eyton rapidly resumed her knitting with a kind of flurried vehemence. "Oh, dear, George would be so annoyed if he knew I'd said this, but really I am so worried. Something has happened, and I can't imagine what it is. I suppose I'm saying something I oughtn't to. Veronica, go with Enid and take Flossie for a run. Peter, I want you to go with Tommy over to Mr. Salomon's and ask for two pounds of his tomatoes. Say Mother said the last ones you had were the nicest Mother's ever tasted, but look out he doesn't give you any more over-ripe ones. There's no reason why he should give us his throw-outs, even if he does let us have them below market price. When will those children learn to close the door after them! Thank you so much, dear. Really, I can't knit, I'm so worried. You know I keep on having it on the tip of my tongue to tell George he *must* tell the police, but I simply daren't. But I know he ought to, because it is quite impossible that it could be anything. And yet he knows something. I am so afraid he's shielding that awful woman. But there, I oughtn't to have said that; perhaps she's a friend of yours. Though goodness knows she was no friend to her husband, and he did do a lot for you, dear, didn't he? I've often heard you say so. I'm sure you agree with me about her really. But I do think he ought to tell the police. Otherwise he might get into such trouble."

"I think George is on the point of getting into very serious trouble," said Sandy.

"I knew it. Oh, dear, do the police know something?"

"They know about the revolver." After all, that was a fairly safe bet, if there was anything at all in Mrs. Eyton's meandering. And if there wasn't, it didn't matter very much whether she was told about George's trouble or not.

"Oh, they know! Then I must make George tell them. I must! It will be so terrible if they hear any other way. That awful woman will tell them her own story, and I'm quite sure that she won't have the slightest compunction in making up a story, *any* story, to save herself."

"What really happened?"

"My dear, absolutely nothing really. But you know when I was so frightened of burglars after they had them in at Mrs. Murples' place, and you remember the burglar got caught by one of the boxers and brought an action because he was incapacitated for life—well, my husband bought a revolver. He said we needn't keep it loaded, but if we just had it in a drawer and could take it out, that would be enough to scare them away. We always kept it in the left-hand top drawer of his desk. Well, that was more than a year ago, and then a few weeks before the murder I was tidying up the room and looked in that drawer and saw it was gone. George was in the room, so I asked him where it was. He just answered casually, 'At The Turrets.' Well, Mrs. Mullins called round the evening before the murder quite late, and the next morning I could see George was worried about something. However, he went to the office as usual, but he was late coming back. I don't remember much that afternoon; it was so upsetting having that fire and people rushing round, and no one knowing what was going to happen next; and of course Veronica couldn't be found anywhere, so that I was scared out of my wits until I found she'd been driven into Peppering clinging on the back of the fire-engine. And would you believe it, they'd given the poor child *beer* to drink, and of course she was sick and fractious all the rest of the evening, and the children started dancing round me singing 'We want beer,' so I hardly knew where I was till the evening. Then I looked in the drawer without saying a word to George, and there was the revolver back again! Well now, ever since that moment George has been worrying, and it's so transparent; and what's worse, he is acting all the time trying to keep cheerful, so that I know he doesn't want me to guess something."

Sandy reflected. Taken alone, the story was significant in only one respect—that here was a revolver which had been at The Turrets. But taken with what she already knew, it had various possibilities.

"It seems very strange," she said at last. "What do you think?"

"My dear, isn't it obvious? Of course it sounds a terrible thing to say, but I feel absolutely sure in my own mind that he lent that revolver to that Mullins woman. Oh, don't try and reassure me. I may be a fool, but I know what's going on under my nose, and goodness knows enough kind neighbours have helped to point it out to me, but I must say you've been good in that respect, Sandy. But of course George is so kind-hearted that he'd do the most awful things, or so they'd seem unless you know him as well as I do. I know it's all nonsense and merely that he happens to be sorry for the woman, but of course other people misjudge him. And it's perfectly plain that that woman borrowed the revolver from him with goodness knows what story. Probably said her husband beat her—you know what women are of that type and how men will believe them, though anyone kinder than poor Mr. Mullins it would be impossible to find, as you know, my dear; and of course he gave Tommy that new air-gun, which I had to confiscate because, after all, cats are all very well, but when it comes to Muscovy ducks one must draw a line, though I must say they are such odd-looking birds that one can hardly blame a child for shooting at them, can one? But I promised to let him have it back on his next birthday, and I always say, whatever happens, never break a promise to a child. Well, I'm absolutely positive in my own mind, though I won't accuse anyone, that that was the revolver that killed him, and she's told my husband to take the revolver back and told him some cock-and-bull story, so that the police will never find the weapon. And I don't believe even George is so simple not to guess, but of course he's too good-hearted to give the game away. But I say he must, for if the police find out for themselves he's an accessory, I believe they call it, and they can even send you to prison for that, apart from the unpleasantness and the scandal which is bound to occur anyway, as far as I can see. All I say to myself is, thank God he was away at the office on the day the murder took place, for goodness knows what the police might think and say if they knew that he'd been anywhere near The Turrets when it happened. I really think it wicked sometimes the way they accuse these wretched people, though of course if they've done it they deserve it. By police I don't mean anything against Mr. Sadler, of course, for he's hardly police, as one meets him socially. I mean, I always think of him as an officer, and really those helmets are not half as absurd as a bearskin. But, Sandy, what do you think I ought to do? Should I tell the police?"

Sandy thought. "If I were you I should wait a little. They know quite a lot already, and the next thing you'll know is that they'll be round here and you can tell them your story."

"Perhaps that's the best way. Really, the sooner I see them the better, for I am on tenterhooks all the time wondering what that awful woman might do. For really I do think she's capable of anything. But, my dear, you aren't going without any tea, are you? It will be in here in two ticks. Please stop."

"Sorry, I really can't stay. Another time."

"Well, of course, if you must you must. It was awfully good of you to come in and talk to me. And be an angel, dear, if you see Tommy and Peter, tell them to hurry home with the tomatoes, and not dawdle, because they're wanted for dinner to-night. I mean, tomato is the one thing a salad must have, don't you think?—except, of course, those funny salads. I think once a salad starts getting away from lettuce and tomato, it's like a woman who starts going off the rails, you know, it might end absolutely anywhere. What a pity you must hurry off. One of these days we'll have a chat."

11

"Really, Sandy, this is the most diabolical and ruthless thing I've ever heard of! You've simply been worming your way into people's confidence in order to get evidence against a friend of yours." Laurence stared at her in amazement.

Sandy blithely continued with her task of rubbing up a saddle. "You ungrateful puppy. Here have I presented you with promotion in a bag, and you look it in the mouth, or whatever it is."

"A pig in a poke is the proverb you're looking for. But really, Sandy, are you serious? Eyton of all people!"

"I never did like him," said Sandy calmly. "I never did like those weak creatures. Oh, good-tempered enough, I admit. Sort of bulky-looking and nice to have about the house with a pipe in its mouth. I know the kind. I've had horses like them. Not with a pipe, of course. They're awfully good and obedient and husky-looking, but they'll founder in half a day's hard riding. Whereas if you get a bit of blood that's bad-tempered with a wicked look in his eye, he'll kill himself before he'll give in. It's just the silly sort of thing Eyton'd do to go and murder someone just because a woman like Pat asked it as a favour with tears in her eyes."

"My dear Sandy, as soon as you say it you must realize how impossible it is. Eyton is a stout fellow, and the idea is absolutely absurd!"

"Well, I hope it is. Anyway, it'll do him good if you go round there and scare the wits out of him. A night in prison wouldn't do him any harm, either. It'll spoil his pose of the model husband. And if the idea isn't so absurd as you think, then remember, Laurence, that Mullins is dead, and save your pity for him."

"I think you're absolutely vindictive, Sandy. However, we'll see. I shall call in on Mrs. Eyton to-morrow morning, when hubby's gone."

Laurence did, and had no difficulty in securing the revolver and a rather more highly coloured version of the story Mrs. Eyton had told Sandy. And Inspector Trenton looked grave when he heard that story.

III

Two days passed. The play-pen was finished and six grubby children were to be seen any day digging furiously in the sand. Lord Overture had told Laurence proudly that it had not, after all, been necessary to hire them. A mere rumour that he had dropped half a crown out of his pocket into the sand when making it had proved sufficient to lure Peppering's poorer infants.

No word came from Eyton during that period, although Sadler expected indignant protests as a result of his visit to Mrs. Eyton and the borrowing of the revolver. Filson, however, looked a little brighter, and started to paint. Blows thudded cheerily in the garden of the New House. Venables of the *Mercury* refused to take the slightest interest in the Affair Mullins, in spite of imploring and seductive letters from his former fellow undergraduate. Holliday wrote again to Samson on a matter of business, still from Spain, but still giving no address, and making no reference to Trenton's request. And on the third day Inspector Trenton showed Laurence a letter he had received from the Home Office.

"INSPECTOR TRENTON,
THAMESHIRE COUNTY CONSTABULARY,
QUEENSBRIDGE.

"DEAR SIR,—We have now received Mr. Samuel Entourage's report on the bullet and revolver sent under cover of your letter of the 18th instant. He reports as follows:

"'After microscopic scrutiny I have formed the opinion that beyond all reasonable doubt the bullet was fired at some date by the weapon enclosed. A fuller report of the investigation is being forwarded at a later date, with the usual affidavits, which no doubt your correspondent will require.'

> "I have the honour to be,
> "Your obedient servant, etc."

"That," said Trenton, "makes it rather simple, doesn't it? So it was Eyton that shot Mullins after all Laurence, present my compliments to Miss Delfinage."

Chapter Fifteen

AN ARCHITECT IS ARRESTED

"Y ou have, I think, Mr. Eyton, been cautioned that anything you say may, at a later date, in certain eventualities be used in evidence against you." Inspector Trenton gave the formal warning while he studied the man keenly.

George Eyton nodded. His heavy, good-humoured face was a little grey; probably, thought Laurence, due to lack of sleep.

"You wish, however, to make a statement?"

Eyton shook his head sullenly. "I don't want to make a statement, as you call it. I have nothing to make a statement about. I want to know what on earth has given you this utterly mad idea. It must be some absurd misunderstanding, and if only you will tell me what it is, instead of badgering me about my movements, and this thing and that thing, I should be able to clear up the whole silly business."

Trenton took a revolver out of his desk and laid it on the table. "This is your revolver, Mr. Eyton?"

"Yes. It seems to be!"

"Then perhaps the first misunderstanding you can clear up is how this weapon came to kill Antony Mullins."

Eyton shook his head. "It didn't. I tell you Mullins could not conceivably have been killed with that revolver."

Trenton shrugged his shoulders. "You will have to take up a more constructive attitude than that if you wish to help yourself. We shall bring forward evidence in good time that will remove any doubt on that score. So again I ask you, Mr. Eyton, how this impossible thing happened, and this weapon belonging to you discharged the bullet which killed Antony Mullins?"

Eyton exploded. "Look here, I don't know what your game is. I tell you you are wrong. I will tell you exactly what happened to that revolver. A year ago I lent it to Mullins. He wanted to shoot a dog of his that had got spinal meningitis; I remember him saying jokingly, 'It's just like one of the biggest makers of armaments in the country to have to borrow a revolver to shoot a dog.' I ought to explain that I had originally bought the firearm because my wife was scared about some burglary that took place near us. So I got her this, but of course took jolly good care that it was never loaded. Mullins said he could run into Queensbridge and get some ammunition the same day. Well, I forgot about the revolver, and the day before the murder Mullins gave it back to me."

"What time would this be?"

"Oh, it would be about ten in the evening when he looked in. Well, I put it in the drawer of my desk the same evening, and as my wife will tell you, it was still there the next evening."

Trenton consulted his notes. Then he looked up. "Thank you, Mr. Eyton. Your wife certainly says that the revolver was there in the evening. The point is that no one has come forward to tell us that it was still there at the time of the murder."

Eyton hit the table. "Yes, but who possibly could take the risk of going to my room and taking away the revolver in that short space of time and replacing it again?"

"Who indeed, Mr. Eyton, but yourself."

"Damnation. I know whether I killed the man or not, don't I?"

"Come, come, Mr. Eyton," said the Inspector, with irritating kindness, "surely you must see the import of your story? In effect, since the evening Mullins returned it to you, no one but yourself had access to it."

Eyton had been watching Trenton's face closely. He realized at last that there was not the slightest doubt in the Inspector's mind that the murderer was sitting opposite him. Laurence, who was unobtrusively taking notes of the conversation, saw the man square his shoulders and attempt to get a grip on himself to meet the danger. He spoke now coolly, but tension was clearly audible in his voice.

"I see the trouble, Inspector. You start from the assumption that your expert evidence about the revolver and the bullet must be right. Now I know experts. I'm one myself. I'm an architect, and before now have had to pronounce on the age of a building. Another architect will give a different opinion. Mind you, we're both genuinely and sincerely convinced that we are right. But obviously one of us is wrong. It's the same with your expert. He's wrong, but at the moment there is no one on my side with the knowledge to prove it. But that is the last sort of evidence you ought to apply to judge all the other facts of the case. I say, 'The revolver was in my desk all the time.' You say, 'Then, as that revolver shot Mullins, you must have shot him.' But don't you see," said Eyton, leaning forward earnestly, "that you ought to say, 'I have such and such evidence that Eyton shot him. Therefore that revolver in the desk may have been used.' Then your expert evidence would come in."

The Inspector smiled thinly. "Thank you for the lecture on Evidence. But where is this leading us?"

"To this," pursued Eyton, still with a sort of desperate calm. "How could the revolver have shot Mullins, who died at midday, when nobody could get at it but I, and I was away in London all day?"

Laurence felt compunction at the candour of Eyton's falsehood. It took a really honest man to tell so transparent a lie.

The Inspector was on him like a flash. "Indeed, Mr. Eyton, and how can you account for the fact that you left for lunch at one o'clock sharp and that your colleagues did not see you again until three-thirty?"

"I happened to have a long luncheon interval, that is all," answered the architect stubbornly.

He did not yet realize that the policeman was merely playing with him.

"Of course you lunch at the same place each day. The waitress would remember you?"

Eyton made a gesture of remembering. "Well, now I come to think of it, I tried a new place that particular day. The Tamworth."

"H'm," the Inspector grunted. "Unfortunate. They serve about five thousand meals a day there, I believe, so the chances are they wouldn't remember you."

"No, I suppose they mightn't," answered the other with an attempt at cheerfulness. "But after all I could hardly know I would need an alibi that day. Otherwise I could have gone to my usual place to feed."

"No doubt. I am afraid that doesn't quite clear the matter up." The Inspector paused cruelly. "The ticket-collector at Peppering Station, by whom I happened to be standing yesterday morning, identified you as a man who came back on the 1.30 p.m. from London on the day of the murder."

The confidence died abruptly from Eyton's eyes. "Nonsense, the man's mistaken!"

"The man is not mistaken, Mr. Eyton, as you very well know," said the Inspector quietly. "Although he doesn't know their names, he knows all the season-ticket holders by sight well enough. But this is a small point. At a quarter to two, Mr. Eyton—a quarter of an hour after this train got into Peppering—you were at The Turrets."

The colour went again from Eyton's face. "I deny it," he said.

"No doubt," replied the Inspector smoothly. "I expected you would. It doesn't, however, depend on your word but on that of trustworthy witnesses, who will not only testify to the fact of your presence, but to the agitation you were in at the time."

Eyton's eyes turned from the Inspector's face to Laurence and then to the windows. When at last he spoke it was in a voice that had an undertone of panic.

"I see. I've been a fool to suppose you wouldn't find this out. And of course the ticket-collector! Somehow I never thought of that. I ought to have told you the whole story from the beginning."

The Inspector smiled. It reminded Laurence of the smile of the tiger, returning from his walk with the Nigerian lady. "Much better, sir," he said seductively, "to tell everything from the beginning."

"It really goes back a long way," said Eyton slowly, his brow wrinkled in thought. "I know it is going to be difficult to make you see exactly what happened. It goes back to months ago. You see I have known the Mullinses and I have seen what is going on there." He turned to Laurence appealingly. "Look here, Sadler, you've seen Patricia Mullins. You know the kind of woman she is. Do you think it was her fault that the life of those two was a hell at The Turrets—and everybody who knew them will tell you it was a hell? Oh, I know I was a fool, but no man who had any guts could help feeling pity for her from the bottom of his soul. I would have done anything for her. But she never gave me the slightest encouragement. Not the slightest. I don't believe I should have ever known what was going on there if I hadn't come upon her in an unguarded moment and I almost forced the truth from her. After that she confided in me more often, and I think, perhaps, it made her feel a little better. But it was never anything but grudging, wrung out of her by her loneliness and distress. I tell you that swine Mullins was a fiend incarnate. It is charity to say he must have been mad. He seemed to spend most of his waking hours doing nothing but to devise some means of hurting her. She confided in me once that she thought he was trying to make her mad so that he could lock her in an asylum! I Imagine the pitch things must have got to for her to think that! But it was during the last six months that he was most devilish. Pat said she felt sure sometimes that he had the thought of murder in his mind. He had kept on hinting at it, not clearly but in an obscure way. The moment afterwards he would act as if he had been joking. But, Pat said, there hadn't been any joke about the look in his eyes. And all the time there had been the terrible uncertainty of it. At first she thought he was only waiting some opportunity when he could kill her safely. It grew to such a pitch that she made Bridget always sleep within call, and she refused to eat anything unless it had come straight from the kitchen. And all the time he was watching her, seeing this going on in her mind, and enjoying it enormously. But just recently she gave up this idea. She thought he had some still more horrible plot." Eyton paused. His eyes were a little dazed. "Now I see what it was, but we never guessed it then.

"On the evening he returned that revolver to me he was in one of his strange moods. But he said nothing out of the ordinary until he turned to go. Then it was as if he was unable to resist the urge to speak. He said (and I remember the exact words because I repeated them later over and over again)—he said, 'I feel quite guilty about taking your revolver, Eyton. It would be so compromising, wouldn't it, if your revolver was implicated in some horrible happening at our house?' Then he laughed and went away...

"I thought nothing about it at the time. But as I was going up to town I suddenly recollected his words. 'Supposing something horrible happened!' As I said the words to myself I remembered the gloating look in his eyes. And the more I thought of it, the more full of sinister possibility it seemed. Why return the revolver to me after keeping it so long? Why pay a special visit, late at night, to do so? Why those strange words, almost wrung out of him as if against his better judgment? I had a horrible premonition that Pat's worst fears had come true. That Mullins had killed her. Of course I tried to tell myself I was a fool, but there had been something indescribable in his face… All the morning I wrestled with the thought. I spoiled ten sheets of paper with the one elevation I was working on. At last I couldn't stand it any longer. I went out, caught the train to Peppering, and dashed straight up to The Turrets. There I asked for Pat."

His eyes were alight with the recollection. He glared at Trenton. "By heavens, Inspector, if a hair of her head had been harmed, there would have been some justification for your charge. For I tell you, I should have killed the devil with my bare hands."

He pulled himself into calmness with an effort. "But she was all right. I went back to the office laughing at my lack of balance. Of course it was ridiculous. And only in the last two days have I realized the diabolical purpose of the man."

"Indeed," said the Inspector coldly. "I'm afraid we ourselves are still in the dark as to that."

Eyton leaned forward imploringly. "Don't you see what the madman has done? He's killed himself. That was the wicked plot he was hatching. He's committed suicide in such a way that it looks like murder. Don't ask me how he did it. How he locked the door and got rid of the weapon. To his ingenious mind a thing like that would not be difficult. Why else did he draft that will, throwing suspicion on his wife and Holliday? Answer that, for even you don't suggest Pat had a hand in the matter."

"But the revolver," interposed the Inspector gently. "Your revolver!"

Eyton banged the table violently with his fist. "Can't you put two and two together? What evidence have you that my revolver fired the bullet? Your Home Office expert! He applies his tests and he says the bullet must have been fired by my revolver. But don't you see the test is only valid if the man who fired the revolver doesn't know about the tests. But here you have a man whose business is firearms. He's a genius at his dirty game. Do you think he couldn't fool your expert and make him think that it came from another revolver? Particularly"—Eyton leaned forward—"particularly, remember, when he'd had my revolver for nearly a year to experiment with before he returned it to me! Do you think in that time he couldn't fake it to fire a bullet exactly like that fired by some other revolver? And if so, wouldn't it confirm my theory that he returned the revolver to me the very evening before he committed suicide? To give me no time to get rid of it, of course. That was his plot, to involve Pat, and myself, and perhaps Holliday, in his murder! To smirch his wife's name utterly and for ever."

The Inspector looked at him curiously. "So this is your statement, Mr. Eyton? You have nothing more to tell us?"

"I have told you everything."

There was a silence broken only by the rasping of Laurence's pen. At last he had completed the statement, and Eyton signed it and initialled each page in silence. Then Inspector Trenton rose.

"You will appreciate that the law must take its course. George Eyton! I arrest you for the wilful murder of Antony Mullins! Here is the warrant."

Chapter Sixteen

AFFAIR OF A FALSE BEARD

"So you were right!" said Laurence.

"So I was," said Sandy abstractedly.

"Do you feel proud?"

"I don't feel proud," answered Sandy thoughtfully. "I suppose it *is* certain that Eyton killed Mullins, and therefore I ought to be pleased that I'd found the evidence that put him where he is. The trouble is the other people that get dragged into it."

"Mrs. Eyton?"

"Yes. It's terrible. She's tearing round like a mad thing. She's been round to see Pat. That was one awful scene. Then she went round to poor Filson. Another scene. Of course she rushed round to me at once."

"Inspector Trenton got it too."

"Well, he's only a dried-up old hen, so it didn't worry him."

"My superior, Sandy. Kindly speak respectfully or I shall be compelled to take action."

"I withdraw. But it's rather awful for the children."

"More awful if their father was a murderer and it wasn't found out."

"I wonder. Do you know, sometimes I think we take murder too seriously."

"I say, old thing, be careful. I can't allow this sort of thing."

"No, don't be funny, Laurence. It isn't at all humorous. Wouldn't it be terrible if I were wrong?"

"Just like a woman! No imagination. You entice Eyton into the snares of the law, and then when he's there you feel sorry for him."

"Well, I do. I feel like that awful man with the red beard."

"Captain Kettle?"

"No, no! With the pieces of eight. Don't be aggravating. You know who I mean."

"Long John Silver? He had the pieces of eight but not the red beard."

"You really are infuriating, Laurence. You know perfectly well who I mean. I remember *now*. Jonas!"

"I see. I gather you mean Judas. There's no need to hang yourself. After all, you only precipitated matters a bit. I knew Eyton had a revolver, and as soon as I had collected it and sent it to the Home Office expert, he would have spotted it was the fatal weapon. Then the rest would have followed automatically. In fact, old thing, to all intents and purposes you've only taken a short cut and dashed in ahead of us unfairly. And it was only luck that the short cut proved and took you to the right place."

"You men are all the same," said Sandy angrily. "You simply refuse to admit women have any brains, and if we ever do discover anything, you always rack your petty brains to try and find some excuse to show that we don't really deserve any credit for it."

"All right, have it your own way," said Laurence resignedly. "It'll be all your doing when Eyton gets strung up."

"Laurence, don't be perfectly abominable!" exclaimed Sandy furiously. "Speaking in such a ghastly way about a man I know. You are trying to make me out a sort of—one of those knitting creatures."

"Eh!"

"Don't stare at me like that. You know who I mean. One of those ghastly French Revolution women who knitted while the heads dropped into the tumbril."

"They travelled in the tumbril, old thing. But I get the idea."

"Yes. You see, you knew perfectly well who I meant. Now listen. I've been doing some more detective work."

Laurence gave a hollow groan. "Good God! My dear Sandy, with what earthly object, when we've got this case perfectly tied up in a bag?"

Sandy smiled complacently. "This detecting business grows on one. Besides, the first murderer is never the real one. It is generally the third. Or the fourth."

"What on earth are you talking about?"

"Poor Laurence!" said Sandy pityingly. "Have you never read any detective novels?"

"Good Lord, no!"

"That explains it. No wonder you've been so hopelessly staggered by the mystery. Now listen! I've been up to London."

"London. Why on earth London? I suppose that's part of your theory. Mullins was shot in London, went back to The Turrets, and then suddenly found he was dead."

"No, silly, I'm after my first suspect."

"Really, dear child, you've had so many that I can't possibly remember at this date who the first was."

Sandy refused to be annoyed. "Constant, of course. The horrid little Secretary fellow who came into all Mullins' money."

"He didn't come into all Mullins' money," Laurence pointed out wearily. "The Society of which he is secretary came into it, which is a little different, though of course one could hardly expect a woman to see the difference."

"You're getting a perfect cat. However, there it is. I'm hounding Constant down."

"Really, Sandy, this is a bit too thick! You mustn't go about hounding people. Poor little fellow! Good Lord, you know that he was at the office all the day of the murder. Why, even if he came to us and confessed he'd done it we'd just laugh at him, his alibi is so perfect."

"Very suspicious that. Anyway, I had a long chat with him, and I discovered one terribly sinister thing about him."

"You've actually interviewed him! What on earth excuse did you give?"

"Naturally one needs tact for this game. Knowing he was a friend of Mullins, I simply typed out a little testimonial to myself, dated it a month ago, signed it with Mullins' name, sent it in, and asked if he would see me about giving me a job."

"Do you realize that is forgery?"

"Silly!" said Sandy tolerantly. "Of course it isn't. Mullins would have done it for me any time, and anyway I was doing it for a good cause."

Laurence laughed sardonically. "And women serve on juries."

Sandy ignored him. "Well, after a great deal of palaver, and my insisting on seeing him, he did see me. Well, my dear, I am sure he was quaking in his boots. He behaved in the oddest manner, I am sure he was trembling."

"With suppressed laughter, I should imagine. He probably recognized the forged signature."

"Don't be hateful. He said he had no vacancies on his staff; and how terrible this Mullins business had been; and all the usual stuff. But the point was, I discovered the most sinister thing."

"Well, hurry up, what was it?"

"I swear he had on a *false beard*! Just fancy!"

Laurence chuckled. "Did it fall off once or twice during the interview?"

"Don't be a fool. No, of course not. But I could see it was false."

"How?"

"Don't be irritating. I could see it at once. I sort of sensed it. I simply longed for the courage to seize it and yank it off. But really one would have felt so silly with the beard in one's hand. One couldn't exactly wave it and say, 'So you murdered Antony Mullins!' It would be one of those Latin things."

"A *non sequitur* possibly."

"Exactly. As long as his alibi is good, of course, one can't do anything. However, I can hang round the office. But that isn't really the most sinister thing."

"You alarm me. Did he perhaps pull off his beard and turn out to be Mrs. Murples."

"Don't be feeble. No, I became perfectly certain that I saw him once on the Estate."

"When?"

"That's just it. I can't for the life of me remember."

"Well, perhaps you did. After all, he was a friend of Mullins and must have often come down here."

"I thought that. So very casually I asked him if he'd ever been to The Turrets. Of course it fitted naturally into the conversation, after we had talked about the murder. And he said he had never been there."

"It's certainly a bit odd."

"Yes, isn't it? What do you think I ought to do about it?"

"Forget it!" said Laurence rudely.

I I

"So you have sent for me after all." Filson, looking worse than on the evening Sandy had called to see him, stared moodily at Patricia Mullins.

She nodded. "Inevitable, wasn't it?"

"I wondered whether it was."

She seemed surprised, and for a moment she scanned his face intently. "I sometimes wonder if you understand me the least little bit, Frank."

He laughed harshly. "I sometimes wonder too. And I think your suspicion is right. I don't!"

"You know of Eyton's arrest?"

"Of course."

"I mean, you know the horrible coincidences that have turned up. So that it seems no jury on earth would think him innocent."

"So I understand."

"Why are you so cold? Surely you see it mustn't take place. You must stop it. You must tell the police everything."

He hesitated. "It isn't very easy for me. Couldn't you—"

"No. Never," she said vehemently. "You must. It is the only way."

Suddenly he became voluble. "I think it is ridiculous," he said suddenly. "I don't know what's come over you the last two or three days. Anyone would think you were a suburban Madame Bovary, with all her petty stings of conscience and absurd remorse. What has changed you?"

"I don't think we're changed," she said slowly. "I think we are opening our eyes and discovering that we are two ordinary, conventional people whose sensibilities have drifted them into false positions. You speak of Madame Bovary, and that is what we are— bourgeois. And for our sort this can only mean a tragic ending."

He made an impatient gesture. "For God's sake don't let's moralize. At least we've avoided that. Darling, if we must be—but it's absurd."

"It must be. And even if I said nothing, if I had never written to you, wouldn't it have happened just the same?"

He dropped his eyes. "As usual, you see farther than I do. If it had gone on, I should have found it ghastly not to—tell! When it was just Mullins it seemed nothing. But George Eyton! Well, I'll see the police to-night."

"I suppose we say good-bye now. And I am afraid it's going to be a rather feeble good-bye. Of course there's hope. There's always hope. But still good-bye."

"Is that all?"

She smiled pitifully. "Darling, I know it sounds cruelly frozen. But that's how I feel—frozen. It is a bitter thing to say now, but you know it's never been love—on my side. That's what makes it so terrible. It has been wonderful—a sort of light in my life. But not the real thing."

"I can't understand you, Pat," he said humbly.

"I don't understand myself," she answered. "I'm afraid I wasn't made for tragic situations. I ought to have fallen in love with somebody incredibly ordinary and have surrounded myself with a perfectly prosaic household. Instead of which I seemed to be hurled about in a sort of devil's theatre. And I can't live up to it. So it's good-bye, and I can't just now say any more than—good-bye."

"Good-bye!"

III

Sandy felt a twinge of pure pity when she met Patricia coming slowly down Oak Avenue. As may have been gathered, they did not get on well together, and Sandy had felt only a passing feeling of sympathy for the woman, in spite of her obviously intolerable position with his murder trial centred round her—always her, however the other pieces were arranged. Now, her face a mask of tragedy, she walked blindly past Sandy without seeing her.

"Good heavens, did she really love Eyton?" Sandy exclaimed to herself.

Patricia did not answer Sandy's first greeting, and the second time she merely stared at her, half-dazed.

Sandy believed in frankness. "My dear, you look ghastly. Are you feeling ill?"

"Very," said Mrs. Mullins with a wry smile.

"Come into my place for a moment and have a drink."

Patricia was in the state when one could more or less steer her, like an inanimate body, where one wanted, and she offered no objection when Sandy sat her in the lounge of "Newmarket" and poured her out a drink.

"You're taking all this business too much to heart," said Sandy. A somewhat banal remark, she reflected as she made it.

Patricia hardly heard her. "Is it never going to stop?" she muttered.

"Really, you know, they say Eyton has a very good chance."

"Yes, he'll get off," said Mrs. Mullins absently.

"Eh?" said Sandy, a little startled. "Is there any fresh evidence?"

"There will be to-night."

Sandy paused a little. Was Patricia, after all, as implicated as she had suspected at the outset? Was she going to speak?

"I'm afraid I don't follow you."

"I really don't know what I am saying," said Mrs. Mullins piteously, staring at the carpet. "I don't know why I should seem to involve everyone in this awful case. First one, then another."

"Well, good Lord, it wasn't your fault!"

"I think it was my fault," said Patricia miserably. "Not in the ordinary sense, but that's not much comfort. My dear, the trouble is, I haven't strength of mind. I ought to have broken right away from all this at the beginning. The first time there was coldness between Tony and me, and I started to get frightened, I should have gone away. But I couldn't. One is so helpless without money, caught in the domestic squirrel cage. Oh, I can't expect you to understand it—free, strong-willed, economically independent. But there it is. And if one is weak enough to stay, one is weak enough to hold one's hand out to people to save one. And instead one drags them in."

Sandy felt embarrassed and murmured something. There was a pause.

"But have they found the real murderer?" she asked.

Patricia looked away. "He is giving himself up to-night."

Sandy started. "Who? Good God, but you don't mean Frank?"

Patricia nodded.

"Oh, but it's absurd," said Sandy urgently. "It's impossible! You must stop him. He's got some wild idea at the back of his mind! It's just the mad sort of thing he would do. But murder, never. You *must* stop him. Do you hear? Or are you in on this?"

"What do you mean?"

"Oh, you know what I mean. Is he sacrificing himself in a noble gesture? It's the sort of damn ridiculous thing he would do," said Sandy angrily. "Don't stare at me like that. Is he doing this for you?"

"You're making this very difficult," answered Patricia. She got up. "We're very nearly of an age, I think, but sometimes I feel worlds older than you. Don't you understand that sometimes these things happen to the most ordinary and nice people? Or are all people angels or devils still in your world?"

"I'm not a child," replied Sandy furiously. "I believe I know the man's character better than you do."

Patricia's face softened. "I shouldn't have said what I did. In fact, I would never have said anything if I had realized."

"Realized what?"

The other woman pulled her gloves quietly on her exquisite hands. "You're the sort of girl who wants to drag everything in the open!" she said, smiling sadly.

"What exactly did you mean?" pressed Sandy coldly, refusing to be side-tracked.

"My dear, I always thought you didn't like him."

"We quarrelled a bit perhaps. But this is different. I must go round and see something is done about this at once. God knows what sort of mess he has got into."

"And see that something is done about it," repeated Mrs. Mullins wistfully. "If only I had been able to say that, in the tone you do, and mean it, all this would never have happened."

Chapter Seventeen

CONFESSION OF AN ARTIST

"**G**entleman called who says he knows who murdered Antony Mullins, sir," remarked Sergeant Vane unemotionally. "Very positive about it."

Inspector Trenton looked round from his desk. "So do we!" he said grimly. "Who the devil is he? Mad?"

"No, sir, I shouldn't say he was exactly mad. Got a very sarcastic way of speaking, but he seems quite sane."

"Show him in," said the Inspector wearily. He turned to his assistant. "What do you make of that, Sadler?"

"The usual looney, or neighbour with a grudge, I expect."

The door opened.

"Good Lord, Filson!"

The artist looked more unkempt than usual. He was wearing a shapeless tweed jacket and a pair of dingy flannel trousers enlivened here and there by a smear of imperfectly removed paint. He scowled ferociously at Trenton.

"Are you in charge of this case?"

"I am Inspector Trenton. Yes, I am conducting the investigation into the death of Antony Mullins. You, I believe, are Francis Filson."

Filson snorted. "Yes, my dear Watson, I am. You deduced it, I suppose, from the clot of clay on my left boot. Bah! It's easy to understand why you damn fools are making such a hash of the case."

Inspector Trenton leaned back in his chair and looked at his visitor severely. "Mr. Filson, we are public servants and consequently prepared to listen to the statements of any witnesses, but I warn you

I do not tolerate insolence. If you have in fact anything to tell us, it will be necessary to be considerably less offensive in your manner."

"I shall be as offensive as I damn well please and you'll listen to me," said the other, who seemed in a state of uncontrollable excitement. "You'll listen to me because I've got something to tell you that you'll want to hear." He leaned forward and the thick hand which gripped the arm of his chair trembled with nervous eagerness. "*We* murdered Antony Mullins."

The Inspector exchanged a glance with Laurence. "Do I understand you to state that you collaborated with Eyton in the murder?"

The artist gave a groan. "Merciful heavens, talk about one-track minds! Why in creation should I wish to collaborate with Eyton? No, I mean, of course, Patricia—Mrs. Mullins—and myself."

The Inspector blinked. "That is a very surprising statement, Mr. Filson. Let me say at once that we have a body of evidence which deeply implicates Eyton. Otherwise, of course, he would not have been charged. Now I must first caution you that—"

"Everything I say may be used in evidence against me," echoed Filson irritably. "Of course. Do you think I am telling you this to while away the hours to dinner?"

"At a later date you may be more interested in these legal formalities," said the Inspector, unruffled. "Now tell us your story, in your own words and your own time, Mr. Filson." He signalled discreetly to Laurence to take the necessary notes.

"Of course," began Filson, "this blighter Mullins ought to have been murdered ages ago." The Inspector's eyes widened, but he merely nodded. "If it weren't for the infernal difficulty of doing it in this country it *would* have been done long ago, I can tell you, either by myself or Pat or Eyton. Though Eyton really was nothing more than a friend of Pat's who was a bit sorry for her and was too much of a family man ever to risk getting put in the dock. But I'll say at once that every time Pat told me something more about the brute I begged her to give me permission to clear the earth of the scum. Drop one of his own foul bombs on him for instance, and blow him to such little bits there wouldn't be an inquest. But she wouldn't. She was too frightened that I wouldn't succeed, I think!

"Well, this went on until the time when Pat began to get scared that he had it in his mind to murder her. As soon as this happened I offered to go and push his face through the back of his head, and generally put the fear of the Lord into him. But that nearly sent her into hysterics. She really thought he was almost superhuman, and that whatever I did would only make it ten times worse. Honestly, I sometimes thought she would have been afraid to leave him even if the angel Gabriel had come down with a fortune in one hand and a safe conduct from the Almighty in the other. So naturally she was even more afraid of anything being done that would infuriate him, and yet leave him enough wits to think out some way of getting back at her.

"When she began to be seriously afraid of violence, and told me some of the nasty hints he had let fall, in his famous manner, I managed to persuade her to do something. I gave her my revolver and told her, if ever he tried to hurt her, to shoot him and make a complete job of it. Then, I said, Eyton and I would lie ourselves pink if necessary to see that she got off on a plea, of self-defence. It seemed to me the likeliest form of murder to get away with, but I must say I still worried her to give me a chance to have a crack at the brute and knock the stuffing out of him. But she wouldn't.

"At last she began to get really scared. The day before he was eliminated she came to me swearing that he was planning something diabolical. Once again I asked to be allowed to have a crack at the swine. No, she wouldn't have it, but she said that she wouldn't part with the revolver for a moment, but keep it in her bag. Then if he attempted to start anything, she would use it.

"Now I don't know if you have learned that Mullins was such a jealous swine that when he went up to town by train he wouldn't even allow his wife to use the car. He used to leave the garage door locked. The cad couldn't bear the thought of Pat driving around the country out of his control. Fact. When Pat told me this I was absolutely furious. So we got round Bridget to get round Dimmock, who's the odd-job man and also cleans the car, and next time Dimmock had the key to clean the car we shoved it on a piece of soap and got an impression. Of course he didn't know Bridget wanted it for Pat. I'm fairly handy with my fingers and from the impression I made a second key out of a blank. So Pat and I often used to have the car out, and, by Jove, we enjoyed those drives!

"On the morning of the murder I suddenly remembered I'd left my gloves in the car. We'd been for a drive the day before. Of course this gave me a fright, and I legged it round as soon as possible to get them back. I popped in the garage, leaned in the car to pick them up, and then, my God, I jumped a mile, for there was something all curled up in the seat with its head shoved under the dashboard and the soles of the feet poking out of the window. I turned on the dash-board switch and there was the head with a neat little hole with blood round it in the back. That was the first corpse I had seen and it turned my stomach for a moment. I had a horrible hallucination that in spite of the hole in the back of the head if I turned the corpse over I should find Mullins was grinning and winking in his usual fiendish way; and then I told myself not to be a fool."

"Did you attempt to see whether life was extinct?" asked Trenton.

"I did not. It would have been too bad if he'd still been alive! I didn't touch him. The horrified feeling passed off and I suddenly thought it damn funny to see the blighter with his head on the floor and his spats in the air and his fur coat still immaculate, but as dead as a door nail. The next moment I felt as frightened as hell. I thought, 'Good God, it's not going to be easy for Pat to prove self-defence with a bullet wound in the back of the head. We must get rid of the body. And how the devil does one do that?' The answer came to me at once. Fire! The garage would burn as easily as anything. First of all, however, I had to make sure Pat didn't lose her head, for the shock must have been pretty awful, once the desperation that made her do it passed off.

"I went into The Turrets and found her. I didn't knock, of course, but went straight in through the side entrance which led to the North Room. She gave a startled cry when I came in the room suddenly and pulled out the revolver. 'My God, this will never do, Pat,' I said. 'Give me that revolver.' 'What do you want to do with it?' she asked. 'Never mind,' I said. 'Look here, Pat, the less you know from now on the better. Go straight into the North Room and stay there until I see you.' I bundled her down the corridor— she seemed a bit dazed—and dashed back to the garage which, of course, I had locked after me. Well, I unscrewed the tap union of the petrol-tank. Mullins' car was one of the huge luxury jobs his firm built when they were making cars, though of course they gave up doing so a little while ago. An old-fashioned job, but went like a top. In fact it was old-fashioned enough to have a dashboard petrol-tank, so when I unscrewed the tap union all the petrol gushed into the car. I don't mind admitting it gave me the shudders, fumbling about with the spanner under the dashboard and every now and then touching the body, but I shut my eyes and tried to pretend it was something else. Luckily there were about ten gallons of petrol in the tank. I emptied out the can of oil which was standing in the garage over the walls and floor, to make a good job of it, because there's nothing like lubricating oil for keeping a blaze going. I peered out of the door to see that the coast was clear. Then I got hold of a bit of string that was in the garage, rolled it in oil to make a fuse of it, and led it away from the car. All I had to do was to light one end, pop out of the garage and lock the door after me.

"I went straight back to my place and hid the revolver in a drawer and locked the drawer. Then I walked to The Turrets. The garage was burning beautifully. Nobody had spotted it yet. I went indoors. The whole business had only taken me about half an hour and Pat was still in the North Room. She was obviously in a state of utter nerves. I took her hands in mine and said, 'Don't worry, Pat, everything is all right. Now listen to me carefully. You know absolutely nothing of anything except that you were in the North Room with me from half-past twelve till now. I was painting your portrait. That will do as an excuse because we've already started it. It'll seem a bit odd that we didn't leave the room for lunch, but we can say we had it in here and that Bridget brought it in. I can fix that with Bridget. But whatever happens you must stick to the story.' Pat was white and scared and shivering, so I said again, 'Don't worry and don't think about it.' I thought she was going to get badly worked up for a moment, but I managed to soothe her. 'Look here,' I said. 'Just think of everything as a nightmare which you've had. It still seems real to you, but you know it isn't.' Just as I was saying this we heard a lot of shouting in the yard. So we went down and mingled naturally with the people. I thought Pat was going to give something away when she keeled over after the body was found, but she's been simply splendid.

"We really thought we'd got away with it, when these blasted coincidences came about and you arrested Eyton. What a damnable position! We could explain everything and yet there was nothing we could do short of confessing. And so, at last, we decided to confess.

"It seems a rather foolish ending," Filson said reflectively, his sullen face now more reposeful than Laurence had ever seen it. "I always imagined Pat to be like myself, quite without scruples, you know, but these last few days she's been nearly driving herself frantic with remorse. I might really have known she was like that from the way she always held me at arm's length, although in her silent, thoughtful way she would listen to anything I said to her. I tried to tell myself it was because she was afraid of her husband, but I might have guessed she suffered from respectability. In fact I realized at last that she would never be able to forget what a moment's panic had driven her to. It's so absurd. I've never given a moments thought to the ethical aspect of it myself.

"When Eyton was arrested I saw that was the finishing touch. Of course she cracked up. And all because you police were so blundering. Can you imagine anything more aggravating, to be betrayed, not by the cleverness of one's opponent but by his bone-headedness! It's all the more ironical because Eyton would have given anything to help Pat if he'd known she'd done this. Well, he probably guessed she had. Instead of which he's unintentionally landed her in this mess."

Inspector Trenton was watching him with an odd expression on his uncommunicative features. He exchanged a glance with Laurence.

"This is a very extraordinary story, Mr. Filson!" he began hesitantly.

"I should damn well think it is."

"We're particularly interested in this revolver. It was the revolver you bought some time ago at Pearson's?"

"Yes."

"Can you tell us how you disposed of it?"

Filson laughed a trifle shamefacedly. "Oh, Sadler here guessed it pretty well. I'm damned if I could think of any way of getting rid of it. You see I got the idea that I was being followed, and every time I started to go to the river and drop it in—which seemed the obvious place—I felt dead certain I was being followed. Guilty conscience, eh? I went out umpteen times to bury it too, and came back with it each time. At last, when I'd taken it out once to bury it somewhere one early morning, I lost my nerve again and started to come back. I got near the cottage and saw a fellow waiting on my doorstep and my heart turned over about fifteen times. I felt certain he was a plain-clothes man and would ask to search the house—and me as well—and that the game would be up. Silly, of course, but there's nothing like a spot of murder to make you start imagining things. I simply felt I must get rid of the darn thing, so I wiped it all over to get any finger-prints off and just chucked it down where I was, which happened to be the path leading to the New House. Then I hopped home as quickly as I could. When I got home my plain-clothes man turned out to be Mrs. Wimpole's husband come to say she was too ill to turn up that day. And I hadn't the nerve to go back and pick up the revolver!

"Well, I thought I must make an effort to cover up my tracks, so I wrote that anonymous letter. I knew the Battling Bantam hung round Bridget. I'd often seen him there. After all, I thought, if I suggest he has something to do with the business it'll send them tearing round a bit after a false scent, and, anyway, it gives an excuse for the revolver being found. And I knew that as soon as they investigated deeply enough they would find it couldn't be the Battler, so it wouldn't really be unfair. A bit weak, of course, but I tell you if I'd had that revolver in the house much longer I should have gone loopy. I gave the most colossal sigh of relief when I found you cheerful fatheads had come to the brainy conclusion that the revolver you found hadn't done the deed."

"No doubt," said the Inspector non-committally. "Now this is a most remarkable story, Mr. Filson, and I am quite sure I never expected to hear such a story told me in my service in this Force. You appreciate, of course, that if true you may be charged not only as an accessory after the fact, but—since you gave Mrs. Mullins the revolver with intent—an accessory before the fact, which is a much more serious matter?"

"What the devil does that jargon mean?"

"It is a question," said the Inspector, "of whether you actually participated in the murder by providing the weapon and inciting, or merely assisted the murderer by concealing the crime."

"Damned if I care! As far as I'm concerned you can charge us both with murder. I'm quite ready to take Eyton's place."

"I don't follow you."

"Heavens, must one say everything twice in a police station? Lock me up and let Eyton go back to his devoted family!"

"Good gracious me!" said the Inspector. "We can't act on the spur of the moment like that. I must consult my superior before we drop the charge against Mr. Eyton. And your story has to be confirmed, you know."

Filson picked up his hat with a snort of disgust, but without the excitement with which he had entered the station. "Of all the confounded red tape! I suppose if I dotted you on the nose, here and now, you would have to send a registered letter to the Chief Constable to find if you ought to take proceedings or get further confirmation."

"I think," said the Inspector with a twinkle in his eye, "that would come into the category of actions in regard to which officers may use their own initiative."

"I'm relieved to hear it, honestly I am! And may I ask what you propose to do if, when you finally condescend to arrest us, you find we've sneaked off to Paraguay?"

The Inspector smiled grimly. "I suggest you try it first. When you have succeeded, ask me again."

Laurence placed a sheaf of papers in front of the artist.

Filson looked at him closely. "Well, what do you think about it?" he said, scrawling his signature to the statement. "You've kept damned quiet!"

Laurence looked him in the eye. "A very decent effort. Honestly, you're a good sport. I'm afraid it's wasted."

Filson flung the pen on the floor. "Is this a madhouse?" he exclaimed. The door slammed violently behind him.

Trenton gently rubbed the palms of his hands together. He looked at Sadler interrogatively. "Well, what do you make of it?"

"Pure invention," said Laurence promptly, "from beginning to end."

Chapter Eighteen

A WOMAN IS SILENT

Inspector Trenton stared speculatively at his subordinate. "No," he said with finality, "that story can't be invention."

"Why not, sir?"

"Because it accounts for certain things. And no other explanation can account for them." Trenton had fallen more and more into the habit of speaking to his assistant as an equal.

"What particular things were you thinking of?"

"The behaviour of these two ever since the murder. The faked alibi. The revolver disposed of in such a crude way. The anonymous letter. Here we have a story which fits those very odd and difficult facts. Surely it must be true?"

"But look at the things it doesn't explain. Two things above all. The time-switch. Filson says he caused the fire simply by lighting petrol with a fuse. And Eyton's revolver that fired the bullet which killed Mullins. Surely those facts are key facts. Unless Filson's story accounts for them, oughtn't one to conclude the story is false?"

"Supposing we believe Eyton's story, as well as Filson's. They fit in together. Isn't that some confirmation?"

"But surely, sir, we would expect them to do that if they'd hatched the stories together. And Eyton's story still doesn't explain the revolver or the time-switch."

Inspector Trenton thought in silence. "Do you think Mrs. Mullins and Filson can have made up this story, knowing it was at variance with the facts, so that as we discovered the true facts we should know their confession to be a lie and release them? I mean, just as a man who'd really done a murder might give himself up, pretending to be one of these looneys who always confess to a murder, and so draw suspicion from himself?"

"That," said Laurence, staring hard at the Inspector, "is rather like the plot of a certain film called *The Blonde Killer*,' which is on at the Peppering Palaceum."

The Inspector looked faintly embarrassed.

"It's a very subtle idea," Laurence continued. "Extraordinarily subtle. Does Filson strike you as being subtle?"

"No," admitted Trenton. "Yet he'd have to be pretty subtle to invent that story with all the bits about the feet hanging out of the window and that kind of thing."

"Is it a fact that the bullet was fired from the back?"

"The skull was too much burned by the heat for that to be certain. There must have been a jet of petrol flame playing against the head."

There was a pause. "Well, there's only one thing for it. We must get Mrs. Mullins' story. If she remembers some detail that he couldn't have known, it'll be some confirmation. On the other hand, we may be able to trip her up."

Mrs. Mullins, apparently, had no intention of being tripped up. She sat in the office, an embarrassing image of frozen beauty, staring straight in front of her, until Inspector Trenton felt completely unnerved and Laurence was looking a little drawn about the cheek-bones.

"Mr. Filson has just made a very remarkable statement," began Inspector Trenton. "It implicates you, madam, in the murder of Antony Mullins."

Mrs. Mullins' thin eyebrows rose a trifle. "The use of the word 'implicates' seems to me a trifle odd in the circumstances."

"Possibly. However, we will use it for the moment. It will explain why we have invited you here. We should like to have your story of what happened on the day your husband was killed, and it is my duty to warn you that anything you tell me may, at a later date, be used against you. I hope, of course, that this will be unnecessary, and that your statement will clear everything up. Please tell us what happened in your own words, just as if you were telling a friend."

"Are you a friend, Inspector Trenton?"

Trenton looked a little disconcerted. "At the moment I am a policeman, and as such I am supposed to have no friends. But even if I were not a policeman, I should find it very difficult to advise you. I can only suggest that things have gone so far you can hardly have anything to fear now from telling the truth."

"I am afraid I am not much good at narrative. Surely Mr. Filson told you everything."

"He told us a great deal."

"Then why are you bothering me?"

The Inspector shrugged his shoulders with a disarming smile. "Only to confirm Mr. Filson's story."

Mrs. Mullins smiled with equal sweetness. "In that case, give me his statement. I will tell you if he is wrong or has left anything out."

"That would be against our regulations, madam."

"I don't believe you, Inspector. Mr. Sadler, is it true? I am sure you, at any rate, do not consider it part of a policeman's duty to trap a woman. I see by your embarrassment I guessed correctly. It is not true, Inspector Trenton, and either I see the statement, or I have nothing to say at all."

"Madam, I will be frank. We want something more than confirmation. We want something only you can tell us."

"And that is?"

"How you killed your husband," he said bluntly.

Her cheeks, which had been pale, flamed with blood. She half rose to her feet, and the horror in her eyes was plainly visible to both her watchers. Then it died away as suddenly as it came. Visibly she forced control on herself, and a smile to her lips.

"I had often heard of police methods of interrogation. I thought they were exaggerated. Apparently not. Well, you have the satisfaction of having made me lose my wits for a moment. Unfortunately, I have recovered them. And I repeat: I insist on seeing Mr. Filson's statement before I say a word."

There was silence for a moment. The two men exchanged a glance. In the Inspector's eyes were doubt and hesitation. "I think we ought to," whispered Laurence.

With a nod of assent the Inspector placed before her the pages of closely typed paper. She studied carefully the signature, and read.

Watching her closely, the two men noticed the exquisite gloved hand which was holding the paper begin to shake. A sound that was strangled terror made the Inspector start. Neither were prepared for the sequel—for laughter which began with a sobbing gurgle, which rose and rose until the whole room was filled with the appalling hysterical laughter of a woman in whom control had collapsed, in whose eyes there was no trace of mirth, only anguish and despair...

I I

Half an hour later two men, sweating under their collars, pulled themselves together.

"God, how horrible!" ejaculated the Inspector. "I thought she was never going to stop."

"I can't make it out," said Laurence, his tanned face looking younger than ever in its bewilderment. "I thought when she calmed down she would say something. But she won't say a word. It's extraordinary. I mean, if she disagrees with the statement, why doesn't she say so? And if she doesn't, why the hysteria?"

"I honestly think she hadn't the faintest idea what she was doing, poor soul. She may calm down when she's had time to think it over. Yet she seemed self-possessed enough when she came in."

"Too self-possessed, I fancy. She's the fine-drawn type of woman that will be as impassive as a statue till the breaking-point is reached, and then she shatters suddenly. I can't imagine what set her off. Some little thing, I expect. Just like a touch on the trigger."

"Um." The Inspector lost himself in thought, his thin, bird-like features melancholy in repose. "There's only one thing for it. You must see this fellow Entourage, and find out if there isn't some mistake. If only it weren't Eyton's gun, you see, it would solve everything."

III

Mr. Samuel Entourage proved to be a hearty soul who took nothing very seriously, particularly a murder in the Peppering district of the Thameshire County Constabulary. "What's this?" he said jovially, a large smile on his massive features. "You've got three murderers for the one murder? Bravo! They do things in a big way in Peppering, I can see. And what lie can I tell to help you, old man? Sit down and have a drink."

Laurence explained his trouble. "You see, the couple who admit murdering the old man used a revolver which you say didn't shoot him, and the fellow who denies it has got the revolver which did."

Entourage closed one eye and dug Laurence in the ribs. "I tell you what, old chap, you've got the revolvers mixed, and sent me the wrong one under the right label, or the right one under the wrong label, so to speak. Have another drink."

"Neither. Neither the drink nor the mistake. Because, you see, we sent off the first revolver to you before we got possession of the other."

"Well, the answer appears to me to be a lemon. I should charge them all with obstructing the police with intent. Ha, ha!"

Laurence laughed, but not too enthusiastically. "What I came here to ask you is this. Is there any possibility of error?"

"How do you mean? Are you suggesting Samuel has blundered?"

"No, we don't suppose you have. But would it be possible for someone who knew all about your little tests to anticipate them?"

The expert whistled. "You must have some hot crooks in Peppering. Perfect Chicago. Of course it would be possible. Look here, old man, between ourselves the simplest way is for you to tell me what you hope has happened, and I'll tell you if you're right."

"Well, what we *hope* has happened is that the first revolver we sent you really did the trick."

"Half a jiffy, then, while I look up the microphotographs."

Entourage hummed gently to himself while he went through his records and examined the disputed investigation. At last he shook his head. "Not on your life. Sorry. I couldn't even make that revolver fire that bullet to save my life, and I'm damn sure no one else could. If they could they can have my job right away, and my humble regards."

"That's some negative evidence, at any rate. Here's another possibility. Could a third unknown revolver, suitably faked, fire the bullet—faked so that people would think it was really the second revolver that was used?"

"You Thameshire people don't half have some ideas, you don't. Let me think. Yes, it is possible. Just possible. But if anyone did that, your search is short, because he's got to be a man who knows the gun business from A to Z and then back again. Yes, sir, it's not a job even I would like to undertake, although I think I could do it. But if so, where's your Peppering expert, for I ought to know him?"

"Could Antony Mullins have done it?"

"Hey!" Entourage looked startled. "I thought he was your corpse. It's not a job a corpse could do, particularly not such a dead one as yours."

"There is a suggestion," said Laurence diffidently, "that Antony Mullins, in a fit of insanity, might have shot himself with a revolver faked to produce bullets which would implicate another man."

The expert smiled. "Three murderers needed for one suicide! I take my hat off to our country constabulary! Well, I won't point out little difficulties like getting rid of the weapon after one's dead. That's your look-out. From the purely technical side I should think Mullins would be one of the few men who could carry it out. Let's have another squint at those photos." He regarded them critically for a few minutes. "It's an interesting possibility, old man. When I start to look at them there do seem some unexplained features... And yet I don't know... I just wouldn't like to say one way or the other. Do have another drink."

"Thanks. And thanks for your help. It strikes me we're between the devil and the deep blue sea. We've got a good case against either party, if the other weren't implicated. But I'm damned if I can see which to go for."

"Cheer up. It seems to me only a matter of changing the labels on the revolvers, and you've got your people who confessed tied up in a bag. Good Lord, if they want to be found guilty, the least you can do is to co-operate with them."

"There's a lot in that," admitted Laurence.

IV

The Chief Constable was a little querulous, and in the circumstances this was pardonable. "I think it's really too bad, Trenton. If ever it comes out that those two have confessed on the top of your arresting Eyton, we shall be the laughing-stock of the county."

"I'm very sorry, sir, but I don't see how we could have acted otherwise than we did."

"That's no excuse," growled the Chief. "No bloody fool can help acting like a bloody fool. The point is, we've got millions of people rushing round claiming this confounded murder, and the only person who says he's not done it is the one we've clapped into jail. Isn't that the position?"

"More or less, sir."

"Well, it's got to stop. Trenton, you've driven me to desperate measures!"

"I am sorry, sir."

"I never thought I should have to do it as long as I was Chief Constable of Thameshire, but there it is. I shall call in the Yard!"

"Very well, sir. I am sure I shall do my best to co-operate with anyone the C.I.D. decides to send me."

Like most people who decide to take unpleasant treatment, it seemed most unpalatable the moment it had been definitely decided upon. The Chief Constable temporized.

"Well, I don't want to be unduly severe. I know you have done your best. I'll give you another four days to sort out this Eyton–Filson–Mrs. Mullins tangle. If it isn't cleared up then, I'll have no alternative but to apply at once to the C.I.D."

"Do you think we might call in unofficial outside help?" asked Laurence tentatively.

"What the devil do you mean?"

"I know a bloke who's an absolute expert at these things. He's cleared up one or two murders that were really more complicated than this."

"Who is he? Sounds like something in a book. I had one experience of an amateur in India. Kept on leaping out at people from behind doors to frighten them into a confession. Never again. Can he keep his mouth shut, this fellow of yours?"

"Well, while the case is going on, of course, he'll be quiet enough."

"Does he want a fee? If so, how much?" said the Chief Constable practically.

"No, not a fee. But after the whole thing was over, he'd want to write it up."

"Do you mean he's a writer?"

"A journalist."

"Good God!" exclaimed the Chief Constable.

"It's Charles Venables, of the *Mercury*."

"Oh!" The other became thoughtful for a moment. "Well, he did clear up those Garden Hotel and Carpenter cases. That is, if he did half he claimed he did, which is doubtful. Charles Venables. Is he any relation to that old boy who's got Tankards, near Much Gaming?"

"The son."

"Really, how odd. Can't imagine his son doing that sort of thing. Still, we all have to earn our living somehow. Family's a bit eccentric, anyway. The mother ran three times round Berkeley Square in her nightdress. Charming woman. Completely fearless. That was in the 'nineties, too. Ridiculous thing to do. Completely did for her at Court. Can't think what put the idea in her head. By Jove, though, I remember now! It was 'Shirty' Gloops who dared her. Now the odd thing about 'Shirty'—H'm, as I was saying, if we can rely on this man's discretion, I've no objection. But remember, four days! Not an hour more."

"Very good, sir. Of course I'm not absolutely certain he can come. But he's cleared up that aeroplane murder now, and he ought to be free."

"Well, there it is, Laurence. Call him in, but results in four days or we go to the C.I.D."

Chapter Nineteen

A SMALL BOY OWNS UP

"Hello, Venables. Damn decent of you to come."

"On the contrary, Sadler. I'm grateful. This case sounds odd. I didn't suspect such possibilities when I first found you sitting on the burning deck."

Trenton was looking at the lean young man with ill-concealed curiosity. Sadler introduced him. "Sir, this is Charles Venables, of whom I've spoken. My chief—Inspector Trenton."

The Inspector was gracious. But secretly he was not altogether sure whether he would not have preferred Scotland Yard, who were likely to be more generous in the sharing of credit.

"Of course. Naturally I know and admire your work, Mr. Venables."

"Very good of you to say so. Largely luck I'm afraid. One can't do much when the luck goes against one. It seems to have done so in this case."

Trenton nodded grimly. "It has, and that's a fact!"

"Well, I hope I shall have my usual mascot effect! But I can't expect it to work always."

The three seated themselves and the Inspector passed round a box of cigars, a recent gift from his wife. Laurence took one. Venables did not.

"I say, Venables," said Laurence irrelevantly, "where's the monocle? I miss it."

"Gone for ever I'm afraid. A reviewer friend of mine who reads all the best books accused me of imitating Lord Peter Wimsey.

Well, I hope I know my place, and since then I have given up the monocle. When necessary, I correct the astigmatism of the right eye by spectacles with lenses of unequal power."

"What a shame!"

"Indeed it is a shame. I feel the lack of some distinguishing mark, so that children in the street may say with awe, 'There goes the great Venables.' Have you any suggestions?"

"A pigtail? Or dundrearies?"

"Both ideas will be considered."

"I am afraid," said Laurence, "that journalism is having a bad effect on the famous Venables' elegance."

"No, that's the contraction of credit one reads about so much. But this is boring Inspector Trenton. Let me know exactly what has happened since the time you discovered that the fire had been started by a time-switch."

"Well, as a matter of fact the fellow who confesses to burning the body says he just started it with a match."

"Oh, that's awkward. Such a crude way of starting a fire! Carry on and tell me how this bloke came to confess."

With occasional comment from Trenton, Laurence explained the various investigations which had resulted at last in the arrest of Eyton and the confession of Filson. When he had finished Venables asked for Filson's statement, and studied it in silence.

"You see," said Trenton, as Venables, hunched up in his chair, still made no comment, "we've got three murderers for one murder. And that, in my opinion, is at least one too many."

Venables was rummaging through the various documents filed with the statements. "Good Lord," he said, without looking up, "you don't want to worry. I was once in a case where there were thousands of murderers all competing for the honour."[1]

---

[1]   Mr. Charles Venables is presumably referring to the Carpenter case recorded in *Fatality in Fleet Street*. If so he is guilty of a slight exaggeration.

Venables looked up from the papers with a sudden flash of interest in his grey eyes. "I say, Filson doesn't mention the time he found Mullins' body!"

"No more he did," admitted the Inspector. "Is it important?"

"I see from Marabout's statement that he saw a short stocky man emerging from the garage with some haste at half-past one. Is that Filson? If Filson, not knowing the exact time given in Marabout's statement, also says he went out about half-past one, it's a confirmation of his story, and a very important one."

"Yes, that's so," admitted the Inspector.

"What's more," Venables muttered under his breath, "it's going to place us in a dilemma, as we shall find in due course."

Aloud he said, "Did you test Eyton's revolver for finger-prints?"

"Yes. Absolutely covered with them."

"Have you the enlargements?"

"You'll find them in the pocket in the cover of that guard file."

"I've got them. H'm, I see you've labelled them. Mostly Mullins', of course. Then Eyton's—which, of course, proves nothing because they would be there in any case. Mrs. Eyton's—not many and pretty indistinct. Hello, what's this small thumb-mark?"

"One of the Eyton kids, we suppose. Too small for any adult."

"Oh, yes, those would be the children mentioned in Mrs. Eyton's statement. You don't know which one?"

"No. I hardly suppose one of them could have done in Mullins."

"Why not? But they could hardly have dragged the body about and put it in the car. Still, for the sake of thoroughness we may as well make sure which infant it was."

He was silent for a space, while he thoughtfully blew smoke rings from his cigarette. The result of this meditation was disappointing to his watchers.

"I wish Filson had said what time he found the body—it worries me."

"Good Lord, we can soon settle that. We'll get Filson up here."

"Do, there's a good chap. I've plenty to think over and I must buzz off. I'd like to have a word with Mrs. Eyton about the kids and settle that finger-print business. Can I use your name in vain?"

"Of course." Trenton hesitated, something obviously on his mind. Then he explained, a little embarrassed. "You know I ought to have told you before. We've only got four days. The Chief Constable wants to call in Scotland Yard. However, he's given us four days' grace. Of course such a time is preposterous for a serious investigation, but although we can't find the murderer in that time, he'd extend the period if we could show any progress."

Venables laughed. "And I ought also to have told you that in six days' time I'm leaving for Iconia—which, I am credibly informed, lies between Bulgaria and Kossovia. The ruling monarch appears to have been murdered, and the *Mercury* is sending me out in the optimistic belief that I can wash the mess up. So Death or Glory in four days' time suits me too."

The matter of the time when the corpse was found was settled easily enough, but not pleasantly. For Filson was, if anything, in a worse temper than on his previous visit.

"Look here, what are you playing at?" he demanded. "To begin with, what have you said to Pat? She's in a state of complete nerves and won't speak to me or even answer my letters. And Eyton's still in jail, with Mrs. Eyton dashing round the Estate worrying everyone into tatters of sympathy. Now I get your message that you would like to settle a small point. Good Lord, isn't my story good enough? Why on earth is Eyton still in jail? Or are you afraid to admit you were wrong?"

Trenton spoke in his most soothing voice. "When we say it's a small point we wish to question you on, we mean that it is a minor issue. But it may have a very important bearing on the case. Here is the question. Can you give us, with any certainty, the time when you went into the garage and found the dead body of Mullins?"

"Is that all you want to know? Why didn't you ask me at the time? Yes, I should think I went in there about twenty-five past one. You see as soon as I started thinking of how to get rid of the body and fake up an alibi I looked at my watch, and it was just about half-past one. And I couldn't have come in more than five minutes before."

"You are sure your watch is accurate?"

"Dead accurate. My father gave it to me. It cost an awful lot. But it's been worth it. Keeps as good time as my mains-controlled clock, but that's not saying much, seeing that the electric power wires on the Estate are always being blown down or carried away by owls or weighed down with snow or something."

"Well, that's very good of you, Mr. Filson. That was all we wanted, and we are glad you have been able to clear up the point so definitely."

"But it's not all I wanted. I wanted to give you my frank opinion of the Thameshire County Constabulary, which is as follows..."

II

The lean young man with the bored mouth but extremely keen grey eyes (or were they green?) did not look like a messenger from heaven. He announced himself, in fact, as sent by the Thameshire County Constabulary. The final result, however, was much the same as that for which Mrs. Eyton had been praying—and seeking—in the last few days.

In the presence of her children she was a little restrained. "I think it is shameful. Why are you still keeping my h-u-s-b-a-n-d in p-r-i-s-o-n? Please be careful what you say in front of the children. Enid, Flossie must *not* chew those slippers! I've written to the papers about it, but instead of publishing my letters they send round the oddest women to try and get me to write my life story. I must say that they offer me a lot for it, but thank heavens we've not sunk to that yet, though goodness knows what we have sunk to with the children's father accused of being a m-u-r-d-e-r-e-r. Don't stare, Tommy. How many times have I told you not to gape at people? Run out and weed your garden. How on earth you can believe that awful woman, I don't know, but she seems to have twisted everyone round her little finger. I suppose if you are wicked enough men like it, but I should have thought the police were different."

"I don't exactly belong to the police," explained Venables. "I've been called into consultation on a point that is puzzling them. I may say they are as dissatisfied with the case against your husband as you are. But you see things look so bad that they simply cannot let him out of quod. Enid looks rather as if she knows what quod means, by the way."

"Run and help Tommy, Enid. You'd better all go. Peter and Veronica, take Flossie with you, you know she can't bear to be left behind! Will those children ever learn to close the door! Thank you so much. Well, it sounds a little rude, but what did you really come to see me about?"

"It seems to me that there are one or two points that have only to be established to clear your husband. Only I want your help."

"Well, of course, naturally. Don't be offended—but you're not trying to trap me in any way, are you? I mean that sounds rather rude, but one knows the police have to ask you things and get you to admit things because it is part of their business."

"I am not trying to trap you," said Venables gently.

"You must trust me that far, anyway. The evidence that might help your husband could come from your children. But it is essential that it should be spontaneous. Will you trust me sufficiently to leave me alone with the children for a little?"

Mrs. Eyton, no bad judge of character, took him into the garden and did so.

Venables, left with four young children, put on his most paternal manner. "Now, children, what do you think I have come about?" he asked.

"The 'stalment on the sewing-machine," suggested Veronica, eyeing him closely.

Venables winced. "No, my dear, I've got a present for you from your father."

"Where's Father?" demanded Tommy.

"In quod," whispered Enid.

"Where's quod?" whined Peter.

"Quod is the other side of London," said Venables hastily. "Near the Zoo," he added with inspiration.

"Have you been there, Mr. Venables?" asked Enid politely. "To the Zoo we mean?"

"Oh, rather. Awfully jolly."

"Please will you take us to the Zoo?" demanded Tommy. "Yes, take us to the Zoo," echoed the other two. Veronica started to dance and yell:

> "We want to see the pelican
> Whose beak can hold more than his belly can."

"Sh-h," reproved Enid. "Mustn't say 'belly.'"

Venables endeavoured to recollect the manner of his governess when dealing with his obstreperous youth. "You won't go anywhere unless you can keep quiet and behave yourselves, children! And you certainly won't get the present Father sent you."

"Did he only send one?" said Tommy. "How lousy!"

"Must'nt say lousy," reproved Enid mechanically.

"Shall!"

"I shall pinch you if you do."

"I shall pinch all of you," said Venables fiercely, "if you don't stop arguing. There's only one present for one person."

"Well, whoever gets it must share it," said Enid.

"Yah, what about those liquorice allsorts Mrs. Murples gave you? You guzzled the lot," hooted Peter.

"You beast, I offered to scramble them."

"Only the ones without sugar on."

The liquorice allsorts affair was evidently a bitter one, and Venables, seeing his only ally, Enid, on the verge of tears, hastily interposed his adult authority. "Shut up, all of you. Here's the present." There was silence while he produced a parcel and unwrapped it. It proved to be a very lethal-looking air-pistol.

"Crummy, a six-shooter!" exclaimed Veronica.

"I've got a six-shooter," volunteered Peter.

"Pooh, you baby, yours is only wood. Whoever heard of a wooden six-shooter!"

"It kills at ten paces."

"Rot. It doesn't even fire caps. You have to say *bang*."

"You cad. I pretended to be dead for you the other day."

"For God's sake shut up!" exclaimed Venables.

"Mustn't swear," muttered Enid under her breath.

He decided to ignore the remark. "Now do you know what this six-shooter is for?"

"How many guesses?" asked Veronica warily. "Will you tell us if we're getting hot or cold? We ought to have three guesses each."

"H'm. Well, I'll tell you."

"Oh, you mustn't tell us," pointed out Veronica, shocked, "if you've asked us to *guess*."

"I think perhaps I'd better tell you all the same. Listen, it's for one of you—if he or she tells the truth."

The children at once looked disturbed. Meanwhile they searched their memories for possible misdeeds. As a result all four looked guilty.

Venables dandled the air-pistol gently in his hand. "Now your father had a revolver in the drawer of the room here, which no one was allowed to touch. But someone did touch it. Now if whichever of you did it will own up and take the consequences, you'll get the air-pistol for telling the truth."

There was a pause. At last Tommy propounded a question off-handedly. "Supposing someone owned up, would Father wallop him?"

"I shouldn't be surprised."

Tommy looked at the air-pistol for some time. After all, the effects of the walloping would go, but the pistol would remain. "I did it," he said.

"When?"

"The day Veronica hung on the fire-engine, and they gave her beer."

"You took it out and played with it?"

"Yes. I couldn't get the darn thing to work. I don't think it can have been loaded. But Mother pinched my air-gun and I wanted to shoot a lion—it wasn't really a lion, of course, it was a donkey—and so I thought I'd have a shot with that."

"When did you take it out?"

"After brekker."

"When do you have breakfast?"

"Eight o'clock," said Enid. "Leastway we're supposed to, but Peter's such a lazy little beast it's generally later."

"And when did you put it back?"

"Well, I popped it back in the drawer lunch-time. Before that really, because I came in first so I shouldn't be seen."

"When do you have lunch?"

"Sharp at one except when Mother has a headache."

"Did she have one then?"

"No. But she's had an awful lot since then."

"Now look here, Tommy, did you have the revolver all the time? Never let it out of your sight?"

"Yep. I was hiding in the jungle all the morning."

"You little beast, so that's where you were," commented Veronica. "Why didn't you tell us?"

"You have to hunt lions alone, Veronica. I thought everyone knew that."

"I shouldn't mistake a donkey for a lion, anyway, fat-head."

"That'll do, children. Well, that's all, Tommy. The pistol's yours. And I hope the walloping will be a light one."

"Yes, gimme it then."

"You should say please, Tommy," said Enid. "Mummy says it's bad psychology to give us bribes for doing what we ought to," she added severely.

Venables groaned. "Heavens, what a generation! Well, Tommy, are your hands clean? You mustn't get dust in the action."

The boy exhibited the palms. Yes, the finger-prints tallied.

Venables gave up the pistol after explaining its working.

"O.K. Just like my air-gun!" Tommy whipped round suddenly and pressed the cold muzzle against Veronica's neck. She gave a shrill scream.

"Stick 'em up, youse guys."

"Don't say guy," said Enid.

Veronica recovered herself with an effort. "Ha, ha! Who's going to be walloped?" she jeered.

Tommy ignored her. "Do you think this would kill a bird?" he asked Venables.

"Certainly."

"A duck, do you think?"

"A duck if you got close enough."

"Crummy!" exclaimed Tommy. He was silent for a minute.

"Please will you take us to quod?" said Enid.

"I am afraid I can't do that."

"Will Father be coming back soon?" inquired Veronica.

Venables felt a spasm of pity. They must be missing their father. "He'll soon be back!"

"Good," said Veronica with relish. "The sooner he's back the sooner Tommy will get walloped, the cad."

Chapter Twenty

A TANGLE IS UNRAVELLED

"Sorry. Eyton's no longer in the running!" stated Venables. He was seated in the Inspector's office in the Inspector's best chair.

The Inspector looked startled. "Not in the running! What on earth makes you say that?"

"Filson's evidence, chiefly."

"Well, what about the evidence?"

"He says he found the body *before* half-past one. At half-past one, as you yourself found out, Eyton was steaming into Peppering station on his train. So he couldn't possibly have got to The Turrets until after Mullins was dead."

The Inspector reflected. Next he objected. "Yes, but look here, you can't have it both ways. Either you believe Filson's statement, in which case you would want us to arrest him and Mrs. Mullins, or you disbelieve it altogether. But now you're picking out bits that suit you. I mean, if Filson is telling the truth, we don't have to work out times to know Eyton must be innocent. Because there can't be two murderers. But the whole point is that Filson's story is incredible. So if you don't trust it how can it exonerate Eyton?"

"Very logical. I wriggle out of it like this. The part of his story that exonerates Eyton is the only part that is independently confirmed. Filson says he left the garage in which he found the dead body about half-past one. Marabout saw a short, stocky man emerging from the garage about half-past one. Filson's story, therefore, is confirmed."

"But Marabout didn't see the body."

"I know. But it is hardly probable that a little incident like that would be independently confirmed unless it was true. So we must believe it, even if we've decided not to believe *all* Filson's story!"

"Yes. I see that. Though I can't see it is definite enough to release Eyton on."

"Wait, though. I have corroboratory evidence. This is where my day's snooping comes in. You know those kid's finger-prints on the revolver?"

"I remember. One of the Eyton children."

"Well, it struck me at the time as a bit queer that they should be superimposed on Eyton's finger-prints. Because so far as we knew, Eyton handled the revolver last. It seemed to me probable that a very odd thing had happened. The infant must have handled it on the day of the murder."

"My God!"

"I found the little wretch and got him to tell his story. Here it is. He pinched the revolver at breakfast-time and never let go of it until one o'clock."

"Um, a child witness."

"Oh, untrustworthy as a rule. But not in a case like this. There's negative confirmation from the other children, because he was hiding, they said, and up to something."

"Well, the child had got rid of it by one. Surely Eyton could still have used it for the murder?"

"No. The boy put it back in the drawer in the room where they all have lunch. I found out from Mrs. Eyton that they were at lunch in that room till two. Then they had lessons till the fire-engine broke up the party in disorder. There were at least two children in the room all the time, so Father could hardly have sneaked in and taken it without being seen."

The Inspector tapped out his pipe with a snort.

"Don't you agree?" urged Venables. "This *must* let Eyton out. Because if the revolver was in the dining-room until the corpse was found, it couldn't have been used for the murder. And as the only real connection between the murder and Eyton is his revolver, the case collapses. The fact that he left the office and dashed back to The Turrets proves nothing. It's explained quite adequately by his own story."

Trenton twisted unhappily in his chair—the less comfortable chair. "Damn experts! That fellow Entourage has let us in for all this muddle. This confounded brat even spoils the possibility that Eyton got to Peppering earlier than we thought, sneaked out of the station, murdered Mullins, and dashed back to go past the ticket-collector with the one-thirty crowd, and so establish an alibi."

"I say, that's a good theory! But Eyton didn't leave the office till one. And although he's next door to Victoria Station, that only leaves him five minutes to get on the one-five, which gets in at one-thirty. So anyway that's not possible, child or no child."

Inspector Trenton gloomily revolved his penholder. "This means apologies to Eyton and more sneers in the Press, I suppose. Look here, Venables, you've had experience of this kind of thing. What do you make of this revolver business? Is the expert just a damn fool?"

"Entourage is not just a damn fool. Be sure of that," said Venables gravely. "It puts a very queer complexion on the whole business."

Trenton was doing little sums on his blotting-paper. Then he looked up. "I say, if Mullins was dead at one-twenty-five, which was when Filson found the dead body, how could he have been in town at twelve-thirty?"

"I checked that up this morning. It can just be done in three-quarters of an hour without taking risks. Mullins' old car had quite a turn of speed, and he would know the road perfectly as he drove up regularly. So he might have got back at one-fifteen. That means the murderer must have been waiting, and shot him at once. But that's only reasonable, for as his body was found in the garage, we can assume he was killed in the garage. So if the murderer was lurking in there, he would shoot Mullins directly he had driven in—before he switched off his engine, perhaps. Minimum of fuss and risk that way. But it makes things look black for Mrs. Mullins and Filson, as the only available suspects."

"Good!" said the Inspector, with the first signs of satisfaction he had shown that day.

I I

"I don't like this confrontation business. It's too American for my liking." Trenton was pacing impatiently up and down his office.

Venables was patient. "It's the only way we can get the truth out of these two *without* using American methods. They're both suspect and they won't speak—or we are assuming that they won't speak. Filson certainly pretends to be frank, but I understand you think he is holding back more than the woman."

"I'm positive of it. Absolutely positive."

"There you are, you see. Well, you're not going to tell me that the woman is going to hold her tongue when Filson tells his garbled story in front of her."

"We'll see. They're in the next room. Damned uncomfortable they look, too. Wondering why the devil they are here. And so am I. Let's go in."

They did. Filson was staring, with a look of furious amazement, at Mrs. Mullins. Patricia was looking with composure, but not at him. The same frozen calm that had impressed Trenton when she visited him also fascinated Venables.

The Inspector's speech was intended to be disarming. "I want you both to understand that we are gathered together here for a friendly chat. Neither of you are charged with anything, though naturally at the moment we cannot say more than that. But Mr. Eyton, I may say, has just been released."

"I should damn well think so!" ejaculated Filson.

Trenton went on smoothly. "I am here, and my assistant is here, because we have had charge of the case from the beginning. Mr. Venables is here because he has consented to assist us, and as an expert he has special knowledge of this kind of case. You will understand from that how unofficial this is, for Mr. Venables is not a member of the Force. And we have also invited you two, because in some way you are involved in this case. Yes, Mr. Filson, although you may think that you have made matters clear, you have, in fact, made them very much obscurer."

Venables, his lean face a trifle Satanic in repose, murmured assent. He now leaned forward. "Mr. Filson, will you tell us again in your own words what happened on the day of the murder?"

"Confound it, you people typed out the whole statement and I signed it! I see you have got the copy there."

"Exactly. But it is a different matter to read a manuscript and to hear the story in a man's own words."

"It's not a recitation. I don't propose to give a performance twice nightly at this place."

Venables looked at him with a sudden assumption of candour. "I'd better tell you the truth. It always pays. We want to confirm your story. You see, we still don't know that your story is true. If in your own words you tell it again, and it doesn't differ in any of the essential facts from the statement, we shall suppose either that you have a remarkable memory, or that your story is true."

Filson seemed a little mollified. "Oh, all right. Thanks for the truth. I'm certainly not afraid of being caught out."

Again he told the story of how he had unlocked the garage door and found the lifeless body of Antony Mullins. Venables, under cover of checking the story with the statement, was, in fact, carefully watching Patricia Mullins' face. It was unchanging. The same look of bored disgust persisted till the end of the story.

It finished and Filson saw her. He gave an exclamation. "Why are you looking like that, Pat?" His brow creased. He looked like a sulky schoolboy. "Why don't you say something?"

She looked out of the window. Her voice, coming apparently from a distance, was cold and resigned. "You don't appear to have left me much to say!"

"Pat! You're annoyed with me! Why didn't you tell me before? Why have you been so distant? Out with it!"

It was still winter where her voice came from. "Need we wrangle in public?" she said with painful distinctness.

"Oh, to hell with that stuff! If you won't speak to me except in public, what can you expect? You're not treating me fairly, Pat. Look here, you must answer me!" His body was taut with nervous irritation. "You looked at me just now as if you hated me!" He laughed sardonically. "I suppose you do! Oh, I can see what's happened. You've regretted your decision! You didn't like Eyton so much as that after all! I suppose you didn't really mean me to tell the truth? You expected me to argue with you and persuade you out of it? Like a damn fool I thought you had as soft a conscience as you said. What a fool I was! I forgot you were a woman."

He stopped. She was silent, her eyes averted. "Well, why don't you answer me? Why are you afraid to tell me you'd like to get out of the business? Tell me what you want. What do you want me to say, eh?"

His eyes only on her, he leant urgently forward. Her eyes were following his gestures now, but she said nothing. "Come along! I'll deny anything. I'll confess to the murder."

His hands gripped the sides of his chair convulsively. "My God, you devil, you're trying to drive me mad!"

When now at last Patricia Mullins spoke, contempt and weariness mingled equally in her tones. "This is revolting. I can excuse you for acting like a cad. You're not the first man of that kind I've met. It's my own fault. I seem to have a bias towards them. But do you really expect me to sympathize with all this self-abasement?" Her hands, showing the emotion she disdained to show in her voice, picked nervously at her gloves.

A wounded incredulity made Filson's dark brown eyes look like those of a dog. But next minute the nervous irritation, which had become increasingly evident in every gesture, hardened them again. "What a fool I was. I see it now. This is the first act in your little game. You've just been leading me up the garden. You never thought I really would confess. You didn't dream that somebody else would care for anything beside his own skin. You never expected I wasn't like you. Never dreamed of it. Gave you a shock, did it, when you heard I'd gone to the police as I promised I would? I'd like to have seen your face when you read that statement. Well, don't worry. I'll back you up. Don't be afraid of wrangling in public! I'll confess in public." He turned to Trenton wildly, shouting, "I did it. I shot Antony Mullins. I've forgotten how, but I'll remember in a moment." He turned to the woman. "And as for you, you're not even a Madame Bovary. You're nothing but a blasted little—"

"Sit down," hissed Venables, jerking Laurence back into the chair from which he had risen. "The thing's working like a charm."

Filson had not noticed Laurence's instinctive movement. Oblivious to there being anyone else in the room, he was glaring at the woman, his face grey.

"Got any brandy?" whispered Venables to the Inspector.

He had. It was often necessary when statements were being taken immediately after a motor accident.

Venables poured out a stiff peg. "Here!" He interrupted Filson in the middle of another tirade. "You're going to pieces; pull yourself together."

Filson stopped suddenly and blinked. He seemed to come out of a daze. "I'm making an ass of myself," he said slowly. He took the glass unresistingly and drained it.

Venables watched him keenly. "If I were you I should stop talking for a little. Also stop thinking. During the last few days you've been winding yourself up, you know. And either you've got to run down for a little or the spring will break. And you can't always mend it. Get me?"

He turned to Trenton and Laurence. "Here. Take Filson in the other room. Talk about the winner of the November Handicap. Or better still, about the winner of the Peppering Flower Show; it's a more soothing subject. I should like a word with Mrs. Mullins."

They were left alone, in an atmosphere where the mental tension had not so much run down as snapped. Venables, indeed, was smoking with apparent ease, slouching a little in a chair, but the woman was tense. Her eyes, still cold, contemplated him for a moment and then moved away.

He spoke to her with elaborate casualness. "And now will you tell me *your* story?"

"I have already made it clear that I have nothing to say," she answered. "Am I allowed to smoke here?"

"Permit me. The lighter, oddly enough, does work. Perhaps you are right. It was unfair for me to ask your story. You see I can guess it—from Filson's."

"Indeed, that is very percipient of you. That saves me even a denial."

"Shall I repeat it?"

"It's rather unnecessary, isn't it, if we both know it?"

"Well, you see, it has one or two trimmings of my own. So perhaps you had better listen, in case, after all, I make a mistake."

The woman made no answer. With an air of smiling confidence, Venables spoke:

"The story begins, I think, earlier than you realize. It begins in the indefiniteness that I am afraid is always between a man and a woman who have confidence in each other. You see they assume each that the other has the same thoughts. The man thinks the woman will make the same allowance for him as he makes for himself. The woman supposes the man must instinctively guess her motives. And on the whole it works. This perilous and absurd confidence that two human hearts can beat as one works extraordinarily well. That is why, when the exception comes along, it is so disastrous.

"Well, this story of yours has been dragged so much into the open that you won't resent my dragging it about a little more. Filson, I take it, knew of all this mental cruelty of your husband. Cruelty which, in the last six months of your husband's life, you really feared would end in physical violence. You discussed it. He offered to intimidate your husband. He used threats. He vowed to do dreadful things. You dissuaded him. But you were frightened of your husband, dreadfully frightened. Filson gave you a revolver. And he credited you with the mental resolution to use it.

"When men and women—ordinary men and women—are driven to the pitch of mental stress where they can at least contemplate so dreadful a deed as murder, they do not contemplate it clearly. Still less do they speak about it lucidly. They grope furtively round these awful subjects. When they think 'kill,' they say 'hurt.' When they think of 'murder,' they talk about 'killing.' And when it is a case of a man and a woman who trust each other both thinking these thoughts, they are so used to wordless understanding that the man doesn't realize that the woman may not follow him. The woman doesn't see that the man may be translating her words all wrong? Do you follow me?"

Mrs. Mullins was looking at him now without antagonism. "I don't," she confessed. "This is not at all what I thought you'd say. It's all true, of course. And I dimly feel there's something important in what you say. But what is it? Why do you tell me this?"

"It's the essential prelude to your story. The prelude that makes it understandable. Now I'll begin your story, and I'll deal in facts now. Filson had been acting very strangely before the day of the fire. You blamed yourself a little, because in your terror you had told him of all the dreadful things you feared from your husband. And then—on that morning we have been over so often—he burst suddenly into your room. You thought it was your husband. The revolver you had kept always near you—it was automatically in your hand. So instinctive had the thought of self-defence become. But it was only Filson. And it was for that revolver he had come."

Venables was looking at her with an odd expression of pity. "I suspect that you've been wondering ever since if what you did then did not of itself make you a murderess. For you suspected what he wanted the revolver for. And you gave it him without a word. Or at least with only a question, which you allowed him to stifle with an impatient reply. He made you go to the North Room, and you obeyed him, almost unconsciously, like someone in a dream. But do not worry. In moments of strain, we act like automatons, like animals.

"I don't quite know what your thoughts were in the North Room. But I can guess that apprehension must have gradually crept over you. When Eyton knocked at the outer door and sent in wild demands to see you, and you heard his incoherent story, you realized that tragedy was in the air. And then Filson came back."

It was an eerie thing to see Venables. For he seemed to see the story he was telling, founded though it was on pure guesswork. She watched him wonderingly. "There was horror in Filson's eyes. But he went about the room quite calmly and efficiently. He spoke to you. He arranged an alibi. He stifled every question of yours. And in your heart you knew he was right. He had done something which it was better you should not know. And in the terrible days that followed that thing remained indefinite. You spoke of it, yes, you had to speak of it, but as ordinary men and women would speak of such a thing. With hints... Indefinitely... Never daring to look at the full terror of the thing. Only once, I imagine, did you appreciate the full horror. That was when you stood by the blazing garage and heard the fireman tell of what he had found in the car. Then you realized that half an hour before that charred thing had been your husband, alive—with Filson. And that you had held the revolver which had killed him. And that now he was dead. Burning... And it seems you fainted."

She shook her head. "Women don't faint nowadays. I am tougher than you think. I did not faint. I guessed what had happened. And I was desperately afraid I should give myself away. So I pretended to faint. But go on. You are amazingly right—just as if you had seen everything." Her face had recovered all its animation.

"Now we come to the most interesting part. Listen carefully. Eyton was arrested. He hadn't a chance of getting off. He had been near The Turrets at the time of the murder. And an expert was prepared to swear that his revolver had shot your husband. It was a ghastly mistake, but how could you expose it? Only by telling the truth. It was almost like the iron hand of Fate. When you met Filson again, still with this awful unspoken guilt between you, only hinted at, you thought you read in his eyes the same feeling. *We can't let Eyton hang!* At a word from you, he proclaimed that he was ready to confess. He said he would give himself up that night. Am I right?"

"Yes. Still right." She bowed her head. "Oh, how could I have been so mistaken in a man!"

"How indeed! For when you were shown the statement he made to the police you saw that, with a treachery, a cowardice almost unspeakable, he had invented a story that implicated you! Moreover it was diabolical in the ingenuity with which it had been framed so that it fitted the facts—but shifted the guilt on you. In the horror of that great betrayal, in your disgust at the black cowardice of a man you trusted, you refused even to attempt to justify yourself. That may have been pure pride, you know. You may not have been able to bring yourself to expose the meanness of the man you had trusted. Or there may even have been a more quixotic feeling. You may have thought that when you gave up that revolver to him without a word, you were as guilty of murder as he was, that some reparation had to be made for the guilt in which you had entangled Filson, for the shame in which you had involved Eyton, for your own dead husband. And as retribution you would accept the blame."

Her head was bowed. One finger was tracing a pattern on her bag. "You know more about my thoughts than I do, I think. Yes, I felt all you say. And so I was silent. Oh, do you want me to tell this dreadful story you have guessed? Don't you see how shameful it is?"

Venables broke into a slow smile. "And you still don't see it!"

She looked up at his change in tone. "See what?"

"Your foolishness! Your blindness! Both of you!"

"What do you mean?"

"Good God! But it sticks out a mile. Don't you see what's happened, you poor self-deluded people? Filson's story *is* true. For when Filson walked into the garage your husband had been *already* shot—shot, Filson thought at once, by you. When he took from you the revolver you were holding, it was to help conceal your guilt. Your husband was already dead. *You* thought Filson then went out to murder him. And all the time since, each of you has thought the other guilty of the fatal shot. All because of the fact that never once have you spoken straight out. It's not surprising, perhaps. Human beings are like that. And so there has been this terrible injustice of yours, this pain, caused by lack of candour, like so much human pain and injustice. Mrs. Mullins, neither of you knows any more of this murder than—to tell you the truth—I do at the present time. It's all the sort of raging misunderstanding that can only come about between a woman and a man. And I think only the woman can make it right again... Filson is in the other room, and I'm calling Trenton and Sadler in here..."

Chapter Twenty-One

HOME THOUGHTS IN ISORB

"**D**o you mean they're innocent?" moaned the Inspector weakly, trying for the second time to grasp the story.

Laurence's eyes shone. "By Jove, sir, Venables is right. It explains everything!"

"But damn it!" went on the Inspector, "when they've practically confessed—"

Venables shook his head. "I am afraid that only makes everything more in their favour. For you see if they were so determined to tell the truth that they would risk being charged with murder, we must still believe their story when we see it exonerates them. We have absolutely no evidence against them except their own story. Even Marabout can't identify Filson positively. And our expert will say Filson's revolver couldn't have done the trick. What chance is there of a conviction, even if we believed them guilty? And I don't."

"I can't believe there isn't something in it," grumbled the Inspector. "I'm positive it's that woman! She's put it across both you young men, if you'll excuse my saying so!"

Venables grinned. "She is lovely enough to turn our heads. I believe she's turned your assistant's. Don't blush, Sadler! But all I ask you to think of is this, Inspector. What sort of case have you got to put up to the Public Prosecutor? It's ridiculous, of course. There's not enough to hang a dog on. Think of it."

The Inspector thought, and certainly it did not look good. He grunted. "Have it your own way!" Then he laughed sardonically.

"You've certainly cleared up the mess! Instead of three suspects, we've got none! Where do we go from here?"

Laurence scanned his friend's lean face hopefully. But it showed no sign of illumination. On the contrary, Venables turned down the corners of his mouth with an expression of hopelessness. "Search me. Quite frankly, after this development, and after reading all the statements, everything seems to point to the innocence of all who've ever been concerned in the case. There are only two things I query—the alibis of Holliday and Constant. Are they really perfect? Because it seems to me that one of those two is logically your man."

The Inspector thumped the desk. "They're water-tight. Oh, I don't pretend to be a C.I.D. man, but it isn't as if they were tricky alibis. In one case his staff swear he was sitting in his office all the day. In the other case there are a dozen accidental circumstances, which couldn't have been arranged, to prove he was in Berlin that day!"

"Well, if those alibis *are* perfect, I'm sorry. For it seems to my poor intelligence that Mullins couldn't have been murdered."

"You think it was suicide?" exclaimed Laurence.

"Can you suggest any other explanation? Mullins was killed by a bullet from Eyton's revolver. But we know Eyton's revolver was not in fact available. We know that Mullins was the only man likely to be able to do the necessary faking. Therefore it seems to be suicide. Mullins is hardly likely to have gone to the trouble of concealing his own murder. Mrs. Mullins' suggestion—in one of her first statements, I think—that he did it to throw suspicion on her, is surely feasible in view of that mad will. Of course it means that the man must have been insane—in the medical if not the legal sense. That isn't what worries me. In fact it's quite likely. What does worry me is how he got rid of the weapon and the key with the door locked. Some quite simple explanation if one really knew."

"Well, look here, Venables, what are you going to do about it?"

"Do? My dear fellow, I am going to clear off to Iconia before my professional reputation is hopelessly compromised. At least I've prevented you arresting the wrong people."

The Inspector stared at him open-mouthed. "Do you mean to say that you—Charles Venables, of whom we have heard so much—have given this case up?"

"Most certainly. Hannibal had his Zama and Napoleon his Waterloo. It was left to Charles Venables to have the cunning or cowardice to avoid his fatal field."

To Laurence, later, he was a little more encouraging. "I won't say that I shan't give this neat little problem an occasional thought in Iconia. Keep in touch with me, there's a good chap. I'll send you my address."

I I

Letter from P.C. Laurence Sadler to Mr. Charles Venables

CHARLES VENABLES, ESQ.,
THE WINTER PALACE,
ISORB,
ICONIA.

DEAR VENABLES,—Have you tracked down your regicide? Apparently not, as I've seen nothing in the *Mercury* about it. Well, in our humbler way, here at Peppering, we've been equally unsuccessful. And we no longer wonder at your precipitate retreat. The *Yard* has acknowledged defeat!

I may say that dear Uncle was perfectly livid when he heard that you had hopped off after clearing the three suspects. He still feels there's a bit of dirty work about it somewhere. Bribery or something. And instantly he heard of it, he sent an SOS to the C.I.D. They sent us down Bernard Bray, who is, I understand, by way of being a pal of yours. Very nice chap, as a matter of fact, and chock-full of tact, which is just as well, for Trenton was quietly bubbling with resentment. As soon as Bray read the statements he said it was simple. There must be a flaw in Eyton's alibi. For if Samuel Entourage said that Eyton's revolver did the murder then it did do the murder, and that was that.

Alas, it wasn't that. Bray nosed around for two months trying to find a hole in Eyton's alibi, and you may rejoice to hear that he wasn't able to. By the way, he also had one or two fleeting suspicions of Marabout, but the old boy was quite equal to him.

The Eyton investigations gave Bray a certain amount of trouble. Tommy pipped him twice with an air-pistol which, I find, was presented to the lad by you. And yet Bray couldn't see the joke! It turned out that Lord Overture was giving Tommy half a crown for every flesh wound.

Talking about Lord Overture and, since you will probably want to hear all our latest news, the play-pen is being turned into a solarium; that is, as soon as the Estate is sufficiently developed. A seedy-looking gentleman in a rusty bowler, whom my practised eye at once recognized as a process server, has been prowling round the lodge, so I am afraid the Estate may liquidate before it reaches the solarium stage.

However, perhaps our local scandals bore you in the regal state in which you live. I confess they bore me. Once again I am wearily pushing a bicycle up hill and down dale in the extraordinary accoutrements that our ancestors designed for the British Police. For my brief career of criminal investigation was not considered a success by Uncle. Incidentally you'll appreciate this story: Uncle was secretly overjoyed when Bray couldn't make anything of the case and reported that it wasn't worth proceeding with the investigation. Uncle said (but the story comes from Bray, mind), "Well, if even the bloodhounds of the Yard can't pick up the trail, we can't blame our own local men, can we?"—at the same time rubbing his hands cheerfully. Bray said casually, "Have you ever heard of a herd of donkeys?" "No," said Uncle, no doubt looking at him suspiciously. "Neither have I!" answered Bray. "So one can't tell what success a bloodhound would have if a herd of donkeys had crashed across the trail he was following." Very subtle and no doubt left Uncle guessing for a bit. Well, cheer-oh, Venables, and don't be shot at dawn for getting familiar with the ladies-in-waiting.

Ever thine,

LAURENCE SADLER,
P.C. 1867 G.B. Div. Thameshire
County Constabulary and all that.

Charles Venables, as he read the letter, yawned lazily. He was lying in the Blue Room, where an eighteenth-century version of the Apotheosis of Hercules (the legendary founder of the Iconian dynasty) sprawled untidily from the ceiling on to the walls. He replaced the letter on the tray of *petit déjeuner* beside him and reflectively buttered a crisp roll before dipping it into the coffee.

"If Mullins did commit suicide all is well, and the problem has very nicely solved itself. But if he was murdered, then I fear the trouble may be only beginning. Bray was bound to fail, of course. And so should I."

Shivering, Venables shot his long legs out of bed and groped for his slippers in the murky dawn of an Iconian winter. "No wonder they have revolutions," he muttered sourly, "if even their palaces haven't central heating."

Chapter Twenty-Two

A BIOLOGIST WANTS BLOOD

"Do you realize," said Miss Delfinage to Police Constable Sadler, "that it is exactly six months since Mullins was killed?"

"Good Lord, so it is! To a day!"

"And do you realize further that the murderer of Antony Mullins still prowls unhung?"

"Unhanged."

"Unhung," said Sandy firmly. "Well, as the guardian of law and order in Hake End, what excuse have you to offer?"

"Venables suggested that he'd shot himself. In which case there ain't no murderer."

"That bright young man was pulling your leg. He must have guessed from hearing about Mullins what I know from having met. Mullins. He was no more likely to kill himself than you are. Now listen. I've earned a holiday, and I've going to take one. If Bessie intends to start a riding school when she leaves me, she can get a little practice right away in running mine. I shall be on the loose for two months. And do you know what I'm going to do on my holiday? A little detective work."

"Might one ask where you propose to begin?"

"Isn't it obvious? Either Holliday or Constant *must* have done it. I admit I can't see for the moment how they took you in with their precious alibis. It probably wasn't difficult, and I'm quite sure one of them did. My money is on Constant—the nasty little man, with his false beard!"

"Is it being too curious if I ask how you will unmask them?"

"You may ask. I haven't the faintest idea. You see, I'm just going to nose promiscuously. Then when I've nosed I shall plan my campaign accordingly."

Laurence smiled. "Aren't you a bit hard on Constant? It strikes me he's been rather decent. For instance, although The Turrets lease has still two years to run and belongs to his Society, he's let Pat stay there as long as she likes. Yet they're paying for the upkeep of the house!"

"Bosh. His stuffy Society has got to do that in any case till they sublet the place. And no doubt they're glad to have someone looking after the place whom they can trust. It's business, that's all. There's no kindness about Constant."

I I

Miss Delfinage had been a little unjust to herself. She had got a plan of campaign more definite than promiscuous nosing. There was a school-friend who lived on the second floor of a house in Bloomsbury. The friend was not an artist or a writer, but a successful biologist, with a hospitable temperament. To those of her woman friends who did not mind finding a dissected arm of a monkey on the mantelpiece or half a dead lizard on the kitchen table, she extended a cordial invitation to "pop in and stay with her, the key's under the mat." It had indeed become a sort of tradition among her friends, and even her friends' friends, so that occasionally people who had never met the girl would "pop in" for a meal or a night. In fact it was credibly asserted that, more than once, coming home late, she had had the door slammed in her face by indignant guests who exclaimed crossly, "Dammit, the place is full enough as it is without any more gate-crashers." The girl's name was Annette Vanguard, known to her intimates as Van, and Sandy thought she might put her in touch with the scientific world in which Constant lived.

"My dear, how too thoughtful of you to write and say you were coming," said Van, when Sandy arrived with a suitcase. "It's absolutely unprecedented. I feel like an hotel or Royalty or something. It is sweet how you have such manners in these little country places, darling. I do believe when you leave you'll write me a nice little note. But there! I'm always careful how I talk to people about leaving, because once there was a queer Scots girl called Frieda— she used to sculpt. And she came in here once and said 'Hello,' and I said 'Hello,' and she said 'Well,' and I said 'Well,' and she stayed for two years. At the end of the second year I said to her *apropos* something, 'By the way, where do your people live?' Then, my dear, she turned absolutely scarlet and said in a strangled sort of voice, 'It's perfectly plain I've outstayed my welcome,' and rushed into the next room and packed her things and dashed out, slamming the door after her. Since when she's been saying the most awful things about me. Which only shows one, doesn't it?"

"You're the most unprincipled liar I've ever met," said a tremendously large woman in a shapeless mustard-coloured garment, who was perched on the end of a settee. She blew out a cloud of smoke and waved a long cigarette-holder. "What does this girl do, Van? Write? Or is she another of your vivisecting crowd of sadists?"

"Neither, dear. She's horsy."

"Good God!" said the fat woman, and relapsed into silence.

The other occupants of the room had taken not the slightest notice of Sandy. They were two thin, pale women, with mousy hair—twins, probably, about thirty-five, but both dressed in very schoolgirlish blue-and-white checks; a tubby, flaxen-haired Germanic youth in violent plus-fours; a placid, olive-skinned

Jewess; and an old lady with silver hair, wearing what looked like a bath-robe with a necklace of enormous imitation-amber beads. Van waved towards them vaguely.

"This is Sandy Delfinage. I've forgotten who half of you are, but you'll have to introduce yourselves..." She turned to Sandy. "My dear, I don't know where you'll sit?"

"Can I sit on that sweet black leather triangular thing there?"

"I shouldn't if I were you, dear. It's a whale's flipper that I'm working on. I am afraid it will be a bit squelchy. Also it smells rather fishy close to."

"Really, you are perfectly barbarous," said the enormous mustard-coloured person. "How you can call yourself civilized with all these dead bits about, I don't know. Come and sit beside me, Delfinage. I used to know a horse once."

A hilarious evening followed, but was ended quite suddenly because the twins seized a pair of brass candlesticks and started to beat the Germanic youth with cries of rage, while for some reason he merely sat quite still with the tears trickling down his cheeks. Van said she allowed almost anything in her flat but fighting, and as a result there was a general ejection. Thus Sandy, surprisingly enough, found that at two in the morning they were alone.

Van started vaguely tidying up. "It's ages since you were up here on the spree, Sandy. If my recollection is correct, last time you won five pounds from Bertie Eidelweiss by riding a cab-horse bareback into the four-ale bar round the corner."

"I didn't really win it, because Bertie's cheque turned out to be a stumer."

"Oh, of course, dear. I ought really to have told you that Bertie's cheques always are. He generally marks them R. D. in the corner when he gives them to you, you know, to save the bank the trouble. Well, I must say that when you country cousins come to town you show us."

"Why you should suppose I live in the country at Fairview Estate, I don't know!"

"My dear, it's quite fifteen miles from Bloomsbury. Do be truthful." She yawned. "Lord, I've got to be at the lab to-morrow at ten. Never mind. The trouble is, you people come up from your rural haunts absolutely bounding with vigour and set such a pace, we wretched creatures are worn to shreds."

"You needn't worry, Van, because this time I'm up for business."

"But how odd, dear. I warn you, though, I can't have any horses in here sleeping on the divans."

"Well, it isn't exactly business, but you remember how Mullins was killed on the Estate?"

"How abrupt the child is! Yes, I remember."

"The police gave the case up, you know. I got very interested in it because I liked Mullins. He helped start me in the school. So I started to nose about, and found it quite thrilling. I didn't find much out; but now they've given the case up, I do think I'm justified in doing a little more nosing, don't you? One never knows, does one? Now that I am on holiday I thought I would take a shot at following up a certain theory of mine, and I can only do it in town."

"How unutterably thrilling! My dear, I am so keen on murders. I simply dote on detective stories. You must tell all your theories to me. So you think the murderer is really in London?"

"That's why I came to you. You see, I think he's a scientist—that is, I think the scientist is the one who really did the murder. But I want to make a few more inquiries about him. And as you are in the scientific swim, I thought you could help me."

Van looked a little startled when Sandy told her the man was Constant. "I say, that's a tall order, you know. He's genuine enough. Of course the Society is mainly interested in physics, so it doesn't come my way, but I know it's doing quite good work. They've got a splendid little laboratory at Wimbledon—the Mullins

Institute—though naturally there's a certain amount of jealousy about an institution with academic ideals that keeps so much away from academic associations. The rumour is, that this man Constant is keeping the Society absolutely under his thumb, which is why the Society is so independent. But no one denies that Constant is a genuine scientist. Good Lord, he's done quite a lot of first-class research work in the last two or three months. I remember hearing Professor Simpkins mention it."

"Why not? He may be perfectly genuine. In fact he must have been to get Mullins to believe in him, for Mullins wasn't a fool. The point is that he's keeping the Society under his thumb because he's that type. I could absolutely see it in his manner when I called on him. All he wants is the power and fame of running this show with all that money at his disposal. Now that type of man is absolutely ruthless. So directly he learned that Mullins had left all this money to him, he made up his mind to murder him as soon as possible. And with the scientific cunning one would expect, he planned it out in detail, and I've got to find out how it was done."

"Scientific cunning! Whoa, there! Why you should suppose, like most laymen, that we scientists are full of cold-blooded intelligence, I don't know. Anything more emotionally fuzzy than a scientist it would be hard to find. We use our emotions so little, you see, that they're all pure and sweet and unspoiled, and simply bubble wildly when they get a chance!"

"That's as may be. But Constant is a nasty little brute, I'm sure. With his false beard! The point is, how can I go round making inquiries about him?"

"I can give you the introductions, I expect. But what are you going to say?"

"That's just it. I mean, one can't surge round saying, 'Look here, So-and-so is a murderer, don't you think—or do you?' They would think one was a bit dotty. Besides, I should imagine it was libellous."

"Slanderous, dear."

"Slanderous, then. Wait a bit, though, here's an idea! Don't you think I might go round pretending to be rich and thinking of endowing Constant's beastly Society? But first, of course, I would be making inquiries to see that it was all it was supposed to be. I mean, that would be quite natural, wouldn't it?"

"You don't look very rich," said Van doubtfully.

Sandy regarded herself in the mirror. "I might make myself a bit more dowdy and depressed. You know—the crushed daughter who's been left her father's fortune after earning it, poor devil, in the course of a long and trying illness."

"Why the dowdiness?"

"Because that impresses people. I mean, haven't you heard A say to B and C, 'Worth a million, you know, and dresses like a tramp,' and B invariably replies, 'Good Lord, old chap, don't you know the real millionaires always look like that? That's why they're millionaires.'"

"I get the idea. There's something in it certainly. I hope, my dear, there are some bloodstains or something. Then my biology would be some use. Or human hair. But, of course, as the corpse has been found, that's not much use, is it? But one never knows. The beast may treasure an odd arm or something, made into a paper-weight, as in a book I read the other day..."

Chapter Twenty-Three

A TEMPORARY ALLIANCE

D r. Augustus Williams, Holyroyd Professor of Physics, looked
faintly surprised.

"My dear—er—Miss Delfinage, that is a very extraordinary
question!"

Sandy nodded. "I propose doing rather an extraordinary thing,"
she said, with unsuspected truth. "After all, if I'm going to part
with a wad of Uncle's money for this Society, I'm entitled to know
something about the man who's secretary and who seems to run it."

"Er—quite." Privately, Professor Williams wondered why
on earth Dr. Dobson had sent this person on to him. In turn,
Dr. Dobson had wondered the same thing about Professor Eliza
Simpkins, who, it need hardly be said, had given the introduction
at the pressing instance of her assistant, Miss Vanguard. "To tell
you the truth, I know very little about the Society, and still less
about its Secretary."

"Have you ever met him?"

"Oh, once or twice in the last year or two. Rather an aggressive
personality. Not quite the scientific outlook."

"What is the scientific outlook?"

"The scientific outlook, my dear young lady, is essentially unego-
istic. Which is not quite the same thing," said Professor Williams,
twinkling, "as saying that scientists are modest. I know too well
that our specialization makes for a certain vanity of character. But
the man's vanity is harmless if the method is scientific. And that is
where I join issue with our friend Constant. I grant him considerable

talents. His last monograph on the electric charge of isotopes was admirable. But everyone who has come in contact with the Society agrees that the excellent research it is doing is far too much under the thumb of its Secretary. It is true he has an ornamental advisory committee, but I doubt if it ever meets. Of course, I grant that the fine research laboratory at Wimbledon is only possible because, as a result of Constant's friendship with Mullins, the Society is now richly endowed; but I still see that is no reason why he should treat it as in effect his own laboratory, staffed by his own assistants."

"You don't seem to like Mr. Constant very much. Forgive me, but aren't you prejudiced?"

"Perhaps I am. There was some discussion, you know, of an endowment of our studies here by a grant from the Society. But the programme the Society outlined as a condition was far too cast-iron for our liking. So the thing fell through."

"Do you really advise me not to put this money up? I know it was Uncle's wish that I should help some scientific society, and it is so difficult to know which." Miss Delfinage appeared really distressed.

"There I refuse to advise you," said the Professor firmly. "You must use your own judgment. I admit I neither like nor trust Constant. But you must allow for the notorious jealousy of scientists."

Sandy thanked him demurely. "They certainly don't seem to like Constant," she reflected. "It's an extraordinary thing, but I haven't been able to find a single friend."

Yet so it was. For though the chain of introductions that clever little biologist, Miss Vanguard, had given her spread its ramifications into physics, into engineering, even into industry—where also this new Society was known, there seemed a universal disposition to treat Constant as an interloper, as an individual clever certainly, but clever in that particular sense which may mean unscrupulous.

But could he conceivably be unscrupulous enough to murder? Stranger still, if he had murdered how had that water-tight alibi been contrived?

Sandy came to the conclusion that Constant's character had been sufficiently blown upon to treat him as a potential suspect. The problem now was how to break down that alibi.

"It seems to me," said Miss Vanguard, in one of the rare intervals when they were alone, "that you've got to worm your way into his office somehow."

"The trouble is that the wretch will recognize me. You know I tried that before, with a forged testimonial, and I am quite sure he suspected something. That shows he must have a guilty conscience."

"I'd do it like a shot if I had any time. Why don't you get one of these sleuths who peer through keyholes to do the job. You know, five guineas per case, *flagrante delicto* extra."

"An excellent idea, darling, but where do you think I am going to get the money? Talking about money, I really can't go on living here without—"

"That is just one of the things that are never under any circumstances said in this place," said Van firmly. "If you realized the deep cunning with which I get all the washing-up done, the place tidied up, and everything else of that kind done by voluntary labour, you would realize there is method in my generosity. So no scruples, darling! It just isn't done."

"All wrong, you know."

"Nonsense. It's my only amusement. Let's get back to your troubles. Here's an idea! Why can't you get your boy-friend who's a policeman to do it? He was investigating the murder, wasn't he? Splendid opportunity. He could surely wangle permission to follow up this suspicious character as part of his job. Combine business with pleasure!"

Sandy looked thoughtful. "Yes, there's always him. Rather a better idea than you perhaps realized. Yes, I think I'll write to-night."

The letter, for some reason, took rather a long time to write. Possibly, however, the fact that there were thirty people sitting round a dish of hot sausages in the room next to the one in which she was writing, all thirty screaming together, had something to do with it.

I I

"Is the boy-friend coming?" asked Van.

"Yes," said Sandy.

"When?"

"Now—this evening."

"Oh!"

Apart from a determined-looking, black-browed girl in the corner, with her back to everyone, daubing at a canvas on an easel with suppressed fury ("Poor thing, her family has forbidden her to paint, so she comes here and does it secretly. It's become a perfect vice," Van explained), the room was empty when Sandy's visitor arrived. There was no doubt he was Sandy's visitor, for he knocked. All Van's visitors pushed open the unlatched front door and walked straight in or, at the most, halted in the lobby long enough to yell to their hostess.

Sandy went to the front door and showed him into the lounge. "This is Mr. Filson," she said to Van. "It was good of him to come so promptly, wasn't it?"

Van gave a perceptible start. "But I thought your policeman friend was named"—a furious glare from Sandy made her falter for a moment—"er—I mean—"

Sandy mercifully interrupted her. "Park yourself somewhere, Filson," she said. "Be careful where you sit down or you may find you're sitting on a monkey's inside or something."

Filson wandered over to a settee. In doing so he passed by the black-browed girl, and glanced over a shoulder at the canvas on which she was working. He shuddered faintly. At this moment the girl turned round and stared at him.

"It's good," she stated. "There's more of me in it than anything I have done yet."

"I don't like it very much, I'm afraid," said Filson, who was a candid young man.

"I don't like you," said the girl, "either," and turned back.

Filson sat down. "Well, that's that," he said cheerfully.

He was looking a little more carefree than he had been for some time. His sulky, don't-care-a-damn-for-anybody personality, which had seemed a little out of place on Fairview Estate, went rather better with the general atmosphere of Van's rooms. It was this train of thought that, rather abruptly, made Sandy remark:

"You know, I often wonder why you live on Fairview Estate."

"Health," said Filson shortly. "Doctor said I must get out of the smoke area for a bit. Lungs, you know. I'm all right now. I often thought of coming back. I'm fed up with Thameshire."

"I am too," confessed Sandy.

Filson raised his eyebrows. "I always thought you were frightfully rural. Horses and so forth."

"Oh, did you?" said Sandy, with a faint trace of irritation. "Well, everybody's got to earn their living. Sometimes I could run down Oak Avenue with nothing on, yelling, out of pure boredom. I love horses, but one can't, after all, get away from the fact that they haven't much conversation."

The artist changed the subject. "Look here, I suppose Miss Vanguard knows all this business?"

"Yes."

"Well, then, Sandy, tell me what all this mystery is. Why on earth should you suppose, as you say in your letter, that I must be interested in finding the murderer of Antony Mullins? It's the last thing I want."

"Indeed. Then why come up?"

"Because I am interested in stopping you finding the murderer. I call the murder of Mullins one of the seven corporal works of mercy, or whatever they are. I should hate anyone to get into trouble for it."

"Wait a moment, though! Do you realize you are still under suspicion? Even though they did say you could go away without a stain on your character."

"That's true enough," admitted the young man, a trifle forlornly. "There's generally some tough-looking egg hanging round near me."

"Exactly! Pretty unpleasant, isn't it? And even more unpleasant for Patricia? Well, if we could find the murderer, that would stop."

"That," remarked Van, "sounds fair enough, Filson."

"Supposing we could prove the murderer to be someone nobody liked—a perfect pest, in fact—what about it then?" pressed Sandy. "It clears you and Patricia, solves the mystery, satisfies my highly developed sense of curiosity, and makes everyone happy."

Filson's eyes rested on Sandy reflectively for a moment. Then he smiled. "Do you really think you are a detective?"

"Of course you'd say that!" exclaimed Sandy indignantly. "Just like a man! But how have all these other detectives got on? The famous Venables, for instance? And Bray from the C.I.D.?"

"A typically feminine argument."

"You'll get your ear tweaked, young man," interrupted Van. "Feminine logic, indeed? Are you really trying to suggest men act on reasonable grounds?"

"Talking about reason, is there anything less reasonable"—
Sandy was about to go on to remind him of the confessions of
Patricia and himself, when she decided that this might be hardly
tactful—"than a man," she added, generalizing.

"Tell us your suspect then?" asked Filson condescendingly.

She told him.

He listened in silence. Then he nodded. "There is something
in it, you know. Quite distinctly. But if, as you say, Constant was
in his office all the time the murder was taking place, how could he
possibly have done it?"

"Masculine logic! Because three or four employees all say their
employer was in the office at a certain time, it *must* be true. But,
good Lord, think how easy it would be to fake it! I mean, supposing
you asked three poor devils whose employment depended on you
to get you out of some little difficulty by saying to the police you
were in the office at a certain time when you weren't, wouldn't
they do it? Supposing they were damned hard up and had a family.
Particularly in these times! It would be quite easy to give some
excuse. Constant might say to them that the police wanted to get
him for some minor motoring offence."

"Yes, he might get away with it that way. Provided the police
didn't say they were thinking of accusing him of murder. That would
frighten a man even if he had sixteen children. It's all assumption. If
one of his employees got frightened, he would be absolutely done.
The fact that he tried to fake an alibi would be damning without
any other evidence. Anyway, if that is what Constant has done,
how do you propose to find out? If the employees lie to the police
they'll lie to you, won't they?"

"That's what *you've* got to find out."

"Here, I say!"

"Simple. All you've got to do is to get a job on his staff."

"How the devil can I do that?"

"Can you type, file, write, lick stamps, answer phones, run messages?"

"No, not really."

"Good God, you are a useless object."

He grinned. "Sorry. Wait a bit, though. He's a scientific Johnny, isn't he?"

"Very much so."

"Well, I studied at the Imperial College of Science in mine early days. Pater wanted me to be an analytical chemist. Of course I chucked it up pretty soon, but I know all the chemical rush—formulæ, laboratory procedure, method of analysis, and so forth. Bit rusty, but one never really forgets. Do you think I could make myself out as ready to do anything to get back into science—you know, work the fingers to the bone for seven and six a week? He might be glad to get me cheap."

"I wonder," said Van critically. "I could give you a testimonial. I could always say you faked it and I'd never seen you, if you were found rummaging in his safe."

"That's the idea! Do you think I could get away with it?"

"You can but try."

Filson looked cheerful. "It sounds quite good fun. I want a change. I'm damned glad to be back in London. It's funny, you know, Sandy, you used to get on my nerves rather at Fairview. You seemed quite different somehow. I didn't realize you fitted into all this atmosphere at all." He waved an arm airily round the disordered room.

Van laughed. "Good Lord, it's Sandy's native stamping-ground. Before the poor dear started earning her living hiring out her wretched cattle, she was most definitely Chelsea's brightest young thing. That was when it *was* Chelsea, not Bloomsbury, as in these times!"

The young man was regarding Sandy critically. "It certainly seems to suit you. You look quite pretty, old thing."

"Odd," said Sandy demurely, "the effect of environment on character. What the devil are you grinning at, Van?"

"Nothing," said the other girl hastily.

Filson rose to his feet. "I ought to be buzzing for a bit. Look up some of my old pals and get put up. I'll be back later. And we'll settle the plan of campaign in detail. Good-bye." He lowered his voice. "Oh, and for God's sake get rid of that painting fiend in the corner. Her work's absolutely pathological. Gets on my nerves!"

As soon as Filson had gone Van pounced on Sandy. "Well, I should never have thought it of you. Of all the unprincipled what-do-you-call-'ems."

"Baggages is the correct word, I believe."

"It certainly is. The effect of environment on character indeed! When even a blind man could see that you spent the majority of this morning and God knows how much money in a beauty parlour."

"One must give oneself a chance, darling."

"You are a secretive little devil though! I thought the policeman was your passion. When did you fall for this young man?"

"Don't be vulgar, darling. I have known he was my fate for some time."

"How?"

"He was the only man who was able to make me absolutely furious with temper. That is the first sign."

"Well, you ought to know. I seem to remember at least twelve fates of yours in the old days."

"Those were mere childishness. This is really serious." She glanced at herself in the mirror. "Queer, to think I used to be quite a success in the old days! Of course, once a girl lets herself go, it takes some pulling to get herself back again. This open-air life enlarges the pores, I'll swear."

"I thought he was madly in love with the victim's wife?"

"Did you, dear? Whoever told you that? Of course *they* thought *they* were. Actually she's fallen for somebody else, if I'm not mistaken. And of course in *his* case it was sheer boredom. It always takes men much worse like that. You see, as they know it isn't really serious, they work themselves up terribly so that they'll deceive themselves that they're suffering from the genuine article."

"You seem pretty sure of yourself."

"There's nothing like the rebound with an accurate fielder. What do you think of him?"

"He's confoundedly rude."

"I always think that's an advantage in a man. You do know what he's thinking."

"I must admit he's got points. Grows on you rather."

"Yes. I shall have to get him out of that habit of smearing paint all over himself. By the way, he paints rather well. Of course the joke is, he doesn't know I know anything about that sort of thing. I always pretended to be the rustic wench. In fact I used to make him almost wild with rage about his painting. Cunning little remarks, apparently innocent, but really rather subtle..."

"Was that wise?"

"My dear, most important! That's how I knew I could collar him eventually, once the Patricia tangle had been sorted out. When they just smile patronizingly at the rudest things, you know you haven't a hope."

This interesting conversation was interrupted by a sound from the corner. The black-browed girl had apparently been listening.

"I think you're perfectly disgusting!" she exclaimed furiously. "It's quite impossible to work in this sex-laden atmosphere." She marched out of the room.

Chapter Twenty-Four

A YOUNG MAN IS TIGHT

"Has that painting fiend gone?" asked Filson, sticking his head in through the door two days later.

"All clear," sang out Sandy.

Filson came in. The young man was dressed in a neat dark blue serge suit, with a restrained tie; and his hair bore traces of having been recently cut.

"Lawks, you look smart!"

"I felt I ought to make a good impression on my future employer."

"And did you? I've been waiting here simply quivering with excitement, unable even to go out."

"You seem to have been able to knock back a pretty good lunch in spite of it. I'm famishing." He leaned over a table spread with a much reduced loaf, a veal-and-ham pie-crust with a little meat still adhering to it, and a partially consumed eminence of tinned salmon. "Why is it that when females eat by themselves they always get together such repulsive meals? Simply slung together."

"Don't be aggravating, Frank. Hurry up and tell me what happened."

The artist scowled. "Nothing. It's a wash-out." He moodily transferred some salmon to his plate.

"How do you mean—nothing happened?"

"Haven't you any vinegar?"

"Are you doing this on purpose?"

"Don't be silly. I can't talk if I'm dying of hunger, can I?" he said reasonably. "And I can't eat this muck without vinegar, can I?"

Sandy fished among some bottles. "This is the vinegar, I think."

Filson started to pour it out and then looked at it closely. He turned a little pale. "There's a dead newt floating about in it," he said.

Sandy examined the bottle. "So there is! Depressed little creature, isn't he? It must be one of Van's experiments. I think perhaps you'd better do without vinegar."

"I think I'd rather."

"Now be an angel and tell me the news. Did you really see Constant?"

The artist nodded. "Yes. That testimonial of Van's got me in all right. Although I should have thought that after your effort he would be a bit suspicious of references. But he was very affable. He asked me what my experience was. I told him that I had a scientific training; that I've been living on an independent income for a time; and that I now had to get a job. And that if he could find a corner for me in the Society I'd come for a nominal wage. Nominal wage sounded well, I thought."

"Sounds fair enough. Wasn't he attracted?"

"That's the rummy part of it. He was quite enthusiastic; and said he thought he had a vacancy for someone like that. He had a long chat with me about it. Asked me if I would be prepared to act as secretary to one of the heads of departments at the research laboratory at Wimbledon. I said 'Yes,' of course. Then he asked me one or two sly questions—obviously to see if I did know anything. Well, I got through those all right, and he seemed quite contented. Then he asked me if I would be satisfied with thirty shillings a week to start with; of course I agreed. Then he asked me when I could begin; and I said at once. Whereupon he started telling me all about the objects of the Society."

"Good Lord! Do you mean to say after all that you didn't get the job?"

"Yes, that's the extraordinary part of it. For after all this, and after he'd been droning on about the Society, and I was saying nothing but 'Yes,' 'Really,' 'Splendid,' he came back to the job again. He said quite casually: 'I don't think I will give you a job after all.' So I said, 'I say, sir. May I ask why you've changed your mind?' And he merely said without a smile, 'Certainly. I don't like the colour of your tie, that's all.'"

Sandy blinked, and then involuntarily glanced at the neckwear. "Good Lord! But it's perfectly ordinary. What did you say?"

"For two pins I'd have dotted him on the nose, the blighter! But I thought that might make investigations a bit strained. So I just swept out."

"I say though, that's wonderful!"

"Eh?"

"Don't you see? It's absolute proof. I mean he *must* have suspected you. And if he suspected you he must have a ghastly conscience. Nothing could have been more innocent than your story. A man might think you were trying it on, or trying to get a job under false pretences, but he'd never act as Constant has done unless he had reason to be terrified."

"There's something in that."

"Of course there is. What did you think of him?"

"Nasty little character. I say, though, there was one damned odd thing. You're right, you know, I'm certain I've seen him prowling round the Estate!"

"There you are. I always said so. And yet he swears he's never been near it."

"I've racked my brains, but I can't remember the exact time unfortunately."

"Did you notice his false beard?"

The artist smiled pityingly. "Good God, no. His beard wasn't false."

"I swear it was. I positively saw it wiggle."

"Absolute imagination. It was as real as your hair. Dash it, you can't tell me I should be taken in by a false beard!"

"I'm afraid you were, dear. I've a damn good mind to wait outside his old office and pull it off with a sharp jerk. However, it would be almost as embarrassing for me as for him. One can't wander about clutching a beard. Well, I suppose we must admit bitter failure. This detective business isn't so easy as I thought."

Filson consumed his salmon in silence for a time.

"Binns may be able to tell you something," he said at last.

"Binns, *Binns*—who the devil is Binns?"

"A long, thin creature with pimples."

"And why should this person be able to tell us anything?"

"Oh, he's on Constant's staff," answered Filson, prodding thoughtfully at the veal-and-ham pie. "Look here, is this really all you've got in the place?"

Sandy gave a little scream. "Stop talking about your food and tell me what you've done! Do you mean you've got a friend in Constant's office?"

"Something of the sort. You see, while I was waiting for Constant to see me I got into conversation generally with the outer office, particularly this Binns person, who seems to run it. He'd got a desk and the other creatures had only got tables, so I suppose he was boss. Anyway, I poured out all my hopes and fears, and the Binns person was quite sympathetic. Then when I came out from Constant's office again I told a pathetic story about how difficult it was to find work when you hadn't had any experience of earning your living. I allowed the little swine to patronize me and give me good advice. Of course I was effusively grateful, and ended up by asking him out to dinner. I thought we might get him bottled and pump him."

"But, Frank, this is absolutely marvellous! You're obviously born to be a detective."

"Oh, I don't know. He probably won't tell us anything. Have you anything to drink in this place?"

"That," said Sandy, "is just the one thing we have got..."

II

Binns was taken to the Venezuelan Restaurant, a once extremely fashionable restaurant which has ceased to be fashionable, and therefore, in the views of Sandy and Filson, would be sufficiently empty to give opportunity for a private conversation. Their presumption was accurate. There were only a dozen people in the Grill Room, and they were able to secure a table out of earshot of any of them.

There was no doubt about it, Binns was pimply. He was probably getting on for thirty, and it was a bit unfair that these accidents of youth should have refused to be banished. Otherwise he was a sprightly youth, and when he saw that the dinner was to be augmented by feminine society—"my sister," Filson explained—his pince-nez glittered as he shot out bright repartees at the slightest opportunity. He did not altogether approve of the restaurant.

"That pirate rig-out is rather cute," he admitted. (The waiters of the Venezuelan Restaurant are, of course, dressed as conquistadors.) "But isn't there a band?"

"The band's upstairs," explained Sandy. "But we didn't want the fag of changing."

"Oh, I'm a great one for dancing. I could easily have donned the glad rags. I don't often miss an opportunity to shake a leg, I can tell you. I think I must have got music in my blood."

"Well, what's in the blood must come out," said Filson, his eyes resting on Binns' complexion.

Sandy kicked him under the table. "We might go on to somewhere where we can dance afterwards."

The arrival of the wine mellowed the party, however. Binns, it appeared, had a local reputation as a raconteur, and after a preliminary bleating about ladies being present, he was soon launched into some anecdotes. By the end of the dinner he had also told them about his business life, his home life, and his love life, and was ready to go off into fits of laughter at any remark, however apparently unhumorous. The two judged that the moment was propitious.

"Do you know who we are?" asked Filson, with a sinister look.

Binns nodded gravely. "Brother and sister. Sister and brother." This remark seemed to him so funny, that he went into roars of laughter and had to be patted on the back before he became articulate again. "Sorry," he said. "I was always a great one for a joke."

Sandy shook her head solemnly. "That's where you're wrong. Look here, Mr. Binns, we see you've got your head screwed on the right way and we're going to tell you the truth." She paused and then leant forward and whispered. "We're detectives!"

"Detectives—defectives, mentally defective!" echoed Binns and relapsed into paroxysms of laughter.

Sandy wondered whether the bottling process had perhaps been carried too far, and Filson signalled for some coffee. But as Binns stopped laughing, the realization of their words seemed to sink into his consciousness. A cunning look flashed into his eyes.

"Oh, you're detectives, are you? Well, let me tell you I don't care that for detectives"—and he flipped his fingers airily. "Not that!"

"Of course not," said Sandy persuasively. "But you're going to help us. It's going to be worth your while to help us."

He gave them a sidelong look through his pince-nez. "Just what he said! The old man's not such a fool as you defectives—detectives I mean—think he is."

Sandy disguised the elation she felt. "So he warned you against us, did he?"

"He told me if anyone came snooping I was to—Here! Who told you he warned me? What are you trying to put across me?"

"Now then, Mr. Binns, we know there wouldn't be any chance of putting anything across you. This is business, and we're all business men."

"That's right, all business men together. Binns and Co. Damn the lot of them! Damn you, too," he added with a hiccup.

Filson produced a wallet casually and pulled out a wad of notes. "Exactly. This is a business matter. Naturally we pay for our information. What about it?"

The young man's eyes widened as he saw the notes. "Here, what do you want to know this for?" He was at the crest of a return wave of sobriety.

"This is a serious matter. The police are bound to take a serious view of it. And I think in your position it would be as well if you worked with us instead of against us. After all, there's such a thing as being an accessory!"

"Police! Did you say police?" He looked decidedly unsettled. "M' Gawd, what's the old man been up to?"

"Murder," said Filson slowly.

Binns was now almost sober. "Murder!" he echoed. "Hanging?" The two nodded in unison.

Binns plucked nervously at his collar. "You'll pay me if I tell you, honest you will?" he said cunningly.

"Yes, if you *can* tell us anything."

"What do you want to know?"

"Where was Constant on the morning of October 18th?"

"What do you take me for? That's over six months ago. How on earth can I remember?"

"I think you can remember, Binns. Because it was a day when Constant happened to be out all day, but he told you to tell the police that he wasn't. Isn't that so?" Sandy shot an accusing finger out in the manner made familiar by many third degree scenes in gangster films.

Binns stared at the finger in a puzzled fashion. "No. You've got it wrong. It's true someone from the police was snooping around asking about what happened on the 18th. But I wasn't there."

"Where were you then?" asked Sandy.

"Why did he tell you to keep quiet?" asked Filson.

"I feel a little ill," answered Binns faintly. He looked it. The inevitable sequel to a wave of sobriety was manifesting itself in a pale green tint in his face.

"Drink up this," commanded the young man, out of his experience, pouring for him a large cup of very black coffee, to which he added a pinch of salt.

Binns drank it miserably. He brushed a lock of hair back from a pallid brow. "I was in Berlin."

Sandy gave a squeak of delight. "At the Atlantic Hotel!"

"Yes, how did you find that out?"

Filson, too, stared at her in surprise.

"We know more than you think!" she said. "You go on and tell us the truth."

"Well, it was the damned funniest thing I've ever known. I had to register under some other cove's name and post two letters. Then at a certain time I had to phone up some number in England he gave me and ask for——" He paused.

"And ask for?" prompted Sandy softly.

But he was staring at her with open mouth and horror-struck eyes. "Mullins," he repeated slowly. "The bloke who was murdered!

The bloke who left the Show his money! I never thought of it before. I swear I didn't. I thought it was just some name the Guv'nor'd made up." He started to his feet. Terror was in his eyes. "You're trying to trap me. I know! But I know my rights. You've got to warn me. You can't catch me like that." Suddenly he sat down limply. "Oh, I do feel so ill," he moaned.

It was impossible to tell whether he was acting. He looked green enough; but it might have been fright. He refused to answer any of their questions with a sly obstinacy.

At last Filson lost his temper. "My God, I'll get you outside and give you the hiding of your life if you don't tell us."

At once Binns' pince-nez flashed indignantly. "You daren't! Don't think I don't know the ropes. I'd go round at once to our Member of Parliament—President of our local Harriers he is, and I'm the secretary—and I'd soon have Scotland Yard buzzing and get you the sack."

Sandy tried guile. "Of course, he's not serious, Binns dear," she said, patting him on the shoulder. "Look here, you've given us quite a lot of useful information. And the more you give us the more friendly we'll be in case of trouble. He stared at her sullenly. "And we'll pay you, as we promised, for what you've told us already." Sandy winked at Filson. "We've had ten quid's worth of information," she whispered.

Filson produced the notes with an ill grace. He still looked threateningly at the bowed figure. Binns' pince-nez flashed again as he observed the notes. He looked at her cunningly. "There's something else. There's no harm telling you! The boss wears a false beard."

Sandy shot a triumphant glance at Filson. "That's worth twenty quid."

"How do you know it's false?" asked Filson truculently.

"'Cos it half came away from his face once when I was in there.

He looked as mad as hell and shot round to see if I'd noticed. I pretended to be busy doing something else. Oh, it's false all right." He gulped down the brandy which had been ordered at the second return of his illness and dully watched Filson count out another five pounds.

The wave of sobriety was passing. "Good old 'tectives," he said thickly, patting Sandy on the hand. "Gotter do her duty. All gotter do our duty. Always a great one for doing my duty, I am. You want to know too much, that's your only trouble, see. Too nosy. Too inquisitive. Get me?"

The remainder of the evening passed without incident. Indeed for the latter part of it Binns slept heavily...

Chapter Twenty-Five

A YOUNG MAN IS FRIGHTENED

S andy and Frank were sitting in the "Purple Beggar," a road-house placed conveniently for a halt after they had dropped the comatose Binns at Mertlesham in Filson's ancient four-seater.

"What the devil has Constant been up to?" the artist asked gloomily. "It's all gibberish to me—all this Berlin hotel business. What the devil does it mean?"

"We've got him on toast," crowed Sandy joyously. "It's a cert. It's a cinch. It's a wow."

"But, damn it, I don't see—"

"Listen. This is how Holliday's alibi was faked. There was a Berlin call from Holliday through to Mullins on the day of his murder. Also, there were two letters posted the same day from Berlin in Holliday's handwriting, referring to that same phone conversation. The police checked it all up and found that a young man *had* stayed at the Atlantic Hotel and *had* phoned Mullins. So that—with the fact that the letters referred to what was discussed on the phone—proved Holliday's alibi. Obviously 'Holliday' was really Binns!"

"Wait a moment, though. There are one or two snags. If friend Binns phoned Mullins, Mullins would have recognized that Binns wasn't Holliday."

"Perhaps Binns belongs to a local amateur theatrical society. After all, he is secretary of the local Harriers."

"You can't get away with that, old thing. No, it's objection number one. Here's another. If the letters from Berlin were in

Holliday's handwriting, how did Binns manage to imitate it? Do you think he is secretary of the Mertlesham Forging Society as well? Thirdly, what the devil does it matter to Constant if Holliday ever had an alibi or not? Finally, why the false beard?—I say, what's the matter with you, Sandy? Have you seen a crocodile?"

"I've got an idea!"

"Damned painful process, apparently."

"I've got an idea. A splendiferous idea. My God, everything fits in! I'm positive it's true! If so, Constant is absolutely the world's outside edge in criminals!"

"Well, let's have the idea then."

Sandy shook her head. "No. It'll be so darned foolish if I'm wrong. I want to wait a bit."

"Well, you are a secretive little devil. I thought we were partners."

"Never mind. As soon as I've got some confirmation I'll tell it you. It's only a matter of hanging on to little Binns and squeezing some more information about him. By the way, it was decent of you to fork out to him."

"Rot. Cheapest fun I've had for ages. Anyway, we've done enough sleuthing for to-night. What about trying the 'Purple Beggar's' dance-floor?"

I I

The hunt rested for a while the next day. Van was giving her Annual Working Party. For this famous affair a suite of rooms over a public-house in the wilds of King's Cross was hired. It was known as a Working Party, because all who were invited were in theory people who worked for their living, and were expected to turn up in the costume appropriate to their profession and trade. Barristers in wigs and gowns, youthful professors in doctor's hoods, and surgeons terrifyingly masked, gave the party a wild air. Occasionally the thing was carried a little too far, as when a well-known model left her clothing in the cloak-room and strolled casually in. She claimed reasonably enough that this was her working dress.

"Nobody takes off their clothes at my party," said Van firmly. "At least, not at the beginning."

Sleuthing was abandoned for the day while Frank and Sandy assisted Van in last-minute preparations for the party. And both turned up—Filson in paint-stained overalls with a beret, Sandy in riding-breeches and a stock.

They were both absorbing the party spirit at the cocktail bar when they were aware of a heated discussion between their hostess and a peaky-faced small boy.

"I tell you there's no Mr. Armitage here."

"Please but my brother says I must find him!" said the small boy, whimpering.

"If he's here he's a gate-crasher. Whatever makes you think he's here, anyway?"

"Well, my brother says as how Mr. Armitage was living at 21B Anise Road, and I went there—"

"You scandalous little monkey, how dare you suggest Mr. Armitage was living there! That's my flat."

"Well, anyway, I went there, and there was only a girl painting or something in the corner—"

"My God," groaned Filson.

"—and she said she'd never heard of Mr. Armitage, but if it did happen as how he was living there, and goodness knows it would be quite possible, he'd be at the party, so she sent me here. Oh, please, do find Mr. Armitage."

Filson stepped forward. "What do you want him for?"

"Please, I've got a letter from my brother for him."

"All right, give it to me."

"Are you Mr. Armitage?"

"Yes, that's all right. Here's half a crown. Run away and buy yourself some acid drops."

The boy's eyes sparkled. "Coo. I shall be able to buy myself some more model aeroplane elastic."

"You're not the secretary of the Mertlesham Model Aeroplane Society, by any chance, are you?"

"Yes. How did you guess?"

"What a family! Well, run off and get it."

The small boy trickled off.

"Are you deceiving that unfortunate boy?" inquired Van. "Or is Armitage one of your aliases?"

"That's the name I applied for the job under."

"It's very nice of you to give my address. So good for one's reputation."

"A biologist has no business with a reputation."

He opened the envelope.

"I might have guessed that was a young Binns," said Sandy reflectively. "He has the family complexion. What's in the letter?"

Filson whistled. "I say, your friend Constant's a swift worker. Look at that."

"DEAR MR. ARMITAGE,—I am very much afraid that Mr. C. has somehow got to know of our conversation of even date. He called me into his office this morning, and said that he had been thinking over my future very seriously. He had come to the conclusion that my present job was a blind alley, and that it was time I entered on the Wimbledon end—that is the research side, you know. Of course they pay bigger salaries there. But it strikes me as fishy, because I have no training for that sort of thing. Then he said he was too busy to discuss it further in office hours. Would I call on him at nine o'clock in the Aerodynamics Section (where he has been working in the evenings lately), and we would discuss it quietly with no one there. Of course I couldn't refuse. It would have been too suspicious. But I can't help being afraid he has some funny business in mind. So I should be grateful if you could come with me and wait outside in case anything happens. I shall be at Wimbledon Underground at a quarter to nine. If you have not turned up at nine I shall go home and make him some excuse, for frankly I'm scared.

"THOMAS LLEWELLYN BINNS."

Filson looked at his watch. "I'm sorry, Van! We must dash. Most urgent pressure of business. Our murderer is about to do another murder. Come on, Sandy. You'll have to tear round Wimbledon as you are, breeches and all."

III

"The next small boy who asks me where I lost my horse will have his neck wrung," remarked Sandy vindictively.

They had been standing outside the side entrance of the Mullins Institute for an hour, and in her breeches Sandy felt a conspicuous object. Filson, bareheaded, and his paint-stained overalls covered by a mackintosh, looked more conventional.

"How long have we been hanging about?"

It was, in fact, an hour since the imperfectly reassured figure of Thomas Llewellyn Binns had vanished into the side entrance of the white-tiled block, which gleamed garishly in its setting of old trees. The main block was in darkness, and here and there at the side, panels of light showed, but which was Constant's room and which were merely corridors the watchers were unable to decide.

Quite suddenly their reflections were interrupted by a high, thin sound.

"What's that?" exclaimed Sandy, abruptly ceasing from her restless pacing.

"Sounds like a scream!"

This time it was unmistakable—a cry of agony that made both watchers' hair prickle.

They rushed up to the door through which Binns had passed. It had been on the latch, and Binns had purposely left it so when he passed through to find Constant. But now it was locked.

"That's extraordinary," said Filson. "I'll swear that was open a few minutes ago!"

They listened for a moment; but there was no sound. Yet the scream had been shattering. Filson knocked on the door.

They knocked for three minutes, and there was no answer. Filson left the door for a moment and tried the other doors and the ground-floor windows, working round from the wing to the central block. The doors were locked and the windows were all barred, with the exception of two, which were unglazed and covered with heavy mesh. He came back.

His eyes were angry. "I'll get an answer somehow," he said, and started battering violently at the door. Not to be outdone, Sandy kicked emphatically at one of the panels with her riding-boots.

They were interrupted by the light of a torch, shone in their faces. "Here, here! What's all this?"

This remark is made by only one class of person, and though he was invisible behind the unwinking eye of the electric torch, Sandy replied without hesitation, "Officer! There's somebody being murdered in here."

"Now then, miss, what makes you say that?"

"We heard a most awful scream."

The policeman laughed. "Well, a sight more people scream than get murdered. The row you're kicking up is enough to scare any murderer. Do you know who's in there?"

"Of course we do! He's a friend of ours who went to see a man here. And he was afraid the man would be violent, so he asked us to stay outside. Then we heard an absolutely petrifying scream. And now we can't get in."

At this moment the door opened. All three people jumped a little. Constant stood in the light which streamed from the door opening. There was an expression of pained surprise on his face.

"Good God, what is this awful noise? I thought there was a street fight outside."

The law detached itself from the fringe of darkness and entered the light. "What's all this about screaming?"

"Screaming?" Constant stared at him. "What do you mean?"

"These two said they 'eard an 'orrible scream."

Constant stroked his beard with a smile. "Really, officer, but this is preposterous. They must be drunk."

The policeman wheeled about suspiciously and scrutinized the two. They endeavoured to look dignified while he peered into their faces.

"They're not drunk. There is a distinct smell of alcohol to be observed on their breaths, but their pupils is not dilated. Besides, they're steady on their feet."

"Look here, officer, you must go inside. Naturally he pretends to know nothing about it. You don't expect him to admit he's got a corpse in here, do you?"

Constant looked at Sandy with surprise. "What is this all about? Corpses? Has Wimbledon gone crazy?"

The policeman coughed. "They said as how you were murdering someone."

Constant laughed. "Really. And do they know who I am murdering? Or is it supposed to be just a habit of mine?"

"Don't try and bluff us. Where's Binns?"

Constant's eyes never flickered. "Good Lord, is it little Binns you're looking for? I am glad to say I can reassure you. I showed him out of this door in perfect health about half an hour ago."

"That's a damned lie," said Filson. "We've been watching this door for the last hour, and no one's come out of it."

"Your attention evidently relaxed for a moment. Watching is a weary business."

"Well, this is a funny show," said the policeman, scratching his head. "People accusing each other of murder! In Wimbledon of all places, too!"

Filson came forward and put his foot in the door. "Look here, we've got good reason for what we've said. When Binns went in here we promised we'd see him safely off, and I'm not going to budge until I've been over this place—every inch of it."

Constant leaned negligently on the door-post. "Of course, I should be delighted to show you all over it. It is frequently my duty, as Secretary of the Society for the Promotion of Scientific Research, to conduct organized parties over this building, and it is generally admitted that I make a capable guide." His voice filled out with the resonant enunciation of the public speaker, but his eyes never left Filson's. "This building, ladies and gentlemen, represents the first step in the realization of an ideal! Its defects, I assure you, we know, but I want you, if you will, to consider some of its virtues. It is the only institute in the country..."

"Shut up," said Filson, whose sense of humour was eliminated by his anxiety. "We're going to turn this place upside down till we find what's happened to Binns."

They did. Although the Institute was a comparatively small building compared to some of the bigger research institutes, its thorough search took some time. Constant, a smile on his face, flung open every cupboard and door. Filson, as grim as Constant was casual, pried into everything, and the policeman gave an air of expertness to the proceedings by marking with a piece of chalk the door of every room they had searched.

At last their task was ended.

"Well, unless he's all in little pieces, your friend isn't here," said the policeman. He shook his head reproachfully.

They were now back in the room to which Constant had first taken them. As this room had then been lit, it was presumably the one in which he had interviewed Binns. In place of the sinks, retorts and test-tubes which connoted laboratory to Sandy, there were glass-covered balances, pumps, and odd-looking conglomerations of piping, springs, and gearing, to which she could not put a name. A large sheet of squared paper was laid out on the central table, on which some graph was in process of being plotted.

The smile left Constant's face. He sat on the table. "Now look here, officer. I've treated this as a joke up to now! You've satisfied yourself that there's nothing in this ridiculous accusation. But what I want to know is, what the devil was it made for? I recognize these two. I recognized them the moment I saw them, but I thought I'd give them a bit of rope first." He shook a finger at Sandy. "That girl came to me months ago and asked for a job. I don't mind telling you I had reason to believe the letter of recommendation she brought me was forged." He half turned and indicated Filson. "And this young man came nosing round in the same way to get a job from me. There's something fishy about it all, I warn you, officer. I shouldn't be in the least surprised if they intend to burgle this place, and this is just a scheme to find all they can about the lay-out of the building."

The constable's eyes narrowed. "You hear what the gentleman says? Well, what have you got to say for yourself? What's your reason for accusing him in such a way? Murder, too! And might I ask what your name is, sir?"

"Certainly. My name is Constant. And I'm the Secretary of the Society which owns this Institute. But I should like you to ask the names of our friends here. This young man, for instance. He once gave his name to me as Armitage. But I shouldn't in the least be surprised if it is something else. Ask him to produce a card or a letter or something to establish his identity. And here's my card."

"That's very reasonable, sir. Now then, you two, your names and addresses, please."

Filson exploded. "I'm damned if we will."

Constant gave an expressive shrug.

The policeman looked stern. "Come, come, this won't do! You can't go round accusing respectable citizens of felony and then withholding your names. There's such an offence as obstructing the police, you know! You've got to stand behind a charge if you make one. Otherwise I'll have to trouble you to come round with me to the station."

With an ill grace, Sandy gave her real name and Van's address, and with an even worse grace Mr. Armitage gave his false name and the same address.

"And I hope you'll look up those names and addresses," said Constant waspishly. "I may want your evidence in an action for defamation."

"Don't you worry," said Sandy. "You won't lose touch with us. The first thing to-morrow morning we go round to Detective Inspector Bernard Bray of the C.I.D. and tell him the whole story."

The policeman looked surprised. "Oh, you know Inspector Bray, do you?"

"Certainly."

"Well, this is a rum thing to happen. In Wimbledon, of all places. I must say, Mr. Constant, you've acted very well over it; very well indeed. It isn't everyone who'd take it the way you do." He shot a reproachful look at Sandy and Filson. "All I can say is, it's lucky you've not been drinking. I should like to hear what Inspector Bray would say of your goings-on. If I were you I'd hop it now, before you start hearing any more murders. Murders, indeed!"

Outside Sandy gazed ruefully at her companion. "I am afraid we are not very good detectives, are we?"

"What about this?" said Filson, stopping under a street lamp. "I found it shoved away in a corner in the room in which Constant was working. I snaffled it when his back was turned."

From under his mackintosh he produced a crumpled linen bundle. Odd stains among the crinkles made Sandy's eyes widen. He shook it out.

It was a white linen overall, and down the front was spattered the equivalent of a pint of blood.

And when Filson touched the stain gingerly with his forefinger, it came away crimson.

"Recently spilt!"

Chapter Twenty-Six

A BIOLOGIST GETS BLOOD

"My dear, but how extraordinary," said Van—with an animation remarkable in anyone on the night after a party. "This is amazing!"

"I suppose it *is* blood?" asked Sandy with a little shiver.

"Oh, it's blood all right! Look here, let me take it to the lab to-day and I'll do an analysis on the crystals for you."

"Don't you think we ought to take it to the police?"

"Nonsense. I'm as good as any of the blasted C.I.D. pathologists. Besides, I'll treat exhibit X very gently and only take the littlest sample."

"All right. I must say it makes me sick to look at it."

"Where's Filson?"

"He's gone round to the Binns' place to see if Thomas Llewellyn has come back yet. He hadn't at eleven o'clock last night, because we dashed over there immediately after we'd left the Institute."

"And supposing he still isn't back?"

"We go straight to the police."

When Filson returned, his face was grim. He threw his hat on the table and dropped into a chair.

"There's no sign of Binns at home!"

"Good God! Does his mother know where he is?"

"She hadn't the faintest idea. But a letter came from him this morning which stopped her worrying."

"A letter!"

"Yes, and this is the most sinister part of it, I think. It was just a typewritten slip of paper—even the signature typewritten—and enclosed with it were two ten-pound notes. It read: 'Don't worry. I'm away on business for a time. Enclosed will keep you going. Will write later. Don't let the neighbours know.—TOMMY.' She'd have been worried if it weren't for the two notes. She said they looked so crisp and new she felt it must be all right."

"Did you tell her anything?"

"Good Lord, no! It's no use upsetting her until we know for certain. But it looks bad. By the way, I took the numbers of the notes, just in case."

"You're getting a real detective."

"Am I? All the same, I think it's time we placed everything in a real detective's hands. This amateur business is all very well in its way. But now it's getting serious."

It was easier than they thought to get into New Scotland Yard and see Bernard Bray. The mention of the Inspector's name and of the Mullins case, and a quick scrutiny by the doorkeeper, secured a direct entrance into the Inspector's cubby-hole.

Both had met Bray when he was down at Fairview engaged on the investigations. An intelligent fellow, Bray, and one of the younger generation, who might or might not prove better than the old guard who had learned their jobs in the ranks. He had the grave eyes and close mouth of the barrister. His manner was friendly.

"I didn't expect to see you two in London. To be frank, I had almost forgotten about the case. And now you are here, what can I do for you?"

"First of all, are you still interested in the Mullins case? Or have you given it up?"

Bray smiled. "You have perhaps heard the legend that the Yard never gives up an investigation? In a measure it is true. Every so often I or my predecessor will turn up this file "—he shot open a drawer and after a moment's hovering selected a substantial guard-file stuffed with papers—"and scrawl against the date, '*No further action possible.*' Routine inquiries will, of course, be made. They still are being made. Any other action is limited by the circumstances. I have fears that this folder will be handed down to my successor, to remind us both of the limitations of the criminal investigator. Fifty years hence we shall assume that the criminal has appeared before a higher court than the one we deal with, and the file will disappear into our archives."

Filson shook his head. "I don't think that will happen. Because we've got important evidence now. Look here, Sandy, it was your scheme. You'd better tell your story."

Sandy explained how her suspicion had made her come to London; how she had tried to find something out about Constant; how a lucky chance had brought Filson into contact with Binns; of the story Binns had told...

Bray's eyes were keen and animated when he had heard her out. "I can't commend your taking the investigation into your own hands. Forged letters of recommendation indeed! It was clumsy of you to do it twice. If there is anything in your theory, we would be dealing with an amazingly astute man—and he's not likely to have been taken in. But perhaps there's something to be said for your methods after all. You don't seem to have been hampered by any considerations of legality. And it sounds as if a word with our friend Binns would be informative. Though I don't go quite as far as you in my suspicions."

"That's the terrible part of it. Binns has gone!"

The detective dropped his guard-file in astonishment.

"Eh?"

"He's gone. Disappeared."

Sandy told him of their message from Binns; the visit to the laboratory; the bloodstained overalls; and the mysterious message.

Bray looked concerned. "Why on earth didn't you come to me at once when you'd got that story from Binns instead of trying to carry on by yourself? Don't you see that if Constant was what you suspected, his first suspicion would be that you had tampered with Binns? And directly he had discovered that you had, don't you see the danger?"

"I do now. But I never thought he'd have the nerve."

"Good God, you have to have nerve for a murder. And that's what you've been trying to tell me he did. Now look here, I don't take so grave a view of it as you do. I shall try and get into touch with Binns; I shall trace, if I can, these notes that you took the number of, and then this afternoon you can turn up here and we'll see what more can be done. I think meanwhile you'd better get all your facts in order, so as to make a full statement. I shall devote the morning to reading up the records. And for the Lord's sake get those overalls from your friend. The very thought of that exhibit kicking round loose makes my hair curl."

I I

When they turned up again later in the day Bray was stern and worried.

"This seems like business. Those two notes were drawn out on Constant's bank account yesterday. I found this as a result of a confidential talk with Constant's bank manager. There is no sign of Binns at the office—I sent a man round who pretended to be a friend—and all the staff there are puzzled about it. Meanwhile I have been trying to think out some way in which establishing Holliday's alibi could help Constant, and for the life of me I can't think of one. And yet Binns' evidence seems to point to that being the clue to the mystery."

"If you won't laugh at me," said Sandy hesitantly, "I should like to tell you my theory."

"I certainly won't laugh at you, Miss Delfinage. You have shown yourself able to pick up a trail which none of us suspected. It is quite possible you can guess where that trail will lead."

"Well, this is what I suspect happened. I think that Constant arranged with Binns to ring up Mullins. Then when the call from Berlin had come through to Mullins, and had been properly registered against Mullins' account, as evidence, Constant himself rang up Mullins. (Of course I assume for this, that somebody in Mullins' office is in Constant's pay.) Then Constant was put through by this person to Mullins as 'Mr. Holliday calling from Berlin,' and Constant carried on the conversation as Holliday, running it on such lines that it would fit one of the letters with which he previously had provided Binns."

Bray laughed. "That brings us back with a bump to my point. Why should Constant trouble to provide this alibi for Holliday? Anyway, Mullins would surely have recognized that Constant's voice wasn't his?"

Sandy leaned forward dramatically. "No! because Constant is Holliday!"

"What?" exclaimed Bray and Filson simultaneously.

"Don't you see, it explains everything! Holliday has always hated Mullins. So some time ago he disguised himself as Constant and started to lead a double life. In the person of Constant he persuaded Mullins to put up money for the Society and finally make it his legatee. Then—after carefully arranging an alibi for himself as Holliday—he shook off the Holliday personality and reverted to Constant."

Bray shook his head. "It won't do, my dear Miss Delfinage."

"But Binns says he had a false beard," she persisted.

"Well, it's conceivable that he wears a false beard from vanity. He may be unable to grow a full-sized one himself, or it may turn out an unfortunate colour. Beards do. I admit a lot of what you say. The double personality is an old criminal device. I admit it might explain the careful preparation of an alibi for Holliday. But it explains nothing else. It involves the difficulty of bribing someone in Mullins' office. It demands the improbable coincidence that the telephone conversation did match up with the letters. This seems to me unlikely. In fact I see from my notes that Samson, who was in the room, heard Mullins raise a point apparently *of his own accord* which was dealt with in Holliday's letter. And the letter was all in Holliday's handwriting. And Holliday you say is Constant and therefore was in London when the letter was posted in Berlin."

Sandy looked cast down. "It's unlikely, I suppose. But I still don't see that it's impossible."

"It isn't impossible. It's in fact more possible than you realized in one respect. For Constant *is* a bit of a mystery man. When I was investigating the affair I naturally looked up his history, and like you I tried to get a line on his past, and found it impenetrable during the years before he came to live in London. I formed the conclusion that he was a doctor or scientist who had got involved in some disgraceful affair and changed his name to start life over again. But against your theory is an awkward obstacle and a complete barrier. The obstacle is that Constant (as you yourself found), has managed to acquit himself, not only in writing, but in conversation with scientists, as a man of scientific attainment. And this when the scientists were mostly antagonistic to him and would have been only too glad to show him up as a charlatan. Now we come to the complete barrier. The fact is that Constant did *not* murder Mullins because he was undoubtedly in his office at the time."

"Couldn't his staff have all been backing him up like Binns?"

"No. I can't believe that any man would take the risk of letting so many people in his confidence. Even then, you can't coach ten people of average intelligence so that when cross-examined about a man's action at a particular time they all give accounts which agree. I examined the staff myself during my investigations, to check up Trenton's work, and I firmly believe in that alibi. You can't get round it!"

"Well, Inspector," interrupted Filson, "how *do* you explain Binns' visit to Berlin?"

"Quite frankly I don't. I can't, yet. There can be no doubt that he was establishing Holliday's alibi. Two English people did not make a stay at the Atlantic Hotel and put a phone call through to Mullins' office, and post a letter to Mullins and to the company's Berlin agent in one day. So I think we can take it that Constant in this respect was acting as Holliday's agent, and took care to cover himself also by a perfect alibi. But how can we get hold of Holliday now he's skating about the Continent under pseudonyms? And how can we trap Constant without Binns' evidence? I think before the trail goes cold, we'd better go round and see Constant, and get his explanation of the story. I think for the moment I shall be justified in not cautioning him, for I don't in the least think he is the murderer of Mullins. In fact it's impossible."

"What about poor Binns?"

"The less I think about Binns the happier I am. It looks bad. Will you come with me, Miss Delfinage? Confrontation is often best in a case of this sort. You may be able to say what I cannot say."

"I'll go too," said Filson.

"I don't think I need trouble you too, Mr. Filson."

"No trouble at all. I should be delighted to go."

The Inspector looked a little embarrassed. "All the same, I think it would be better if you didn't."

Filson looked at him keenly. "Oh, I see. Still under suspicion, am I? I thought when those blighters stopped dogging my footsteps soon after I came up to London that you'd given me a clean sheet. Well, I take the hint without offence. See you at Van's later, Sandy."

III

When he saw his visitors, Constant was as unperturbed as he had been the preceding evening. "So you have gone to Scotland Yard, young lady, have you—after all? Well, Inspector, I am sorry to see they have dragged you into this practical joke—if it's nothing worse."

The Inspector wasted no time on fencing. "I have been told an extraordinary story. I should certainly not be doing my duty if I did not investigate it further. An employee of yours, Binns by name, has told two of our informants, of which this lady is one, that you gave him certain instructions, namely to register under an assumed name at the Atlantic Hotel on the day when Antony Mullins was murdered, to ring up Mullins' office, and to post certain letters."

"What the devil has this cock-and-bull story to do with me? Why the hell should I send one of my employees—an indispensable office manager, Binns—gallivanting off to Berlin? What good would it do me?"

"The point is this. Mr. Holliday (whose movements on the day of the crime were traced as a matter of routine) had his actions accounted for in this very way—namely, he stayed at the Atlantic Hotel, he phoned up Mullins, and he posted two letters in Berlin."

"Again I ask, what the devil is it to do with me? Holliday, if I remember rightly, was Mullins' nephew, and why you should ever have listed him as a suspect at all I don't know. But no doubt you have good and sufficient reason. But what is it to do with me? I've never even met him."

"It might be suggested that you were acting for Holliday."

Constant jumped to his feet, glaring. "Indeed, Inspector, might it? But not by you, I hope—not on the evidence of what my employee is supposed to have said to this young lady, or to her friend, or for that matter to any number of persons. You know the elementary rules of English justice, I hope, Inspector. You are familiar surely with the laws of evidence. This is hearsay evidence you are putting forward!" He hit his desk violently with his fist. "I demand your evidence! Bring Binns here! Let me hear his story! Hear it yourself! As for me, I deny it, root and branch. I say you are being victimized by these two young people, who appear to be engaged—to put the most charitable interpretation on it—in some distorted form of practical joke."

The Inspector was unruffled. "This brings us to the next point on which I would like to question you. This person Binns, whose evidence—as we both agree—would be so valuable, sent a message to this lady and her friend, asking them to escort him to an appointment with you. For some unspecified reason he was afraid. We have that letter here, and that letter, Mr. Constant, is not hearsay evidence. I am informed that they watched outside the building, but there was no sign of Binns again. And now he has disappeared completely."

Constant smiled. "I noticed he was not at the office this morning. But his mother phoned up to say that she had had a note from him, and it seemed he had gone off on some scheme of his. Naturally I was very vexed, but at least we don't have to put on the matter the serious interpretation you do."

"It is a pity the note was not in his writing. However, perhaps you can explain what you saw him about on that evening?"

"Certainly. One of the heads of the departments at Wimbledon wants a research secretary. A much better paid job than Binns has here. I have always had a high opinion of his abilities, and I asked him down to see how he reacted to the surroundings of the Institute and whether he was the proper man for the job. He showed an intelligent interest in everything, and I offered him the job. He accepted."

Constant gave a sidelong glance at the Inspector, and a faint smile was on his lips as he went on. "He staggered me by taking the opportunity of asking, as a special favour, for a month's wages in advance. He did not state the reason, but I supposed that perhaps he felt his new job would require rather better clothes. Quite a mistake, as scientific workers are the shabbiest of creatures. But it was a natural mistake. I did not, of course, take the risk of wounding his feelings by inquiring further. I happened to have twenty pounds by me which I had drawn from the bank that day, and"—again he gave a sly sidelong glance at the Inspector—"I suspect that was the money which, his mother tells me, was enclosed in the note. Why not get the number of those notes from my bank manager, Inspector? If they were to agree with the numbers of the notes in his letter to his mother, it would prove the authenticity of the letter."

The Inspector snorted.

"Of course," went on Constant, "it might also show that I'd written the letter." He laughed. "But that at least I hope is not alleged against me?"

"Oh, isn't it?" said Sandy hotly.

Constant gave her a furious glance and then swung round from his desk and faced Bray.

"Inspector, this is intolerable! I'll be frank. Brutal if necessary! You've come into the office and as good as accused me of murdering, first my old friend Mullins, and secondly my office manager, Binns. Here and now I demand to be definitely cleared by Scotland Yard of these absurd suspicions. I murdered Mullins, did I? I demand you to probe my alibi to the very bottom. Examine every member of my staff to your heart's content. Here's another idea. We keep here a list of all telephone numbers. Turn back the records for that day. Search out everybody I phoned. See if they didn't recognize my voice. I demand that you use every possible means to test my innocence. I shall not rest satisfied until you come to me and say

'Mr. Constant, your alibi is water-tight!' And as for this ridiculous Binns affair, it must be plain to you that this highly strung young man has gone insane. Oh, it's nothing more than a variation of the sort of complex that makes people confess to murders, I expect. He's invented this absurd story and then vanished to give himself importance. But here too, I demand to be justified. Search the laboratory and its grounds, and these offices and my house. For an accusation of murder I may claim at least the previous formality of a corpse. Send out a wanted message through your excellent police system, and when you've got hold of this unfortunate lad, examine him for yourself. I am confident of the result."

Sandy so far had managed to contain herself with comparative calm, beyond an occasional exclamation. But this was too much. She got to her feet menacingly.

"If you are so damned good at explaining, explain this!" she shouted, and, grabbing hold of the man's beard, she tugged at it with all her strength.

Constant gave a piercing scream of pain and flailed the air wildly with his hands as he bowed over, following the beard. With an exclamation of horror Sandy released it.

"My God! It *is* real after all!"

Purple with rage, Constant pointed a shaking finger at the door. "Get out," he yelled with fury. "Get out. Before I forget myself."

I V

"What the Superintendent will say when he hears this, I don't know," said Bray, when they were outside. His voice was grave but his eyes were twinkling with laughter. "You must have hurt the fellow diabolically, I've never heard anyone yelp so loudly."

"I'm sorry. I simply couldn't stand it any longer. Damn that fellow Binns. Why the devil did he say Constant had a false beard? Do you think he has been leading us up the garden?"

Bray smiled. "It looks uncommonly like it, doesn't it? You know it's always dangerous to pay for information you want. The person to be paid may take care you get it, right or wrong. But it's odd he should have vanished like this. I'll put out a wanted message to-day, and I guarantee to have him in in two days if he's in this country. At the same time, I shall take Constant's tip and search the Institute and so forth, and also go into his alibis again."

"Well, there's one thing. There's still the bloodstained overall."

"Yes, I didn't say anything about that. And I was rather surprised he didn't say anything about it either. For if he's as clever as he would have to be if he's not innocent, he'd surely have found an explanation for that."

"Perhaps he hasn't missed it."

"That's possible. But unlikely. Will Miss Vanguard be home now?"

"I should think so. Call in there with me."

Sandy introduced Bray to Van. Van looked at them solemnly. "Well, I've analysed your overalls. This is a serious business! It *is* blood all right! It looks like a big tragedy!"

"Good Lord! Tell us."

Quite suddenly Van burst into laughter. She collapsed on to the sofa. "It's no good," she exclaimed breathlessly. "I can't keep it up. Your blood is the"—she struggled helplessly with another fit of the giggles—"is the blood of a donkey!"

Chapter Twenty-Seven

A TEMPORARY ALLIANCE
BECOMES PERMANENT

"We've found Binns," remarked Detective Inspector Bray, "alive and well."

Sandy looked startled. She was sitting in Bray's little office in Scotland Yard. The air of self-confidence with which she had swept into it a day or two ago was gone. And now she met Bray's news, shattering her theory of murder, with resignation.

"The little beast! I'd like to twist his head off."

"You're still quite positive about that story he told you?"

"Of course."

"And you are still sure that it couldn't have been the result of your unconscious prompting?"

"Certain. Binns reeled off the whole story directly he got a bit sozzled."

"Odd." Bray scratched random figures on his blotting-pad while he reflected. "There must be *something* in it. I'm blessed if I can make out what it is. Look here, will you come up with me and see Binns?"

"Where is he?"

"At Inverness."

"What an extraordinary place. Really, one would think he had gone as far from us as he could."

"One would," said Inspector Bray with a significant expression.

In the *Flying Scotsman*, Inspector Bray explained to Sandy the result of his fresh scrutiny of Constant's alibi. It was four days since the day when Sandy had found her suspicions about Constant's beard were unfounded. "It had become a perfect monomania," she explained to him in justification. "I built my entire theory on it. I swear it *looked* false. It must be the silly way he cuts it."

Since that time Bray and his assistants had turned the staff inside out, in examination. They had also communicated with the recipients of all phone calls from Constant's office on the day of the murder. They had also obtained from the post office a list of all phone calls inward on the same day. The net result was to establish beyond all doubt that from one o'clock till the evening Constant was working in his office, seen almost continuously by his staff, and speaking to various acquaintances—all with such a cloud of witnesses that his alibi was indestructible.

"If he confessed," ended Bray gloomily, "we could do nothing but get him certified. For as sure as I exist, which is the only other fact of which I can be as certain, Constant *did not* kill Mullins."

"I suppose it would not be possible for us to be wrong about Mullins being alive at twelve-thirty. I mean, that depends on the evidence of Samson—the manager fellow."

Bray shook his head. "I thought of that when I first investigated the case. Unfortunately, the date doesn't depend upon Samson's evidence alone. It depends on that of about thirty members of Mullins' staff. No, I am driven back more and more to my first view, that Holliday had a hand in it. His absence on business is such a splendid excuse to avoid answering awkward questions. And it is in answering our innocent questions that suspects generally give themselves away—more by what they can't say than by what they will. Whether I can do anything depends on Binns' story. If he'll only pass the responsibility for faking Holliday's alibi on to Holliday, it establishes the chain we want. Then I shall go full out for Holliday—and get him."

Binns was staying at the Loch Hotel. He met them with a curious mixture of defiance and embarrassment. The lounge was empty.

Declining Binns' wave towards a settee, Bray seated himself sternly on a straight-backed chair.

"I suppose you know what we've come for?"

Binns' furtive eyes slid from Bray's face to Sandy's. "No. Really I don't."

Bray allowed one of those pauses to follow which seem endless. They heard the clattering of silver in the restaurant. Binns wriggled.

"You made certain allegations to Miss Delfinage. They were extremely serious allegations, for they show that you are in possession of evidence that concerns the murder of Antony Mullins."

Binns smiled palely. "Oh, I say now, Inspector. Evidence, indeed! Really, I don't know what you are talking about."

"What were you doing in Berlin on the day of Antony Mullins' murder?"

"Me in Berlin? On the day... What *are* you talking about? Is this a joke?"

Bray smiled sardonically. "You don't agree? You were at the office perhaps? The staff would, of course, remember? Or you stayed at home? Your family would remember?"

"Come to think of it, I took a day off then."

"Where did you go?"

"Oh, just roamed around."

"How odd! Have you a passport, Mr. Binns?"

The other's eyes became wary. "Yes, I have."

"I should like to see that passport, Mr. Binns."

A look of comprehension dawned in the youth's perturbed face. "Oh dear, I *am* sorry. I haven't got it with me now. I lost it only the other day. It'll come to hand, I expect. Then I'll let you know."

"I should be surprised," remarked Bray, "if it does. Do you really deny making a statement to the effect that you went to Berlin to Miss Delfinage?"

"Well, really I can't rightly say what I told them. I was just a bit blotto, you see. And I might have told them any silly story. I was always a great one for joking."

"You little beast!" burst out Sandy furiously. "Do you mean to deny that you told us in absolute detail how Constant told you to go to Berlin, and you were to stay at an hotel and ring up a number? And didn't you say you did it? What's more, didn't we pay you for the information?"

The young man cowered slightly, but he continued to smile thinly. "I must have been tight, and that's a fact! There now, I wondered why I had all that money in my pocket when I came home. Couldn't guess where it came from."

"What did you mean by telling Miss Delfinage this story?" asked Bray sternly.

The other dropped his eyes before the detective's sharp scrutiny. "Can't I have my joke, same as they did? Didn't they come pretending to be brother and sister and asking the Guv'nor for jobs? And then telling me they were detectives and asking all sorts of silly questions. Why shouldn't I have my joke too, that's what I'd like to know."

"Why, in that case, did you write the note you did to these two, and then disappear completely—without even letting your employer know?"

"I wanted a holiday. Can't I have a holiday if I want one? I wanted a rest and didn't know what to do, so I came up here to see if I could find the Loch Ness monster. As for Mr. Constant, I knew Mother would tell the Guv'nor I'd gone on holiday."

This was too much for Sandy. "You damnable little liar. Do you expect anyone to believe you? After writing that letter to us how dared you steal away without a word!"

"Well, the fact I'm alive shows there wasn't anything in it, doesn't it? Why should I be persecuted because I had a harmless little joke? Can't a man have a joke? I saved up for a holiday, and I'm going to have a holiday, and I want to be left alone."

"Let's get this straight," said Bray coldly. "The investigation doesn't rest here. I shall follow it to the end. Do you refuse to make a statement? You are, of course, entitled to refuse, but if you do you cannot be surprised if we put the worst possible construction on it. And should you be concealing any material fact from us, it would render you liable to prosecution as accessory after the fact."

"I don't know what you are talking about, really I don't. If you don't stop badgering and bullying me, I'll complain to our local Member of Parliament. And here are some of the residents coming in. Whatever will they say if you carry on like that? Please remember I'm secretary of the Loch Hotel Guests' Entertainment Committee, and I've got a reputation to lose."

They left him with a final caution from Bray. As he explained, there was nothing else to do but leave it until further evidence was forthcoming.

"It's baffling. Holliday's alibi stinks now. But still I don't see the link between Binns and Holliday. Directly I get back I'll send out our 'Wanted for Information' message and I'll get authority to make Samson give up any addresses that'll be likely to find him. And when we do trace him there'll be a very intimate little heart-to-heart talk."

But the weeks passed, and Holliday was still "somewhere in Europe"... Or had he, as Samson suggested, gone on to South America? No one knew.

I I

"I may not be much of a detective, but I've had a good holiday," stated Sandy.

"Why 'had'?" asked Filson. They were in Van's flat.

"Because duty calls. Because I've no money left. Most important of all because my poor dears are suffering from various horsy complaints. Nobody ever does look after things like oneself. So once again—back I go to Fairview Estate."

"Leaving the mystery unsolved?"

"Leaving things considerably more obscure than before. You know I'm still furious with Constant, but I believe in a month or two I shall be able to laugh at it. I think he's a wicked old devil with a sense of humour. He must have known at once who we were and why we had come, and simply went to some trouble to pull our legs. I can imagine him screaming diabolically in that wretched Institute to curdle our blood."

"Anyway, you got a bit of your own back when you tweaked his beard."

"Yes, I never heard anyone yelp quite so loudly. It was a horrible feeling. I thought I'd pulled his head off for a moment. Well, it's all over now. And I'm going back."

They were silent. Van's room, for once, was deserted and the silence seemed full of their thoughts.

"Have you heard anything of Patricia lately?" asked Sandy at last.

The young man looked up. "No. We've rather drifted apart, you know." He laughed a little bitterly. "I say, Sandy."

"Yes?"

"Did you think I was a bloody fool?"

"Sometimes. Why do you ask?"

"Oh, I was just wondering. You know you're infuriating sometimes. Do I ever infuriate you?"

"Often. Again why?"

"Well, I was only anxious to know if I affected you the same way as you did me."

"I rather suspect you've known that for some time."

"I had only hoped. I'm glad it's true. And will you marry me then?"

"Darling, of course! Thousands of times if you like!"

The black-browed girl, coming in to get on with her painting, slammed the door again in a temper. "Disgusting! The cold-blooded way in which she angled for him!

"I wonder how she brought him to the scratch?" she added reflectively...

Chapter Twenty-Eight

A CHASE ACROSS EUROPE

L aurence lacked advancement.

His uncle had not been pleased with the outcome of the Mullins case. The Chief Constable had had the optimism to suppose his nephew would play a leading part in the solution of this mystery. The fact that the problem was apparently insoluble in no way caused him to modify his criticism. So Laurence was again pushing his bicycle wearily up the slope of Oak Avenue (formerly Bog Lane) on Fairview Estate (once Hake End). His brief career as a plain-clothes criminal investigator was ended, and as he pushed the bicycle he cursed the heat of his uniform in the early summer sun.

But Laurence could hardly help having a friendly feeling for Fairview Estate itself. There was a tie between him and many of its residents. Lord Overture waved to him cheerfully out of the play-pen, in which he was now feeding six goats. The episode of the shot-gun was a bond between them. Besides, Lord Overture had had two inquiries for a plot on the Estate in the post that morning. Mrs. Murples also waved an umbrella in greeting as she passed him. By her side, stooping to listen to her, was "Slim" Murgatroyd, whose huge frame was plainly in the heavy-weight class. The "Battling Bantam" had won his battle, and this was his successor.

Laurence pushed his bicycle a little farther up the hill. Dr. Marabout was busy photographing his front lawn for the illustrations to his new book, *The Unreason of Common Sense*, which was, of course, to be a sequel to *Clouds of Witnesses*. He had lately been blessed by the visits of fairies to his garden. Although they pulled up most of his carrots and onions, he did not grudge their visits, for they left behind evidence of their revels in the form of a fairy ring, which he was now photographing. Laurence did not disturb him, but walked on.

The four Eyton children were playing in their garden. Holidays again! When Laurence saw that Tommy had his air-pistol with him he pushed his bicycle past the garden as rapidly and inconspicuously as possible...

He passed "Newmarket." Sandy was still not in residence. He turned to go down the road to The Turrets. There he met Patricia Mullins.

Against all regulations, he took off his helmet and hung it over his bicycle. The helmet always made him feel foolish in her presence. Besides, it was hot. Patricia turned to speak to him and he halted beside her.

"The large person who used to follow me everywhere has vanished!" she said. "What does that mean?"

"It means that my uncle has at last agreed with my frequent memoranda. He has called off the plain-clothes men he appointed for your special protection."

"Protection is an excellent way of describing it. Anyway, it is just as well because I am going away."

"Going away?"

"Yes. To-morrow."

He looked at her more closely. She seemed worried. "You are wise, I suppose. A change would do you good."

She looked down thoughtfully. "I don't feel ill. Yesterday indeed I felt better than I had felt for years. Perhaps it sounds callous, but it was because for the first time in many years I felt free."

"You say this was yesterday. Do you mean that since then—"

"I mean that I find, after all, one never does get rid of obliga- tions. Why is it the past always puts one in its debt, and nobody seems to think we owe the future anything? Do you owe the past anything?"

"Not a farthing. I think it owes me a little. And it must owe you a lot. You know you speak as if you were years older than me. Yet actually you are the younger."

She smiled at last. "Indeed. And how do you know it?"

"Firstly, you look it."

"Surely that should be enough. What is the 'secondly'?"

"Secondly, it's in our records."

"How frightfully prosaic. Do you always remember to be a policeman?"

"I shall have fewer opportunities of forgetting it after to-morrow."

"Why after to-morrow? Oh, I see. Thank you."

"You haven't really told me why you are going, you know. What did you mean? Of course I can understand your wanting to get away from this place, with all its associations. But you meant something more than that, didn't you?"

"I did."

He hesitated. "Will you think me very presumptuous if I say that you seem to me to admit debts a little too easily? It's always bad business. Perhaps your life would be much easier if you didn't."

"I don't think you presumptuous but very—discerning. And now good-bye."

"Not even *au revoir?*"

"That depends on a great deal of things. By the way, are you asking that in an official capacity? Don't look offended. I was only joking."

"I hope you won't remember me only in my official capacity."

"No, in a very human capacity, I assure you. But whether we meet again depends on other things, not on me."

"On what?"

"Oh—on what the debt is exactly. I don't know yet..."

I I

Charles Venables received a letter. At the time he was swinging lazily in a hammock in the gardens of the Royal Palace at Iconia, during one of the hot, airless afternoons for which Iconian summers are notorious.

The letter was Sandy's last contribution to the solution of the Mullins mystery. Before she finally withdrew from that struggle, chastened and humiliated, she wrote to Venables a full account of the remarkable events revolving round Binns and Constant, not omitting even the affair of the pseudo false beard and the interview in the Loch Hotel.

He skimmed through the letter; read it through quickly again; and then studied it paragraph by paragraph. When the Vice-Grand Chamberlain, who was pulling a garden roller over the Palace lawn to get his weight down, passed near him and made a remark about the weather, he answered it only with an assenting grunt. The swinging of his hammock had ceased. He was thinking.

Suddenly he started swinging again. A possible solution occurred... He turned over the other evidence. Did it fit in?

An hour later he waved away the scarlet and gold flunkey who offered tea. Still later he waved away the frock-coated valet who brought him a rug, to keep at bay the cold winds for which Iconian midsummer evenings are notorious.

At dinner that night his right-hand neighbour, the Deputy-Mistress of the Wardrobe, rebuked him playfully for his abstraction.

Next morning he sent a telegram.

The telegram managed to survive the usually fatal transmission by several Continental telegraphists and reached Police-constable Sadler, when he returned for lunch to Peppering Police Station, in a coherent form. Though coherent indeed, it was hardly comprehensible.

"HAS ANYTHING MORE BEEN HEARD FROM HOLLIDAY aaa EXPECT HE MAY ASK MRS. MULLINS TO MEET HIM SOMEWHERE ON CONTINENT aaa PLEASE MAKE INQUIRIES AND LET ME KNOW WITH GREATEST POSSIBLE SPEED aaa THIS MOST URGENT—Venables."

After considerable thought, Sadler replied as follows:

"NOTHING HEARD FROM HOLLIDAY OUR END BUT MRS. MULLINS LEFT SUDDENLY TWO DAYS AGO FOR EUROPEAN DESTINATION WHICH SHE REFUSED TO GIVE aaa DO YOU THINK THIS WAS RESPONSE INVITATION HOLLIDAY—Sadler."

Laurence received the following telegram in answer sent at triple rates.

"MRS. MULLINS IN GREAT DANGER aaa TRY AND PICK UP TRAIL ANY MEANS AND FOLLOW ALL POSSIBLE DISPATCH aaa LIFE AND DEATH MATTER aaa WHEN FOUND DO NOT LEAVE UNTIL I ARRIVE aaa WIRE ME INSTANTLY WHEN FOUND aaa HURRY HURRY HURRY—Venables."

This not too lucid cable had the effect, as Venables calculated, of stirring Sadler up to instant and immediate action. He went round at once to The Turrets and asked for Bridget. She was, he was told, packing her mistress's things. He demanded to see her. She came down resentfully.

"Where are you going to?"

"I'm going back to Ireland."

"Are you taking your mistress's belongings with you?"

"Of course. I'm taking them back to her mother's."

"Where has she gone to?"

"Sure, won't she be going back to her mother too?"

"That's what I asked you!"

"Well, I suppose she will."

"I don't believe she is!"

"That's for you to say, sir. All I know is she told me to pack her things and take them back with me."

"Look here, Bridget, I believe you know where she's gone to. You must know!"

She gave him an ox-like stare. "How should I be knowing?"

"Bridget, this is most important. You must believe me. Your mistress is in great danger."

The earnestness in his voice made her pause. "You wouldn't be trying to blarney me, would you?"

"I swear it's the truth. Bridget, answer me this. Has your mistress's going away anything to do with Mr. Holliday?"

She nodded.

"Then you must tell me where's she going. I'm telling you the bare truth when I say she is in danger."

Bridget reflected. Laurence watched her in silence. Then her eyes cleared of suspicion. "I do believe you then when you say you're a friend of the mistress. For she's spoken softly of you many a time. And it's true she had a message from Mr. Holliday. It's my belief she'd rather not have gone, for she's been nothing like so cheerful since she got it and started planning to get away. Though why she should mind I don't know, for Mr. Holliday was a nice gentleman with a civil tongue. But there, I've never understood her, not though I've known her since she was only a baby and I little more. Her heart always seemed to pull one way and her wishes another. But there, you say it's urgent. Well, sir, she didn't tell me where she was going, except that it was to France, but I heard her book a room over the telephone, and it was at the Hotel Tally something or other."

Laurence at once thought of that respectable caravanserai, the Talleyrand.

"That would be the Talleyrand. Thanks, Bridget. I must hurry. You won't be sorry for doing this."

Sadler demanded instant leave from Trenton to follow Patricia. When Trenton asked him what the devil he expected to find on his wild-goose chase, Laurence threatened to resign, run away, desert in the face of the enemy, do anything in fact; but he was determined to go. For Venables wouldn't send a telegram like that without the strongest reasons.

After all, he was a relation of the Chief Constable, Trenton reflected. And theoretically the investigation had not yet been abandoned. He gave Laurence three days' leave of absence and a warning that his expenses would be paid by himself.

Thus it was that P.C. Noakes was pushing a bicycle up Oak Avenue while Laurence, having drawn out his available bank balance, was hurrying to Croydon.

He caught the French *Golden Clipper* service, and felt some satisfaction in speeding to Paris at two and a half miles a minute. His satisfaction was short-lived. In response to his pressing inquiries, the reception clerk told him that Madame had indeed stayed one night at the Talleyrand, but she had left the next morning. No, he had no idea where she had gone to.

The affair seemed romantic. This young man, a passionate type, certainly, inquiring so desperately about the woman. Would it be the husband? If not, why had the pretty lady fled? The sympathetic young man bestirred himself and sought aid from the staff. And the hall porter remembered that she had asked the taxi-driver to drive to the Gare de Lyon—even remembered the time.

Laurence did not stay to satisfy their curiosity. His not too fluent French and unofficial position would handicap him in any questioning that had to be done. But the Sûreté were cordiality itself, once satisfied of his genuineness by his warrant-card. There were three main-line trains leaving the Gare de Lyon likely to be caught by Mrs. Mullins, on the basis of the time she took the taxi. And the ticket inspector of one of them remembered an English lady answering Monsieur's description who got on the *Rapide d'azur*. Her ticket was for Cannes.

The questioning had occupied most of the evening, but first thing in the morning Laurence was able to catch the Air-France machine for Lyon and Cannes. He got there early in the afternoon and provided himself with a classified telephone directory. After he had telephoned twenty-four hotels he struck oil.

"Yes, Madame has been staying here. But she has left."

He went round to the hotel. Here the fair-haired and seemingly agitated young Englishman aroused the same sympathetic interest. They were desolated to be able to give him not the least help as to Madame's destination. She had been so silent; so determined. She had telephoned from Paris and booked the room; she had come; and she had gone. There you were.

Laurence drew blank after blank. No scrap of paper in her room; no overheard conversation. She had not used the hotel telephone. She had paid her bill at twelve in the morning, but she had left the hotel later than that. As to the exact time no one knew.

At last, reflecting on her wild progress across the Continent, he reflected that she had twice before booked her rooms by telephone. But she might not always know the telephone number of her next destination. In that case she would, she decided, telegraph. As she was obviously trying to disguise her destination, it might occur to her also that a phone call could be overheard.

The letter of introduction with which the Paris Sûreté had provided him worked wonders. An official accompanied him to the post office nearest to the hotel where Patricia had stayed—it was, in fact, the next most conspicuous building in the street. To send a telegram, she could walk out of the hotel straight into the post office.

The search was fortunate. He turned up her telegram forty-second in the batch for that day. It was addressed to an hotel in Rodriad, Catalonia, a town whose name meant nothing to him. It meant nothing to most people at Cannes, but at last it was identified on the map—a little industrial centre in Catalonia, about thirty miles from Barcelona and ten from the coast.

After an interchange of courtesies with the police authorities Laurence went back to Cannes aerodrome. The machine had left for Barcelona. And there was not a single machine, as it happened, available for charter.

The official he saw could do nothing. He could wire Marseilles, but it was unlikely. Le Bourget was too far. Lyon was rarely helpful. Could he produce *des pilotes* and *des avions* from nothing?

They were arguing outside the manager's office and Laurence strove frantically, with every French adjective he could remember and every gesture he could invent, to explain the importance of the occasion. A slim and dark-haired young man with a look of boredom on his suntanned face, wearing a bright yellow cardigan, was watching his efforts with faint interest.

"It seems an affair of importance this," he said, strolling up. "Why must you have an aeroplane? Is it a matter of money?"

"No."

"A lady?"

"Well, yes."

"It explains itself. And where do the conditions of the romance demand that you hasten to?"

Laurence unfolded his map again and pointed out his destination. The bored young man might be an ally. He took the map thoughtfully. "A four hours' flight. We could clear Customs at

Barcelona. There is no aerodrome at Rodriad but one should find a field. Is there an adventure at the end of this wild chase of yours? And a story behind it?"

"An adventure possibly. A story certainly."

"Then I will fly you there. My machine is that blue monoplane on the tarmac—a Farman *de tourisme*. We will seek the adventure; and on the way you will tell me the story."

"You have to thank," introduced the relieved official, "the Vicomte de Grandlieu."

Even Laurence had heard of the Vicomte de Grandlieu. Had he not flown solo to Saigon, then to Dakar, then to the Cape, and finally to Singapore, on each occasion arriving at his destination sleepless, dishevelled, but still bored and every time but one in possession of a new light aeroplane record?

Shouted in the Vicomte's ear, his own story sounded excessively odd.

"It appears," admitted his pilot, "that we might expect anything."

To this Laurence agreed.

They cleared Customs with unexpected promptitude. The Vicomte could make officials hurry in twenty languages—a remarkable gift. They found their field near Rodriad at dusk. The Vicomte's perspicacious eye had noticed a farmyard beside it, and after haranguing in Catalan the six labourers who hurried up, the Vicomte succeeded in persuading them to push the machine, its wings folded, into the gate and into the farmyard. Here, surrounded by sheds and a wall, it had a reasonable chance of being safe.

"In these rural districts one must be so careful. When a cow chews up one's ailerons it is sufficiently annoying. My special hate is reserved for small boys who cut off pieces of wing fabric with their pen-knives for souvenirs."

They rode into Rodriad on a bullock cart laden with produce for to-morrow's market. The Vicomte appeared slightly less bored.

They found the hotel. Yes, Mrs. Mullins was there. A Mr. Holliday had gone up to see her. Her room was No. 23. "Give me the master-key," said Laurence peremptorily. Surprised, the reception clerk surrendered it.

They went up. Laurence unlocked the door. Patricia was stretched on a sofa apparently asleep. But Laurence at first could only stare incredulously at another man who was kneeling down beside the fire, his face half turned towards them.

The man jumped to his feet and in a second a revolver was in his hand. Laurence was momentarily too bewildered to act. It was the Vicomte who hurled a chair with sufficient precision to throw the man off his balance, and it was the Vicomte who jumped on him like a cat and secured the revolver.

"The affair grows interesting already," said the Vicomte.

Chapter Twenty-Nine

A MATTER OF IDENTITY

I t appeared that the room had been made as air-tight as possible. Newspapers had been jammed into the cracks of the window and pasteboard had been gummed to the door so that when it was closed the cracks would be overlapped. Stretched on the couch, Patricia breathed heavily in a deep anæsthesia. Five minutes later, the man on whose writhing body Laurence and the Vicomte now sat, would have turned on the gas, thrown the key of the room on to the couch, closed the door, locked it with his duplicate key, and walked quietly away.

Next morning a Spanish hotel-keeper would have found that an English lady had had the ill grace to commit suicide in his hotel. Would the Spanish authorities trouble their heads about it further than that? Would the world, and in particular the English authorities, want to investigate further? Nothing could be more natural than for the wretched widow of Antony Mullins to creep away to an obscure Spanish tavern to end her life by the method so notoriously affected by English widows.

Summoned by the bell of No. 23, an astonished maid entered, flew out again, and returned with the *padrone*.

Meanwhile the Vicomte had looped the man's thumbs together behind his back with a length of string, secured by a running knot, tied to a similar knot round the ankles.

"It is sufficient," stated the Vicomte.

It was.

Laurence had given his main attention to the unconscious figure on the couch. His inexperienced nose could not detect the anæsthetic that had been used. Not chloroform at any rate. Perhaps ethyl gas. Once or twice Patricia turned uneasily and groaned. Then, with the instinctive gesture of the anæsthetized, she placed one hand to her head. Laurence parted the short golden hair delicately. The scalp was bruised. She had perhaps been stunned before the anæsthetic was given.

She slept soundly. He made no attempt to awaken her, but the servant was again sent out for a doctor.

At least Laurence now understood more. One glance at the man's face had been enough...

The *padrone* returned with a Guardia Civile, an enormous man decorative in red and gold, with a sword and fierce moustache. "Tell them," answered Laurence of the Vicomte, "that I am an English policeman."

"Enough," said the functionary at once. "I understand the English. In due course you will produce your papers. Meanwhile what happens here? This man—is he a criminal?"

"I charge him with the attempted murder of this lady here. I shall also charge him at a later date with the murder of one Antony Mullins in the County of Thameshire, England. My superior will be informed at once and will arrive at the earliest possible date to complete the formalities of extradition.

"The man's name is James Constant, of London."

I I

Laurence sat by Patricia while she returned to consciousness. It appeared later that she knew nothing, absolutely nothing, of what had happened. She remembered drawing off her gloves before the mirror and afterwards sitting down, and that was all.

Perhaps this was because the chair in which she remembered sitting had its back to the door.

Laurence supposed that Constant had approached very quietly from behind, stunned her, and then given her the anæsthetic. The blow was risky inasmuch as it would leave a mark on the scalp. But Laurence knew it was a necessary preliminary to giving an anæsthetic to a healthy woman. It is only in Victorian romance that a pad soaked with chloroform pressed to the nose causes the victim to fall senseless to the ground without a sound.

The risk of detection was very slight. Apart from his master-key there was only one key to the room, the *padrone* would have assured the police. The door would have been locked. The one key would have been on the bed beside the dead woman. How was the *padrone* to know that the man he knew as Holliday (who had occupied that room for a time and afterwards moved out but had asked him to give it to his English lady friend shortly arriving)—that this man had taken the opportunity to make himself a duplicate key?

The facts were so simple. This poor lady, a widow, even suspected by the police for a time of the murder of her husband—wrongly as it happened, but that explained the matter more tragically—would it be surprising that she went to this lonely place and killed herself?

Laurence thought of all this as Patricia tossed restlessly in the bright-eyed stupor of semi-consciousness, and his heart contracted within him as he thought how narrow her escape had been. If it had not been for the Vicomte... But perhaps these affairs were conducted by Fate.

He had wired Trenton and Venables and he wondered how soon he could expect them. Iconia was a good way away. Two days? Three days? He longed to see Venables to clear up with him the mystery that still involved the case. It now seemed certain that Constant had killed Mullins. But why? And above all, how? And why had this attempt to murder Patricia been the sequel?

He was still ignorant that Constant's alibi, probed by Bray to the utmost, had proved unshakable. Otherwise the mystery would have seemed to him deeper still.

When at last Patricia came out of the shadow of anæsthesia—so oddly terrifying and unreal—he told her something of the story.

"I can't understand it," she murmured. "Where is Ralph? How did that awful man get here? I have never seen him. Why should he want to hurt me?"

"All that will be explained in a little while. No one knows where Holliday is at the moment, but he knows no more about this than you. Constant used his name to get you here."

She thought, and when she looked up a strange flash of pleasure was in her eyes. "So Ralph did not want me after all!"

"You mean—"

"That the debt doesn't exist. It was only in my imagination..."

I I I

Next day after luncheon the Vicomte hired an ancient car and bumped out of Rodriad to the field where he had left his aeroplane. "I had better see that the pigs haven't rooted up the pickets," he explained.

He returned an hour later. He sat down in a chair beside Laurence and Patricia, who were reflectively disposing of something cool in long glasses, as the burning heat of noon began to lift from the dusty roads.

"It commences to rain aeroplanes in that field," remarked the Vicomte.

"Good Lord! Do you mean somebody else has arrived?" exclaimed Laurence, jumping excitedly to his feet.

The Vicomte languidly waved a hand. "The famous British phlegm! Control yourself! Yes, several have arrived. They will be here soon. There was a proper-looking old buffer who first made an excellent landing in one of your elegant Leopard Moths. His young pilot is a friend of mine, with whom I spent an enjoyable evening in Cairo. A little while after there came a military machine, a two-seater trainer, but of an age which is incredible! Figure to yourself, a rotary engine! This was piloted by a gentleman who is at least a general in the Air Force to which he belongs, if his uniform is of any significance. He wore a large parachute. A necessary precaution, one imagines. His passenger was a lean and melancholy young man, but with a distinguished air. Both asked for you."

"By Jove, I believe it's Trenton and Venables!"

It was. A little later the ancient car halted outside the hotel. In it were Trenton, Venables and the two pilots.

"It was sporting of you to fly here," said Laurence to his superior.

"It was," agreed the other heavily. "I'd never have done it if Venables hadn't phoned me up from Iconia and talked me into it. I must admit it wasn't so bad. Except just at the end when we kept on falling miles and miles with sickening drops. Still a Channel crossing makes me ill for weeks, so I mustn't grumble."

The pilot, a quiet little man with mouse-coloured hair who looked about sixteen years old, laughed.

"We had perfect weather! Bit bumpy off the Pyrenees, that's all."

Laurence did not remember hearing him speak again except when from time to time he called for beer, which he drank peaceably in enormous quantities.

Venables dropped into a chair. "Phew, it's hot. We had a perfect trip, thanks to the brilliant piloting of Squadron Leader Yalinoff, and the kindness of the Iconian Government, which put at my disposal

the best machine in the Iconian Air Force." Venables winked surreptitiously at the Vicomte.

"Do not believe my friend!" said Squadron Leader Yalinoff, a
tall, pale individual with black hair. He spoke with great gravity
in slow English. "That was not the best machine in our Air Force.
Please do not get such a low opinion of the Force as that! Our other
machine is much newer but our Air Marshal crashed it on Sunday.
It was very regrettable. The Marshal, as senior officer, insisted
on landing the machine, although Group Captain Ferenov, who
was with him, had repeatedly explained that modern day bombers
cannot be glided in at 30 m.p.h. 'There is no such word as can't in
the vocabulary of the Iconian Air Force!' said the Air Marshal, just
before they crashed. 'The man is indomitable!'"

Laurence wondered anxiously whether to smile or not. The
Vicomte was roaring with laughter.

"You will get used to the Iconian sense of humour in time," said
Venables. "I must say I was a little peeved when I asked Yalinoff
how my parachute worked. He told me not to trouble myself. They
were short of parachutes in the Iconian Air Force, he said, and my
pack only contained blankets. They had a surplus of these, and the
result looked as well in the newspaper photographs."

Yalinoff laughed, and insisted on ordering drinks...

By the time they had finished the drinks it was the hour when
Spanish officialdom might be expected to attend again to business.

Trenton, Venables and Laurence went round to the town hall.
Constant was produced. He looked tired and dishevelled, but he
confronted them defiantly. There was an odd air of furtive apprehension in his attitude.

The *alcalde* studied the credentials produced by Trenton, looked
over his own records of the affair and then turned to the prisoner.

"You are charged, it appears, with the attempted murder of a
lady, Señora Mullins. It further appears that these gentlemen propose

to lay a charge against you for the murder of Antony Mullins, an extraditable offence."

The look of apprehension died out of Constant's eyes. He laughed mockingly.

"Ridiculous! I can prove my innocence to the hilt. I shall call an Inspector of the English Criminal Investigation Department as witness to my innocence of this absurd charge. Murdering Antony Mullins indeed!"

Venables, a faint smile on his saturnine features, raised his eyebrows.

"There appears to be some mistake," he said in slow but good Spanish. "This man is not charged with the murder of Antony Mullins at all but that of one Ralph Holliday.

"He *is* himself Antony Mullins, *alias* James Constant."

Chapter Thirty

HOW IT WAS DONE

The extradition proceedings turned on the question of identification.

Patricia had been warned of what she had to face. It was Laurence who told her that her husband was no longer dead, and she looked at him as if he had told her that Antony had risen from the grave, the clothes still round his charred body. And he told her too of the man her husband had killed, and she bowed her head in fear.

"What have I done? Oh, God, will it never end?"

"It has ended," said Laurence, and took her to the mayor's office.

The man that had been Constant looked his wife in the face with a strange and passionate expression, which made the *alcalde* stare at them both unbelievably.

Then the man who was Mullins laughed horribly.

Patricia turned her eyes slowly from him and looked at the magistrate. "This is my husband."

She walked out; her eyes were dazed.

The extradition was difficult. The attempted murder of Mrs. Mullins was committed on Spanish soil and therefore within the jurisdiction of the Spanish Courts. The British authorities wished to obtain the possession of the body of Antony Mullins to try him, however, for the murder of Holliday on British soil.

Again the extradition proceedings were held up for an identification, this time of the body found in the garage, presumed to be that of Holliday.

It was exhumed. The unconsumed teeth of the corpse were compared with a chart in the possession of Holliday's dentist. The dentist deposed on oath that the teeth were identical.

The Spanish authorities therefore adjourned *sine die* the charge of attempted murder, and the extradition proceeded. Meanwhile, her evidence having been given, Patricia was allowed to return to England.

"You had better see her safely home, Laurence," said Inspector Trenton.

Trenton remained on during the wearisome course of the proceedings.

The Iconian Major had long ago flown back alone to Isorb. Two days later the Vicomte flew thither with Venables, with whom he had struck up a friendship. Their proceedings there are no part of this book.

Venables had declared his intention of returning to Barcelona after the extradition proceedings were over.

He did so. Thus it was that Trenton, Venables and the accused man went back together. With no personal interest in the matter, Trenton and Venables were able to take a perhaps cold-blooded interest in the affair. The third, with the very keenest personal interest, treated the matter with even more callousness. Perhaps the perennial self-confidence and optimism of the murderer sustained him.

Thus nobody would have realized that of the three men who travelled under assumed names, one was accused of murder and the other two were his keepers. At the most, fellow travellers remarked on the friendliness which made the three inseparable.

The authorities had decided that it was safest to bring Mullins back by water. Thus it was that night found them in a deserted corner of the saloon, their dinners settled by a glass or two of old brandy. In an awkward pause Trenton pressed Venables to tell him of how, in Iconia, he had been led to penetrate the secret of this most amazing of murders.

"Do, my dear chap," pressed Mullins coolly. "For the life of me I can't see how you did it."

Venables scrutinized the brandy swirling in his glass sardonically.

"The case could have been solved on the facts known at the very outset of the investigation. Every fact and clue we needed was given us. It was like the fairest possible detective story in the world, in which the reader is let into every material circumstances needed to enable him to guess the solution.

"And yet I couldn't guess it! It is something to be ashamed of."

"I hardly think you are being fair," protested Mullins. "My alibi was surely cast-iron."

"The most dangerous kind of alibi, because it is so brittle. As you will find, my friend, when you stand your trial! Now listen to the facts, Trenton—the facts as we had them before us in statements at the very beginning of our long investigation. And tell me, if you can, why we didn't see at once what happened.

"At twelve o'clock Mullins is alive. At a quarter to three his burned body is discovered. It is identified mainly by means of the remnants of the clothes and belongings. He is then discovered to have been shot; the door is locked, the revolver is missing; and the time-switch is found which has been arranged to start the fire. These facts were discovered at once. Obviously a case of murder.

"Suspicion pointed at first to two people—Holliday, of whom Mullins was rumoured to be jealous; Constant as having most to gain by Mullins' death.

"We examined their alibis. Constant's was perfect. From twelve-thirty to six he had been in his office, seen by all his staff. Holliday's also was perfect, but more complicated. Half an hour before he was last seen in his manager's presence, Mullins had spoken over the telephone to Holliday in Germany. Letters posted in Germany that afternoon referred to this telephone conversation with Holliday. The letters were written, one in Holliday's hand, the other in typewriting but signed by him. A young Englishman staying in the Berlin hotel which Holliday was supposed to have gone to had phoned Mullins. Presumably he was Holliday.

"The alibi therefore was complete. Who but Holliday could have posted those letters in Berlin—for they were in his handwriting and referred to a phone conversation with Mullins in England two or three hours earlier?

"This was confirmed by the fact that a young man had stayed in a Berlin hotel and phoned Mullins at the exact time in question, and no other German calls had come through to Mullins."

"I still don't understand how that was done," said Trenton.

"Nothing easier. The clue was in our hands. Cast your minds back to the report of our graphologists. They said that one letter was entirely in Holliday's writing except that if the body of the letter had not been indubitably authentic they would have suspected the signature. The signature to the typed letter was genuine."

"I still don't see."

"This was how it could be and probably was done. The graphological experts *were* right. Holliday, you remember, stayed on to talk to Mullins after that conference at which Samson was present. We may suppose the clerical staff was gone. Suddenly Mullins remembers a letter he wishes to write. He turns to Holliday, 'This is a letter which must go off,' he might say. 'It must go off first thing to-morrow to catch the air-mail, and I shall be late at the office to-morrow morning. Look here, do you mind writing it down while I dictate it, and then I'll leave it to-night on my secretary's desk to type and sign for me and send off before I arrive to-morrow.' He tosses Holliday a sheet of the firm's note-paper and dictates the letter. Holliday copies it down—irony of ironies—his own alibi and yet his own death warrant. Of course he does not sign the letter. Mullins can think of no stratagem to make him do so. Thus he later has to forge the signature. What does that matter? The body of the letter is genuine. However, it would be as well to have some authentic signatures of Holliday's. So next day Mullins might remind Holliday, before their final leave-taking, that he is a partner who is going away for a long journey. Oughtn't they to have a few signatures for formal documents? Holliday is hardly likely to refuse—he was only a junior partner and as Mullins might jokingly reassure him—any money which was misappropriated under his signature would be Mullins' own, for he held practically all the assets of the business. So Holliday signs his name on a few sheets of the firm's note-paper, and from time to time Mullins uses these, with typewritten letters above them, to create the illusion of Holliday's continued existence. A letter from Spain or Roumania, posted by unsuspecting agents, the final communication to Patricia—oh, I've no doubt the signatures were invaluable.

"Holliday's alibi is now complete. All that is necessary is for Binns to be sent to stay at the Atlantic Hotel, and to phone up Mullins any time before two—actually it was just before noon. Mullins then discussed with him in Samson's presence the contents of the letters which were in fact already written, telling him to write them, and impressing the conversation on Samson's mind by consulting him in the course of the telephone conversation.

"Think of the dramatic irony of the situation. The previous evening Mullins had gone out to the garage with Holliday ostensibly to drive him to Peppering station. Instead of doing so he had shot Holliday in the garage—with a silenced revolver no doubt. And while Holliday's body was still lying stiff and dead in his locked garage, he was busy concocting a perfect alibi for a corpse, and concocting it brilliantly.

"Is the cleverness of the alibi so surprising? Had he not been brooding over this murder since the day he first suspected Holliday, when this insane jealousy first possessed him and turned his mind? For over a year he had been preparing an alias—a fictitious person named Constant. For days, for weeks, when no doubt he was thought to be absent on business, he was turning up at the offices in Victoria Street, in a false beard and thick glasses, creating James Constant. He created a congenial character—created him lovingly, and provided him with this dummy Society as a congenial environment. I call it a dummy Society with reason, for if you look up its constitution, you will see its government is vested entirely in its Secretary who is created for life. One day this temporary alias would be permanent, when Mullins would die to the world and slip into the character of Constant for ever.

"With him he must take his fortune. But this very legacy might throw suspicion on Constant. And Constant was as yet too suspicious a character to have the police probing into his past, finding that he was only a phantasm. How could he prevent it? Only by giving himself an alibi so simple and perfect that the police would never dream of looking beyond it—so strong and foolproof that no intelligent person could doubt it for a moment.

"And such indeed was his alibi. From a few minutes after the time Mullins was last seen alive—just long enough in fact for him to slip in somewhere—probably into the lavatory at Victoria Station, and change into his beard and spectacles—from that time until long after 'Mullins' was found dead an hour's journey away, Constant sat among his staff, and spoke to them and carried on his normal business. Here was the perfect alibi. It would take nearly an hour to get Mullins, alive or dead, from where he was last seen alive to where he was found dead. But Constant had been in London since ten or fifteen minutes after Mullins has last been seen alive. Thus it was that Constant–Mullins sat in his office and waited—secure.

"I am filled with admiration at the security of his position. To begin with, he might reasonably hope that body, car and garage would be so completely burned that there would be no question of anything but an accident. Well, it didn't work. We were lucky enough to find the time-switch, and the bullet in the corpse, and suspect murder.

"He had foreseen this and prepared a triple line of defence. First, alibis for victim and murderer. Secondly, a will designed to throw suspicion on his wife and make it seem likely that Mullins had always feared murder. Thirdly, and most cunning of all, he had used Eyton's revolver, borrowed long before, with which to kill Holliday, and had given it back so that it would be in Eyton's possession during the time 'Mullins' was presumed to have been murdered.

"No doubt his mad jealousy had already noticed Eyton's friendship for his wife. And what could have saved Eyton except the accidental playfulness of a child?

"That, of course, was where we were inexcusably obtuse. That was where we should have seen the inescapable deduction. Eyton's revolver shot the dead man we found in the garage. The revolver could not have been used between the time Mullins was last seen alive and was last seen dead. But the revolver *was* used to shoot that dead man. Therefore the dead man could not have been Mullins. But we missed this.

"Consider again the brilliance of this man's invention. First he deluded us as to the man who was murdered. Next he deluded us as to how and when that man was killed. Thirdly, he provided fictitious alibis, not only for himself in his new personality, but for the man whom he had murdered.

"These alibis were the crowning stroke of his genius. He saw at once that Holliday would be suspected of the murder of 'Mullins.' The police would then start to search for him. They would at last find that he was nowhere; that no mortal eye had seen him since he left Mullins' house the day before the murder. And this might have awkward consequences. So he diverted suspicion from Holliday completely and also maintained the illusion of his continued existence.

"Now the amazing thing is, that this scheme was betrayed, not by our cleverness, or his foolishness, but by the absurd suspicions of two blundering children—that irresponsible person Sandy, and her artist friend. But before that happened he was almost betrayed by the merest accident. Mullins had always supposed that he had the only key to the garage. Thus although Holliday's body had to be left in the garage overnight, it would be safe against any intrusion, with the door locked and the one key in his possession, until it went up in flames.

"But all the time Filson had a duplicate key. Think of the narrowness of Mullins' escape! At twenty-five past one Filson went into the garage and saw Holliday's dead body. But because the corpse was dressed in Mullins' clothes, and because it was lying face downwards, huddled in the driver's seat, Filson did not turn the body over. He assumed that this dead body, in Mullins' clothes and Mullins' car, *was* Mullins. The sight of the body made him sufficiently ill without wanting any further investigation. And the mystery therefore remained inpenetrable, although by this odd chance Mullins' ingenious time-switch actually never came into operation. Before it did the garage was burned down by Filson.

"This was where we all gave up the mystery in despair. Except Sandy. Do you believe in feminine intuition? She was confident Constant was a murderer. It may well be that when she first saw him he was nervous of being recognized. She said she noticed his nervousness. Here we come to the most interesting point—Mullins' gradual perfection in his rôle as Constant. At first, of course, he had worn a false beard. He felt certain that his alibi was so good that suspicion would never fall on him and he would never be confronted by those who had known him intimately. Sandy saw him, but in a dark office, disguised by a beard and spectacles and because she never expected to see a man whom she thought dead, he survived her scrutiny. But old acquaintance with the disguised man affected both her and Filson. They both felt sure they had seen him before. Of course they had, but not as 'Constant.'

"Six months elapsed before Sandy took up the trail again. During this interval 'Constant' had evidently gone for a holiday and grown a real beard. For now he was to be permanently Constant. Meanwhile he subtly altered his features. You know how the gradual change of face in a man through age or illness, while instantly obvious to somebody who had last seen him many years before, is unnoticed by his intimates? So it was with Constant. Gradually he changed as far as he could the Mullins characteristics in his face. He plucked his eyebrows to alter their shape; trimmed the eyelashes, treated the forehead to loosen and wrinkle the skin, removed certain fatty contours of the face with diathermic treatment. At last he felt secure from detection by those who had only known the clean-shaven Mullins, while his staff probably hardly noticed the difference.

"Of course he could not have survived the scrutiny of anyone who knew him intimately. His wife, for instance. Or Samson, his former manager. But he kept out of the way of these.

"His one mistake was to take those amateur detectives, Sandy and Filson, at first too frivolously. Secure in his new identity and confident of his alibi, he laughed at them. He ought at once to have shown he knew who they were, claimed police protection from their intrusion and frightened them off. He discovered too late that they were after all to be taken seriously. Perhaps more by luck than judgment, but none the less dangerously, they had discovered the part Binns had played in establishing Holliday's alibi. Binns was his weak point—a somewhat foolish young man, who could be trusted to obey his employer's instructions without overmuch reasoning, and who, of course, never suspected the real identity of James Constant.

"At once 'Constant' realized there was only one thing to be done. That was to shut Binns' mouth and make fools of the amateur detectives. He shut Binns' mouth when he invited him to the laboratory and there no doubt offered him a large sum if he would disappear at once and talk no more about his Berlin visit. Binns agreed. Meanwhile Constant hoaxed Sandy and Filson into thinking there had been a murder. The scream and bloodstained overall were sheer impishness. Bray found that the Institute had been investigating the properties of blood glues, which, as you may know, are largely used in carpentry work where structural strength is required—in aircraft construction, for instance. They therefore had large quantities of animal blood, and 'Constant' was unable to resist the symbolism of using donkey's blood, and leaving the overalls in a place where Filson was likely to find them. Meanwhile, of course, Binns had gone out inconspicuously through another entrance some time before.

"'Constant' felt that they would thus make such utter fools of themselves that they would give up the investigations. In this he was right. But before Sandy gave it up she wrote me a full account of everything that had happened just in case there was anything in it. Also she told me Constant had gone to the Continent on business. Directly I heard Binns' story, the whole thing clicked into place like a kaleidoscopic pattern. And I cursed my foolishness at not seeing it before. Never, I assure you, shall I consider myself a criminal investigator till I have forgotten this affair.

"As I turned it over in my mind, and saw that Mullins was alive and Holliday dead, I wondered what next might happen. And I feared. Was Mullins' hate fully gratified? All men kill the thing they love. That at least is psychologically true of the murderer. In his insane jealousy of his wife, had not Mullins attempted to involve her in a charge of murder? He had failed, but would he end there? I did not like this absence of Constant on business.

"I suddenly saw the horrifying ease with which he could murder her. Supposing he lured her on to the Continent with a message from Holliday. With her odd generous loyalty, which I saw sufficiently even in my short stay, I thought she would come. I doubt if she ever really loved Holliday. He was a friend; a kind friend; and God knows under that roof she needed friends. He loved her certainly—died because of it. And I think that afterwards, when the innocence of Filson was proved, Patricia Mullins suspected in her heart that Holliday must have murdered her husband. Perhaps he had even threatened to. Let us suppose she suspected this. Then when out of the blue came a call from Holliday, how could she fail to answer it after what he had done for her? And would it not only confirm her suspicion, and make the debt more certain, if Holliday told her in the letter to come in such a way as not to be followed? To go to an hotel at Paris, then on to one at Cannes, and finally to the address he had given her in Rodriad. And so it happened. So cunningly her husband had read her mind.

"For you see now she was the one perfectly safe victim and he the one perfectly safe murderer. 'Constant' and Mrs. Mullins had never met each other. He had nothing to gain by her death. No one therefore would even suspect him. In addition he would stage the murder so that it appeared a suicide—he was still cautious—but supposing they discovered it was murder? Supposing they even suspected that the man who knew the lady and had been staying at the hotel had a hand in it? What of it? That man had registered under the name of Holliday. And what chance had they of ever finding Holliday—a man who was buried under a lying gravestone?

"And when their search for Holliday was in vain, who would be surprised? They would say that Holliday, in his fear of discovery, had vanished from sight for ever, and so they would themselves have coiled up the final clue in the tangled mystery.

"I saw these possibilities at once and my wire to Sadler brought me the answer I dreaded. I dared not wire in reply that Mullins and Constant were the same people. Set down in black and white he would think the message was a joke, or at least would wait until he heard further from me. And there was no time.

"So, I sent the message that I thought would make certain of Sadler following her. For I had formed the opinion that if he believed Patricia Mullins in danger, he would go round the world to her aid. Once he had found her she was safe. And he succeeded. But he succeeded by such a narrow margin that it seems the merest stroke of luck. Yet one may, if one likes, see in it something deeper, the foiling of the malicious genius by something more than hazard…

'… the times have been
That, when the brains were out, the man would die,
And there an end; but now they rise again
With twenty mortal murders on their crowns…'

"It is impossible, as I take it, to conceive a more brilliant alibi and more neatly executed murder than this has been. It has failed not by the romantic brilliance of a storybook detective but by the blind working of events towards this revelation."

"You do yourself an injustice," said Mullins politely. He was leaning back in his chair, and the smoke from his cigar rose in a vertical column.

Inspector Trenton, lost in Venables' narrative, came to himself with a start. Then he looked coolly at his prisoner. "Well, is the story correct?"

Mullins smiled. His beard made his features difficult to read; but he seemed happy and unperturbed. "You do not, I trust, expect

I shall confess? Or make a statement? Good. What I am going to say is therefore in confidence. In the dock, of course, I shall fight you to the end, and I think win. But now we are discussing this affair, as among masters of our crafts, you of the science of investigation, I of the famous art of murder. And I claim that Venables here, in his perspicuous analysis, has yet omitted something."

The lounge in which they were sitting was deserted. Through the glass window they could see the splendour of the Atlantic sky as they swept over the waters, for the moment untroubled, of the Bay of Biscay. The air was warm.

Mullins leaned forward, a strange glitter in his eyes...

"Your analysis is as correct as that of the surgeon, who cuts up the brain and says, 'Here it all is—cerebrum and cerebellum, nerve ganglions, brain cells, cortex and spinal chord.' He omits to mention those invisible matters, the memory, the understanding and the will, without which the brain is no brain, but mere rubbish. You have left these invisible matters out in my case, Mr. Venables. Let me put them in."

Mullins gently disengaged the ash from his cigar. His rather croaking voice had softened and became almost melodious.

"Has a woman ever made you suffer? Have you ever loved and found the object of your love evasive, become frigid, at last hating you? I am a man. But when all the strength of my soul had been poured out to the woman who was my wife, and she had spurned it with her foot, I was turned into something little better than a beast. I became dazed. It disturbed my reasoning powers. It interfered with my business. I implored, I threatened. I went on to my knees to her. I may have ill-treated her, as the world understands cruelty, but it was more painful to me than to her, and so I was justified. Yes, I have knelt to her, and she has treated my abjectness with worse than hate—with fear."

His hand shook a trifle, and the pupils of his eyes contracted suddenly. "When I found myself wandering without thought or purpose wildly about the house all night, yes, night after night, sleepless, not knowing where I was going, I knew she was driving me mad. I could have screamed the names of her lovers to heaven— Holliday, Filson and Eyton. I could hear the whole world whispering behind my back. I controlled myself by sheer will. I never struck her. I never threatened her. I did nothing. She was driving me mad.

"One of her lovers I hated most of all. I have always hated my nephew, Holliday. His youth and charm brought him friends and success when I was thirty-five and still slaving to make my way. Then he was rich and carefree and twenty-one. The years passed. Our positions were reversed. I was rich. He was poor. I befriended him to triumph over his poverty, as one tosses a cur a bone. And then he took from me the only thing I loved. Worse still, Patricia had the cruelty to suspect my jealousy, and to tell me Holliday was nothing more than a friend. A friend!

"She was laughing in my face—turning the arrow in the wound. Lest they drive me mad, and turn me into a sleepless beast, I resolved that he must die, and in due time and course that she must die too. Perhaps she might die under accusation of murder—perhaps by my own hand. But the whole canker must be cut out of my life. I must become a man again and sane. I had been a beast too long.

"What (I thought in those dreadful moments) had I done with my life? With my intelligence I might have been an original thinker, one of those names which are written in letters of light—Newton, Cavendish, Einstein, Faraday, Leibniz and Descartes. Laugh at me if you like, but first speak to some of those who were with me at St. Andrews, where Dumbarton, one of the greatest physicists of his day, predicted for me that I would one day carry on his work and carry it to greater heights. Dumbarton! Laugh now if you dare.

"But I craved too much the material things. I wanted to make money. I prostituted my talents to mere invention. I made guns and explosives and other toys for the children who rule and ruin this world of ours. I became a mere engineer, a petty Kelvin.

"So in these moments, maddened by love, I hated myself and my life. Often I considered committing suicide. And what I planned was at last a kind of suicide. For I was to cut off the limb that was paining me—the woman I adored and loathed. And I would kill Antony Mullins, the engineer, and from his ashes would rise Constant the scientist. And all came about as I planned.

"Do you know that when you arrested me I was on the verge of great discoveries? A year, two years, perhaps three, and my name might have been mentioned with Planck, and Niels Bohr, and de Broglie, and de Sitter. It still will be. For I warn you I shall fight, fight to the end. Let them get me if they can. They will drag me from the dock; they will drag me to the scaffold."

His head sank forward.

"I am tired," said Antony Mullins.

Afterwards, when the door of his cabin had been locked, Venables and Trenton sat talking while the stars still moved slowly across the lovely Spanish sky.

"Yes," said Venables, "as Mullins said, he is after all a man. And there are two things of which no one can persuade human nature— with a jealous man, that there is no cause for his jealousy; with a competent engineer, that he is not a great scientist."

And as he spoke the dawn lightened in the sky.

Epilogue

The public forgot at last the great fight that Mullins had made for his life, and the brilliant defence of Freeth-Jones. The most imposing array of medical witnesses ever assembled at a trial were called to show that the accused was a maniac suffering from a double personality. As Constant he was a Mr. Hyde, a murderer; as Mullins he was a Dr. Jekyll. The Hyde periods were periods of madness. The sheer intellectual brilliance of his scheme of murder told inevitably against him, however.

The public forgot at last about it. And they never knew that the governor, pale and grim, had watched a screaming man dragged struggling to the scaffold and that the chaplain had said steadily amid his screams the last words of the judge's sentence: "May the Lord have mercy on your soul," and that thus Antony Mullins was hanged by the neck until dead, fighting, as he said, to the last.

Time passed; and time heals everything.

Venables flatly refused to accept any credit for the case.

"My dear fellow," he said to Laurence, "there is a limit to what the public will believe. They certainly won't believe I solved the case when, as everyone knows, I was in Iconia all the time. No, I'm content with the inside story for the *Mercury*. You take the credit yourselves—you and Trenton. You deserve it."

"I always knew you had it in you," remarked the Chief Constable. "Splendid, my boy. You're being appointed to headquarters. Another year in the ranks and you qualify for an inspectorship. And now for real news. You've stuck this policeman business well, damn well. I said to myself when I signed your warrant-card: 'If Laurence sticks this for two years I'll make him an allowance.' And now the two years are up. Good Lord, don't thank me. I owe it to Ted's son anyway, but I preferred to make you earn it first and you have."

Which made things easier. Patricia had fallen in love for the first time. And none too soon. She had known that Laurence had fallen in love with her the first time he had seen her.

Yet time had passed—months and months. She had stayed on at The Turrets—spoken to him. But he had steadfastly refused to say anything.

The obstacle in his mind was finance. How could he marry her on a policeman's pay? The idea was ludicrous.

He asked her to marry him that evening after his conversation with the Chief Constable.

"Where shall we be married? Not a 'fashionable' wedding for heaven's sake!"

"Why not at the sweet little church at Great Hake?"

"By Jove, yes, that's an idea."

The banns were read a month later. Lord Overture, a regular attendant at Divine Service, stirred in the Overture family pew when he heard the vicar drone out, after the usual preamble about impediments, the following:

> Laurence Sadler (bachelor) and Patricia Mullins (widow) *both of this Parish*.
> Francis Filson (bachelor) and Sandra Delfinage (spinster) *both of this Parish*.